The last reindeer was crossing th
following closely behind. As the
me, I realized why the reindeer were struggling to pull their load.
Santa had company. Dead company.

Acclaim for the Anastasia Pollack Crafting Mysteries

Assault with a Deadly Glue Gun

"Crafty cozies don't get any better than this hilarious confection...Anastasia is as deadpan droll as Tina Fey's Liz Lemon, and readers can't help cheering as she copes with caring for a host of colorful characters." – *Publishers Weekly* (starred review)

"Winston has hit a homerun with this hilarious, laugh-until-your-sides-hurt tale. Oddball characters, uproariously funny situations, and a heroine with a strong sense of irony will delight fans of Janet Evanovich, Jess Lourey, and Kathleen Bacus. May this be the first of many in Winston's Anastasia Pollack Crafting Mystery series." – *Booklist* (starred review)

"A comic tour de force...Lovers of funny mysteries, outrageous puns, self-deprecating humor, and light romance will all find something here." – *ForeWord Magazine* (Book-of-the-Year nominee)

"North Jersey's more mature answer to Stephanie Plum. Funny, gutsy, and determined, Anastasia has a bright future in the planned series." – *Kirkus Reviews*

"...a delightful romp through the halls of who-done-it." – *The Star-Ledger*

"Make way for Lois Winston's promising new series...I'll be eagerly awaiting the next installment in this thoroughly delightful series." – *Mystery Scene Magazine*

"...once you read the first few pages of Lois Winston's first-in-series whodunit, you're hooked for the duration..." – *Bookpage*

"In Winston's droll second cozy featuring crafts magazine editor Anastasia Pollack...readers who relish the offbeat will be rewarded." – *Publishers Weekly*

"...a *30 Rock* vibe...Winston turns out another lighthearted amateur sleuth investigation. Laden with one-liners, Anastasia's second outing (after *Assault With a Deadly Glue Gun*) points to another successful series in the works." – *Library Journal*

"Winston...plays for plenty of laughs...while letting Anastasia shine as a risk-taking investigator who doesn't always know when to quit." – *Alfred Hitchcock Mystery Magazine*

Revenge of the Crafty Corpse
"Winston peppers the twisty and slightly edgy plot with humor and plenty of craft patterns. Fans of craft mysteries will like this, of course, but so will those who enjoy the smart and snarky humor of Janet Evanovich, Laura Levine, and Laura DeSilverio." – *Booklist*

"Winston's entertaining third cozy plunges Anastasia into a surprisingly fraught stew of jealousy, greed, and sex..." and a "Sopranos-worthy lineup of eccentric character..." – *Publishers Weekly*

"Winston provides a long-suffering heroine, amusing characters, a...good mystery and a series of crafting projects featuring cloth yo-yos." – *Kirkus Reviews*

"A fun addition to a series that keeps getting stronger." – *Romantic Times Magazine*

"Chuckles begin on page one and the steady humor sustains a comedic crafts cozy, the third (after *Death by Killer Mop Doll*)... Recommend for Chris Grabenstein ("John Ceepak" series) and Jess Lourey readers." – *Library Journal*

"You'll be both surprised and entertained by this terrific mystery. I can't wait to see what happens in the Pollack household next." – *Suspense Magazine*

"The book has what a mystery should...It moves along at a good pace...Like all good sleuths, Anastasia pieces together what others don't...The book has a fun twist...and it's clear that Anastasia, the everyday woman who loves crafts and desserts, and has a complete hottie in pursuit, will return to solve another murder and offer more crafts tips..." – *Star-Ledger*

Decoupage Can Be Deadly
"*Decoupage Can Be Deadly* is the fourth in the Anastasia Pollock Crafting Mysteries by Lois Winston. And it's the best one yet. More, please!" – *Suspense Magazine*

"What a great cozy mystery series. One of the reasons this series stands out for me as a great one is the absolutely great cast of characters. Every single character in these books is awesomely quirky and downright hilarious. This series is a true laugh out loud read!" – Books Are Life–Vita Libri

"This is one of these series that no matter what, I'm going to be laughing my way through a comedy of errors as our reluctant heroine sets a course of action to find a killer while contending with her eccentrically dysfunctional family. This adventure grabs you immediately delivering a fast-paced and action-filled drama that doesn't let up from the first page to the surprising conclusion." – Dru's Book Musings

"Lois Winston's reluctant amateur sleuth Anastasia Pollack is back in another wild romp." – The Book Breeze

A Stitch to Die For
"*A Stitch to Die For* is the fifth in the *Anastasia Pollack Crafting Mysteries* by Lois Winston. If you're a reader who enjoys a well-

plotted mystery and loves to laugh, don't miss this one!" –
Suspense Magazine

Scrapbook of Murder

"This is one of the best books in this delightfully entertaining whodunit and I hope there are more stories in the future." – Dru's Book Musings

"*Scrapbook of Murder* is a perfect example of what mysteries are all about—deft plotting, believable characters, well-written dialogue, and a satisfying, logical ending. I loved it!" – *Suspense Magazine*

"I read an amazing book recently, y'all — *Scrapbook of Murder* by Lois Winston, #6 in the Anastasia Pollack Crafting Mysteries. All six novels and three novellas in the series are Five Star reads." – Jane Reads

"Well written, with interesting characters." – Laura's Interests

"...a quick read, with humour, a good mystery and very interesting characters!" – Verietats

Drop Dead Ornaments

"I always forget how much I love this series until I read the next one and I fall in love all over again..." – Dru's Book Musings

"*Drop Dead Ornaments* is a delightful addition to the Anastasia Pollack Crafting Mystery series. More, please!" – *Suspense Magazine*

"I love protagonist Anastasia Pollack. She's witty and funny, and she can be sarcastic at times...A great whodunit, with riotous twists and turns, *Drop Dead Ornaments* was a fast, exciting read that really kept me on my toes." – Lisa Ks Book reviews

"*Drop Dead Ornaments* is such a fantastic book...I adore

Anastasia! She's clever, likable, fun to read about, and easy to root for." – Jane Reads

"...readers will be laughing continually at the antics of Anastasia and clan in *Drop Dead Ornaments*." – The Avid Reader

"I love this series! Not only is Anastasia a 'crime magnet,' she is hilarious and snarky, a delight to read about and a dedicated friend." – Mallory Heart's Cozies

"It is always a nice surprise when something I am reading has a tie in to actual news or events that are happening in the present moment. I don't want to spoil a major plot secret, but the timing could not have been better...Be prepared for a dysfunctional cast of quirky characters." – Laura's Interests

"This is a Tour de Force of a Murder/Mystery." – A Wytch's Book Review

"Lois Winston's cozy craft mystery *Drop Dead Ornaments* is an enjoyable...roller-coaster ride, with secrets and clues tugging the reader this way and that, and gentle climbs and drops of suspense and revelation to keep them reading." – Here's How It Happened

"...a light-hearted cozy mystery with lots of energy and definitely lots of action and interaction between characters." – Curling Up By the Fire

Handmade Ho-Ho Homicide

"Handmade Ho-Ho Homicide" is a laugh-out-loud, well plotted mystery, from a real pro! A ho-ho hoot!" – *Suspense Magazine*

"Merry *Crises*! Lois Winston has brought back Anastasia's delightful first-person narrative of family, friends, dysfunction, and murder, and made it again very entertaining! Anastasia's clever quips, fun stories, and well-deserved digs kept me smiling, and reading the many funny parts to my husband...does that count as two thumbs up in one?" – *Kings River Life Magazine*

"Once again, the author knows how to tell a story that immediately grabbed my attention and I couldn't put this book down until the last page was read.... This was one of the best books in this delightfully lovable series and I can't wait to see what exciting adventures await Anastasia and her friends." – Dru's Book Musings

"This was such a fun quick read. I can't wait to read more of this series." – A Chick Who Reads

"The story had me on the edge of my seat the entire time." – 5 Stars, Baroness Book Trove

"Christmas, cozy mystery, craft, how can I not love this book? Humor, twists and turns, adorable characters make this story truly engaging from the first to last page." – LibriAmoriMiei

"Take a murder mystery, add some light-hearted humor and weird characters, sprinkle some snow and what you get is *Handmade Ho-Ho Homicide*—a perfect Christmas Cozy read." –5 stars, The Book Decoder

A Sew Deadly Cruise
"*A Sew Deadly Cruise* is absolutely delightful, and I was sorry when it was over. I devoured every word!" – *Suspense* Magazine
"Engaging Drama! Brilliant! *A Sew Deadly Cruise* earns 5/5 Upgraded Cabins. Winston's witty first-person narrative and banter keeps me a fan. Loved it!" –*Kings River Life* Magazine

"The author knows how to tell a story with great aplomb and when all was said and done, this was one fantastic whodunit that left me craving for more thrilling adventures." – Dru's Book Musings

"The combo of investigating and fun makes for a great read. The author does a good job of keeping the killer a secret. Overall a fun read that cozy fans are sure to enjoy." – Books a Plenty Book Reviews

"Winston has a gift for writing complicated cozy mysteries while entertaining and educating." – Here's How it Happened

Stitch, Bake, Die!

"Lois Winston has crafted another clever tale...with a backdrop of cross stitching, buttercream, bribery, sabotage, rumors, and murder...with vivid descriptions, witty banter, and clever details leading to an exciting and shocking conclusion. All making for a page-turner experience to delight cozy fans." – *Kings River Life* magazine

"...a crème de la crème of a cozy read." – Brianne's Book Reviews

"...a well-plotted mystery that takes the term 'crafty old lady' to new heights." – Mysteries with Character

"This story is fast-paced with wacky characters, a fun resort setting, and a puzzling mystery to solve." – Nancy J. Cohen, author of the Bad Hair Day Mysteries

"Lots of action, a bevy of quirky characters, and a treasure trove of secrets add up to another fine read from Lois Winston." – Maggie Toussaint, author of the Seafood Caper Mysteries, Lindsey & Ike Mysteries, and the Dreamwalker Mysteries

"The mystery was nicely executed, with bits and pieces of clues here and there as well as humorous interludes that enhanced the telling of this tale. This is another great addition to this engagingly entertaining series and I'm patiently waiting for the wedding of the century." – Dru's Book Musings

Books by Lois Winston

Anastasia Pollack Crafting Mystery series
Assault with a Deadly Glue Gun
Death by Killer Mop Doll
Revenge of the Crafty Corpse
Decoupage Can Be Deadly
A Stitch to Die For
Scrapbook of Murder
Drop Dead Ornaments
Handmade Ho-Ho Homicide
A Sew Deadly Cruise
Stitch, Bake, Die!

Anastasia Pollack Crafting Mini-Mysteries
Crewel Intentions
Mosaic Mayhem
Patchwork Peril
Crafty Crimes (all 3 novellas in one volume)

Empty Nest Mystery Series
Definitely Dead
Literally Dead

Romantic Suspense
Love, Lies and a Double Shot of Deception
Lost in Manhattan (writing as Emma Carlyle)
Someone to Watch Over Me (writing as Emma Carlyle)

Romance and Chick Lit
Talk Gertie to Me
Four Uncles and a Wedding (writing as Emma Carlyle)
Hooking Mr. Right (writing as Emma Carlyle)
Finding Hope (Writing as Emma Carlyle)

Novellas and Novelettes
Elementary, My Dear Gertie
Moms in Black, A Mom Squad Caper
Once Upon a Romance
Finding Mr. Right

Children's Chapter Book
The Magic Paintbrush

Nonfiction
Top Ten Reasons Your Novel is Rejected
House Unauthorized
Bake, Love, Write
We'd Rather Be Writing

Handmade
Ho-Ho
Homicide

LOIS WINSTON

Cover design by L. Winston

ISBN:978-1-940795-46-1

DEDICATION

In loving memory of my oldest and dearest friend Janice Kerr Boot, a woman who epitomized the true meaning of friendship.

ACKNOWLEDGMENTS

Where would authors be without readers? While writing this book, I couldn't decide on a craft to feature. Special thanks to newsletter subscribers Judy Weaver and Faith Creech for their suggestion of greeting card crafts.

I've been to various mystery conventions where auctions are held to raise money for local charities. Readers love to bid on having a character named for them. So I ran a contest for the naming of a character in *Handmade Ho-Ho Homicide*. That honor and a copy of *Handmade Ho-Ho Homicide* went to Robyn Konopka.

Sometimes readers will write to me with suggestions for future books. Awhile back I heard from Nancy Eady. She loved Tino Martinelli from *Decoupage Can Be Deadly* and asked if I had plans to bring him back in a future book. I hadn't thought about doing so until Nancy planted the idea in my head. If you, too, loved Tino, you can thank Nancy for his return.

I'm always grateful for the experts who take the time to answer my questions. Special thanks to Michael Maloof for answering my questions regarding computer security and tracing a remote connection back to the source. Also, thanks to Kia Dennis and Wally Lind for answering my questions regarding subpoenas.

And finally, as always, special thanks to Donnell Bell and Irene Peterson for their superb editorial skills.

ONE

Ira, the unwelcome elf, had struck again. At least, I assumed Ira was the culprit. Who else would fill my postage stamp front lawn with more than a dozen enormous inflatable cartoon characters? I sat in my car and stared out the window in disbelief. The entire Peanuts gang, half a dozen yellow Minions, and a smirking neon green Grinch, all decked out in Christmas finery, swayed and bounced to a recording of "Santa Claus is Coming to Town." The music was so loud I heard it through my Jetta's closed windows—with the engine running and the radio currently giving the four-day weather forecast.

Two-and-a-half weeks ago I'd arrived home from one of the worst days of my life (no hyperbole, given someone had tried to kill me and nearly succeeded) to find my house ablaze with enough Christmas lights to be seen by the astronauts on the International Space Station. Now this.

Enough was more than enough. I'd asked. I'd pleaded. I'd demanded. Nothing got through to Ira Pollack, the half-brother-in-law who'd shown up at my front door last summer and who continued to try to weasel his way into my life with unwelcome gifts.

But Ira can't take a hint, even when you club him over the head with it, and although I've repeatedly asked him to stop, I can't bring myself to go full rhymes-with-witch on him. Being too nice is one of my many failings.

Besides, Ira means well. And I have to admit, albeit grudgingly, I am indebted to the man. Case in point, my used Jetta, which he insisted on selling me at cost when I was forced to put my Hyundai rust bucket out to pasture. Given my precarious financial state, I don't know what I would have done if not for Ira's generosity. However, he's but one more complication I don't need in my already overly complicated life.

My name is Anastasia Pollack. Look me up in Webster's, and you'll find I'm defined as the epitome of the clueless wife.

Speaking of my Jetta, the vehicle's interior filled with light as another car pulled behind me. I killed the engine and stepped out into the frigid December night, my boots crunching on the driveway's packed snow, to find Zack exiting his Boxster.

Zachary Barnes is the one good thing that has happened in my life since my husband dropped dead in Las Vegas last winter—after raiding our joint piggy bank and racking up a Mt. Everest of debt.

In one of my first cost-cutting measures, I rented out the apartment above my garage, formerly my home office/studio, to Zack. He's since become considerably more than a tenant.

"Ira?" he asked, simultaneously hooking his backpack over one shoulder and cocking his head toward the lawn circus.

I shrugged. "Who else?"

Zack crunched his way over to me, and we headed toward the back door. "Seems odd he'd wait so long. I wonder why he didn't include these when he surprised you with the light display."

"Don't know, don't care. I'm pulling the plug as soon as I figure out where it is." Which would probably entail scrambling through the snow-covered shrubbery to find the power source. I'd deactivated more than half the lights first chance I got. I didn't care if they were the eco-friendly LED variety. They'd still run up my electric bill.

"Here." Zack handed me his backpack and retraced his steps to the front of the house. He crunched his way across the snowy lawn and headed for the rear of Snoopy's doghouse. Bending down, he found the spot where the power cord connected to the doghouse. With a quick yank he dislodged the snow camouflaging the cord as it snaked toward the house. He then followed the cord to where it plugged into an indoor/outdoor power strip nestled under an azalea bush. A second power strip sat beside it. Zack flipped the switches on both. The music died, and the characters slowly melted into the snow.

"Thank you, Dorothy!" I said as he retraced his footsteps.

He chuckled. "I suppose that makes you one of the flying monkeys?"

"This flying monkey is freezing her tootsies off. Let's get into the house."

We stripped out of our coats and boots in the mudroom and stepped into the kitchen where I inhaled the inviting aroma of roasting chicken with onions and carrots. At least one of my sons had arrived home ahead of us and remembered the text I'd sent to take dinner out of the refrigerator and place it in the oven at five-thirty.

We found both boys doing homework in the bedroom they now shared, thanks to their father permanently sticking us with his semi-invalid mother, an octogenarian communist who'd never had a kind word for me. Karl Pollack was the gift that kept on giving, though certainly not in a good way.

"Where's your grandmother?" I asked Nick and Alex, noticing her dog camped on Nick's bed. Ralph, the Shakespeare-quoting African Grey I'd inherited from my great-aunt Penelope Periwinkle, kept watch from atop a bookcase under the windows, but as soon as he spied Zack, he flapped his wings and made a beeline—or should I say parrot line?—for him, landing on his shoulder and nuzzling his beak against Zack's five o'clock shadow. Zack reached into his shirt pocket and offered the bird a sunflower seed.

"Haven't seen her," said Alex.

"*Would I had never seen her*," squawked Ralph after devouring his treat. "*Anthony and Cleopatra*. Act One, Scene Two."

Ditto, Ralph. The parrot had an uncanny knack for spouting the Bard's most appropriate quotes for any given situation.

"She wasn't here when we got home," said Nick.

"Did either of you walk Devil Dog?" Devil Dog, aka Mephisto, was my mother-in-law's French bulldog, although she'd named him Manifesto after the communist treatise. However, when he first invaded our home, he acted more like a hell-raising devil. So I dubbed him Mephisto. The boys simply called him Devil Dog.

Lately Lucille has abdicated all responsibility for her pet and spends most of her time with her fellow Daughters of the October Revolution. I suspect she's punishing the dog because he now prefers our company to hers. So be it. Although his nicknames have stuck—mostly because we all refuse to call him Manifesto—

he's mellowed in his old age, which is more than I can say for his owner. I'll take Devil Dog over Lucille Pollack any day.

"I took him out about an hour ago," said Nick. "Those blow-up cartoon characters in the yard scared the crap out of him."

"They didn't do much for me, either. Do you know how they got here?"

"Uncle Ira?" asked Alex.

"That's my guess."

"They were up when we got home," said Nick.

"They're down now, and they're staying down," I said. "After dinner I'm returning them to him."

~*~

Lucille hobbled into the house within minutes of dinner coming out of the oven. Worse yet, Harriet Kleinhample, her mini-me minion, followed close behind her.

So much for a peaceful dinner. Of all Lucille's cohorts, Harriet, who bears an uncanny resemblance to the actress who played Maude's mother in *Golden Girls*, was her staunchest ally. As such, she was second only to my mother-in-law in her contempt for me.

Harriet was also the primary mode of transportation for the Daughters of the October Revolution, all the others having given up driving—either voluntarily or involuntarily—before I met them. Since Harriet had recently been involved in a hit-and-run, she should no longer have a valid driver's license. She probably didn't, but that wouldn't stop her from getting behind the wheel of her ancient, battered VW minibus.

Nick had already set the kitchen table. As he scooped up the plates and utensils to move everything to the dining room table, Lucille poked her head into the kitchen. "Harriet is joining us for dinner," she announced.

"Of course, she is," Nick muttered behind her departing back as I quietly indicated he should leave the plates on the stove.

Luckily, Lucille hadn't heard her grandson. She was already off on a rant about the tacky deflated Christmas decorations littering my front lawn.

"We didn't put them up," I heard Alex tell her. "Besides, they're not staying."

"So, this is the work of that imposter?" she asked. "The lights weren't enough of an abomination? He has to turn us into a sideshow exhibit?"

"If you mean Uncle Ira, probably. We don't know for sure."

"That man is no more your uncle than I am," she said. All evidence to the contrary—including the fact that Ira looked the spitting image of Karl in his younger, thinner, less bald days—Lucille refused to believe that her beloved Isidore had walked out on her and subsequently married and fathered a second son.

According to my mother-in-law, J. Edgar Hoover had abducted and murdered Karl's father. She even once claimed the FBI had buried his body under the goalposts at Giants Stadium. Isidore may have been a union activist once upon a time, but he was no Jimmy Hoffa. Besides, no bodies were ever discovered buried under the goalposts or anywhere else in the stadium—not Karl's father and not Jimmy Hoffa.

Lucille and Harriet settled themselves at the dining room table and waited. "What if you don't serve them?" asked Nick.

Lately I've noticed both boys becoming more intolerant of their grandmother. Not that I blame them. We'd all enjoyed a recent, if short-lived, reprieve when Lucille and her scofflaw cohorts went on the lam and headed for Cuba. Unfortunately, they never made it.

Lucille was never supposed to become a permanent resident of Casa Pollack. Of course, when she temporarily moved in with us, I still thought my husband was a fine, upstanding human being. Live and learn.

I turned to my son. "Really, Nick? I need to instigate World War III over roast chicken?"

"Sorry, Mom. I—"

Before he could finish his thought, Lucille bellowed, "We have no plates, Anastasia!"

"Should I bring out the plates?" asked Alex.

"Not yet," I said.

The last time I'd served family style, Lucille and Harriet had helped themselves to half the food before the rest of us had taken our seats around the table. For a woman who stood several inches shy of five feet tall, Harriet Kleinhample could eat us all under the table and come back for seconds. And thirds. Only Lucille packed away more food at each meal than her diminutive disciple. Tonight I'd turn the tables on them.

As soon as Zack had finished carving the chicken, I placed a slice of breast meat and a normal serving of carrots and roasted potatoes on two plates. Handing one to each boy, I said, "For your grandmother and Harriet. Then come back to help yourselves."

Nick glanced down at the plate in his hands. "They are going to be so pi—angry," he said, before carrying the plate into the dining room.

True, but everyone would have a fair share of dinner this evening.

From the dining room I heard Lucille ask Alex, "What's this?"

"Dinner," he said.

"We're not children," said Harriet. "We can serve ourselves!"

"Not tonight," said Nick.

I heard an undercurrent of grumbling from Lucille and Harriet but couldn't make out what they said.

Nick and Alex returned to the kitchen without engaging further with the curmudgeonly commies. "How much should we take?" asked Alex, picking up a plate and serving spoon.

"As much as you'd like," I said. "Just leave enough for Zack and me." After serving themselves, the boys headed into the dining room.

Zack and I filled our plates with the remaining food and carried them into the dining room. If looks could kill, those octogenarian vultures would be picking at our bones.

Lucille and Harriet maintained a torrent of complaints throughout the meal. The four of us refused to respond until Zack pounded his fist on the table. "Enough! One more complaint, and I take your plates away."

"You wouldn't dare!" cried Lucille.

"Try me." He stood and reached across the table for Lucille and Harriet's plates. Both women grabbed hold of their dishes and held on as if they were in the siege of Leningrad instead of my dining room. Zack returned to his chair. "That was your final warning."

Sullen silence commenced, broken only by the sounds of silverware clattering on dishes. I turned to my sons and initiated normal dinnertime conversation. "How was school today?"

Nick grinned. "Pretty cool, Mom. We learned all about the collapse of the Soviet Union in history class."

I nearly choked on a carrot. Was he deliberately trying to get a rise out of his grandmother and Harriet? I glanced over at the two women. Both had turned a deep shade of purple. At any moment

I expected to see steam shooting from their ears.

"What did you learn?" asked Alex.

Had they rehearsed this act of defiance? If so, it worked. Lucille and Harriet shoveled the last bits of food on their plates into their mouths and stormed out of the dining room. A moment later the sounds of some inane reality TV show blared through the house.

"How much longer do we have to put up with her?" asked Nick.

"'Til death we do part," I said, silently adding *thanks to your father.*

"Can't that be arranged?"

"Nick!"

"Chill, Mom. I'm just kidding." He grinned sheepishly before adding, "Although we do know a guy who knows a guy, right?"

More than one, actually, including Karl's former bookie and my mother's ex-husband. Both now reside in federal prisons on murder convictions.

"This is New Jersey," said Zack. "*Everyone* knows a guy who knows a guy."

Including my sons' father who'd arranged a hit on his mother a year and a half ago, only to have her survive. But Alex and Nick didn't know half of what I'd learned about their father after his death, and if I had my way, I'd take those secrets to my grave.

As for Lucille, she'd never believe me anyway. She refused to accept what little I'd told her about Karl gambling away our life savings and sticking me with debt equal to the GNP of Uzbekistan. In her eyes, Karl was the communist equivalent of a saint—if there is such a thing.

~*~

After dinner the boys, Zack and I bundled up in our winter gear to wrestle the Grinch and his now-deflated fellow inflatables into the trunk and backseat of my car. They barely fit. Leaving Alex and Nick at home, Zack and I headed across town to Ira's new McMansion.

Ira had surprised us a few weeks ago with the unwelcome news that he'd bought a home in Westfield. I didn't care all that much for Ira when he lived on the other side of the state. I'd prefer he lived on the other side of the country. Having him not only on the other side of town, but on the same street as Alex's girlfriend Sophie Lambert and her father Shane thrilled me no end. At least the two houses were about a mile apart.

Ira had closed on his five thousand square feet of new construction last Friday and moved in over the weekend. He'd driven me past the house before he took possession. When he'd called on Sunday to invite us over for brunch and a tour, I'd begged off with the standard sorry-but-we-have-plans excuse, even if the only item on my schedule for the day was to avoid Ira and his brood.

We hit traffic shortly before passing the Lambert house. Vehicles crept along as though we were stuck on the Garden State Parkway in the middle of rush hour instead of the normally quiet residential area. Parked cars lined the curb on both sides of the street for as far as we could see. "What gives?"

Zack shrugged. "Beats me. An accident? I see flashing lights up ahead."

"Must be a bad one. I'm not willing to spend an hour in traffic to return the Grinch and his pals to their rightful owner."

"Agreed. I'll turn at the next intersection."

However, before we inched our way to the cross street, we saw Shane and Sophie standing on the sidewalk in front of their house.

Zack tapped the horn and pulled into their driveway.

"Come to see the show?" asked Shane when Zack killed the engine and we stepped from the car.

"Show?" I asked.

"Can't you hear the music?" asked Sophie.

Now that she mentioned it, I did hear what sounded like a brass band playing Christmas carols. "Is something going on at the elementary school tonight?"

"Not the school," said Shane.

"You don't know?" asked Sophie.

I didn't like the sound of that. "Know what?"

"You have to see it to believe it," said Shane. "Up for a crisp moonlight walk?"

"Is it worth it?" I asked.

"Trust me," said Shane. "You're going to want to see this."

I turned to Zack. "I'm game if you are."

He nodded to Shane. "Lead on, Macduff."

Sophie giggled. "You sound like Ralph."

"They've developed a symbiotic relationship," I said. If Zack and I ever split up, he'll probably sue me for custody."

"I guess you'd better not split up, then," said Sophie. "I'd miss Ralph." When I raised my eyebrows, she added, "And Zack, too, of course."

"Of course."

As we walked up the street, the lights grew brighter, and the music grew louder. Multi-colored lasers arced across the sky.

Several families passed us, heading in the opposite direction. The adults shook their heads and muttered comments like, "unbelievably tacky" and "This is Westfield, not Staten Island." But the children had huge grins on their faces.

"How much farther?" I asked after we'd hiked along the sidewalk for about ten minutes.

"About half a mile," said Shane.

I was beginning to have a queasy feeling in the pit of my stomach. It had nothing to do with dinner and everything to do with my half-brother-in-law. I stopped short and confronted Shane. "Tell me we're not headed to Ira's house."

"I wish I could."

I had no idea Ira celebrated Christmas. Then again, we'd never discussed religion. Perhaps his father had jettisoned the "opiate of the masses" indoctrination and returned to the religion of his youth when he and Lucille split. However, those particular religious beliefs aren't supposed to include Christmas. Since I knew nothing about Ira's first wife, other than she'd passed away, perhaps he'd converted when he married her.

"Didn't he just move in?" asked Sophie. "Dad and I spent half a day decorating the outside of our house, and we only strung lights and hung some wreaths on the windows and front door."

"I'm sure his employees handled the installation," said Zack.

"Or he hired a professional decorating crew," I said.

After the unwelcome surprise he left at my house, it didn't shock me that Ira was a card-carrying member of the Over-the-Top Christmas Decorators Club. Although I suspected his motivation had less to do with impressing his neighbors and more to do with his need to impress his kids. Whatever Melody, Harmony, and Isaac wanted, Melody, Harmony, and Isaac got.

The closer we drew to Ira's house, the louder the music and brighter the lights became, launching a full out assault on my senses. A bass drum keeping time to "The March of the Toy Soldiers" reverberated in my head, nearly drowning out an undercurrent of shouting. Not the happy shouts of excited children in awe of a spectacle that belonged on Main Street in Disneyland but angry adult shouting, interspersed with four-letter name-calling.

We pushed our way through a crowd that had gathered on the sidewalk. More people wandered around the display, even coming and going from the backyard, where I assumed there were more decorations.

Ira stood in the middle of his front lawn. A group of extremely irate adults surrounded him. They wildly gesticulated as they verbally bombarded my extremely perplexed-looking half-brother-in-law.

"Neighbors," said Shane, raising his own voice to be heard over the commotion.

Exceedingly unhappy neighbors from the looks of it. Not that I blamed them. Ira had turned his home into a three-ring circus. Row upon row of multi-colored string lights wrapped around every vertical surface of his house, snaked up and down his roof, and wound around the porch columns and railings. More lights blanketed the shrubbery in front of the porch. If my house had blazed with enough lights to be seen from the International Space Station, Ira's would be visible to aliens in the outer regions of the solar system.

Larger-than-life mechanical nutcrackers festooned with more lights stood at attention, saluting along either side of the path leading to the house. Inflatables of every cartoon character imaginable filled the lawn. Laser lights, choreographed to the music blaring from speakers, shot into the sky.

But the *coup de grace* was the railroad track that encircled the house. At a break midway between the nutcrackers, it crossed over the path leading from the sidewalk to the porch. On it ran eight life-sized mechanical reindeer pulling a sleigh. Inside the sleigh a waving Santa bellowed "ho-ho-ho" every few seconds. And of course, the reindeer, Santa, and sleigh were also covered in hundreds of twinkling lights. Luckily, the reindeer pranced at a slow enough pace that no one heading to the house risked getting trampled—as long as they stopped, looked, and listened before crossing the tracks.

"I've seen enough," I said, turning to inch my way back through the crowd of gawkers. No way was I getting involved in Ira's battle with his neighbors. As far as I was concerned, they had every right to be annoyed with him. What was he thinking? Then again, Ira doesn't think. He constantly acts on impulse, assuming his actions will be appreciated.

I had nearly cleared the mass of onlookers when a bulldog of a man barreled into me and kept going without so much as an "excuse me" or an "I'm sorry." Luckily, he'd shoved me into Zack, who broke my fall.

"Hey!" I yelled, but he ignored me as he continued on his path, shoving aside anyone who didn't move out of his way.

Seconds later the crowd gasped. A woman screamed. All at once the music died, and darkness descended over the house and yard. The night filled with the sound of air simultaneously rushing from dozens of deflating cartoon characters—and blaring sirens growing louder by the second. People grabbed their children and quickly disappeared into nearby homes while others, protectively clutching their offspring, hurried down the street toward parked cars, leaving Ira flat on his back across his snow-covered lawn.

TWO

Zack, Shane, Sophie, and I rushed toward Ira. "What hurts?" I asked as Zack and Shane helped him to his feet.

"I think he busted my nose." A trickle of blood ran from one nostril and dripped onto Ira's ski jacket. I scrounged for a pack of tissues from my purse, removed several, and handed them to him.

Zack pulled out his phone and shined a light on Ira, scrutinizing his face, while Ira gingerly dabbed at the sticky moisture on his upper lip. "Doesn't look like he hit you that hard. Luckily, the snow cushioned your fall. I don't see any obvious signs of concussion."

No concussion and what appeared to be an unbroken nose. Ira's nasal cartilage seemed unfazed by its recent encounter with an assailant's fist. I wondered if he'd even wind up with a black eye. Time would tell. The guy may have had the build of Jake "Raging Bull" LaMotta, but the visual evidence showed he threw a punch more like Ferdinand the Bull.

The front door opened, and Ira's kids rushed onto the porch.

"I called the cops," yelled Melody—or Harmony—I could never tell Ira's pre-teen identical twins apart.

Suddenly the Christmas lights covering the house blazed back on. I glanced up at the porch to find nine-year-old Isaac tapping away on a tablet. The music started playing again. Then the nutcrackers lit up and saluted. The fans whirred, struggling to spring the deflated inflatable characters back to life, but most failed to rise from the dead. Finally, the reindeer resumed pulling Santa and his sleigh around the house.

The guy who'd punched Ira had killed the inflatable characters, but not by yanking the plug on the holiday horror show. Apparently he'd slashed quite a few before disappearing into the departing crowd. Isaac had pulled the cyber-plug on the remainder.

"Let's get you inside," Zack told Ira.

However, before we took more than two steps toward the house, a police cruiser with siren blaring and lights flashing, drove up to the curb, and out stepped Officers Harley and Fogarty.

I first met the local Westfield cops nearly a year ago after Karl's bookie broke into my house. Since then, we've interacted on multiple occasions. At times I've wondered if I've had more face time with both men over the last year than their fellow officers, the police chief, or possibly even their wives—assuming they're married. Neither has ever offered up any personal information, even though at this point they know some pretty intimate details about my family and me.

Meanwhile, the two cops took one look at me and shook their heads in unison. "Didn't expect to find you here, Mrs. Pollack," said Harley, the older, shorter, and stockier of the two.

"That would make two of us," I said.

"Someone called 9-1-1 from this address to report a brawl in progress," said Fogarty. "Looks pretty calm to me."

"It was nothing," said Ira. "My daughter shouldn't have called you. She overreacted."

"I did not overreact!" shouted Melody—or Harmony. She stomped down the porch steps and headed toward us. Her sister followed. With hands on hips, she confronted the officers. "They were ganging up on my father, and one of them slugged him."

Harley and Fogarty stepped around the girls toward Zack and Shane. "Which one of you threw the punch?" asked Harley.

"It wasn't them," said Ira. "They came to my rescue."

"So who hit you?" asked Harley, withdrawing a notepad and pencil from inside his jacket pocket.

Ira shook his head. "I don't know. It all happened so fast. The guy came out of nowhere."

Harley and Fogarty glanced around at the empty street. "Just like that and you didn't notice him until he was in your face?"

"There was a huge crowd of people here at the time," said Ira. "They came to see the light display."

"And all of a sudden the crowd vanished into thin air?" asked Harley. "You got David Copperfield hiding in Santa's sleigh?"

"No, they dispersed after the guy attacked me. Ten minutes ago the street was lined with cars and the sidewalk crowded with onlookers."

"Yeah, we did see more traffic than normal for this time of night as we headed down the street," admitted Fogarty.

"I guess they got scared and took off," said Ira. "I can't blame them. You never know with crazies these days, right?"

I noticed Ira had failed to mention the group of angry neighbors accosting him over his million-megawatt extravaganza.

"I'm confused," said Harley. "Your daughter said *they* were ganging up on you. You claim one person punched you. Care to explain?"

"She's mistaken."

"I am not!" cried the twin in question. "There were all these people yelling about our Christmas lights."

"We were having a discussion," said Ira, "and the guy who socked me wasn't part of the group I was speaking with. I told you, he came out of nowhere."

"I can attest to that," I said. "He nearly pushed me to the ground as he barreled his way through the crowd to get to Ira."

Pencil poised, Harley turned to me. "Can you describe the guy, Mrs. Pollack?"

I shook my head. "Other than his build?"

"Which was?" asked Fogarty.

"Average height. Stocky."

"That's all?" asked Harley.

"He was bundled up in a puffy black ski jacket. So maybe he wasn't really all that stocky but only looked stocky, and he wore a dark knit ski hat pulled low over his forehead."

"That's it?" asked Fogarty. "What about the rest of you?" he asked Zack, Shane, and Sophie.

"We were walking away when it happened," said Zack. "Our backs were turned to Ira. We didn't realize the guy punched him until someone screamed and Ira's kid turned off the lights and music. Everyone else quickly fled the area."

Harley turned his attention to Melody, Harmony, and Isaac. "Which one of you turned off the display?"

The twins motioned toward their brother on the porch.

"Come down here, son," called Harley.

"I'm not your son."

"Get down here anyway."

Isaac took his time walking the several feet to where we all stood.

"Why did you turn everything off?" asked Harley.

"To get them to leave."

"Who?" asked Fogarty. "The people who'd come to see the display?"

"No, the guys yelling about it. It's our house. Why can't we have as many lights as we want?"

"Yeah," piped in Harmony—or Melody. "They have no right to tell us what we can and can't do."

"So who were the people yelling at your father?" asked Harley.

"The stupid neighbors," said one of the girls.

"No one was yelling at me," said Ira.

"They were, too," said Isaac. "I hate this town. Why'd we have to move here?"

"Yeah," agreed one of his sisters. "The people here suck. Everyone loved our Christmas displays at our old house."

Her sister chimed in. "There were contests each year for who had the best display. We did a new one each year and always took First Place."

I suppose that explained all the lights and inflatable characters that found their way to my house. Ira had probably gifted me with some of last year's winning decorations.

"People here hate Christmas," said Isaac.

Harley turned back to Ira. "Who were the neighbors arguing with you?"

"I told you," said Ira, "we weren't arguing."

Harley sighed his impatience. "Let me rephrase, then. "Who

were the neighbors having a *discussion* with you about your Christmas display?"

"They didn't introduce themselves."

"You don't know any of your neighbors?" asked Fogarty.

"We just moved in this past weekend."

"I'm guessing they didn't bring a basket of muffins to welcome you to the neighborhood," said Fogarty.

His partner frowned at him. "So, if you're only here a few days, and you claim there were crowds of people clogging the street and sidewalk," he waved toward the house, "how'd people know about all of this?"

Ira glanced down at his son. "I posted on Snapchat and Instagram," said Isaac.

Why did that not surprise me?

"Were the neighbors upset over the crowds of strangers on the street?" asked Harley.

Ira nodded.

"Nothing else?"

"Everything," said Isaac. "They said it was tacky and trashy."

The officers eyed the display just as the eight reindeer rounded the house once again and Santa waved at us from his sleigh. "Can't imagine why they'd think that," said Fogarty.

Seriously? I certainly hoped he was going for sarcasm. I have nothing against tasteful holiday décor. I've seen some truly elegant, brightly lit displays over the years in our town, but what Ira had created was neither tasteful nor elegant.

"I know," said Isaac, nodding in agreement with Fogarty. "Isn't it the coolest thing ever?"

Sophie looked over at me and executed an exaggerated eye roll. I thought she'd burst out laughing at any moment.

"Getting back to the guy who punched you," said Harley, returning his attention to Ira. "Anyone else ticked off with you for some reason?"

Ira smiled at them. "Of course not, Officer. To know me is to love me." He nodded toward me. "Just ask my sister-in-law."

My jaw dropped as Harley and Fogarty turned to face me. What was I expected to say? The only words that came to mind sounded really lame when I uttered them. "*Half*-sister-in-law. He's my deceased husband's half-brother." Maybe they already knew that. At the moment I couldn't remember if the officers had ever met Ira on one of their many visits to my home.

Meanwhile, my toes had officially morphed into ice cubes. I'd witnessed murder investigations that entailed less questioning. Someone needed to move this encounter along before we all succumbed to frostbite. Since no one else was stepping forward, I nominated myself. "I don't know what more we can tell you, Officers."

Harley flipped his notebook closed. "Not much to go on here, especially if you don't care to cooperate, Mr. Pollack."

"You know what I know, Officer."

Harley eyed Ira skeptically. "Keep in mind perps often strike again. You're absolutely sure you didn't recognize the guy?"

Ira shrugged. "I'm sure whoever it was probably just had too much to drink. Maybe he was on the wrong block."

Right. Too bad Harley and Fogarty couldn't question Santa, the reindeer, the nutcrackers, and the inflatable cartoon characters. They'd probably be far more forthcoming than Ira. Maybe the Elf on the Shelf had been staring out the window and witnessed something.

Before leaving, Harley said, "Mr. Pollack, if you want to

maintain a good relationship with your new neighbors, I suggest you lower the volume on your music and shut everything down for the night at a reasonable hour. You wouldn't want anyone filing a complaint against you."

"For what?" asked Isaac. "We haven't done anything wrong. They were doing all the yelling and punching."

"Disturbing the peace," said Fogarty.

"And keep your son off social media," added Harley. "We don't need an influx of lookie-loos blocking our streets and creating a traffic nightmare."

Too late for that. Once something is posted on social media, it lives forever.

"Who do they think they are?" asked Melody—or Harmony—as Harley and Fogarty returned to their squad car.

"They can't make me stay off social media," said Isaac.

I doubted Ira had enough control over his kids to get them to do anything they didn't want to do. I certainly had never seen any effort in that direction. Melody, Harmony, and Isaac had their father wrapped around their spoiled pinkies. Did Ira realize he could face charges should Isaac's actions jeopardize public safety from the increased traffic?

Isaac stomped off toward the house, followed by his sisters. The last one to cross the transom slammed the door.

"Why don't you all come in?" suggested Ira. "I'll make hot cocoa."

"I don't think so," I said. "It's getting late. I'm sure you have to get your kids ready for bed."

"And I have homework to finish," said Sophie.

Ira looked like we'd just told him there was no Santa Claus. "What about Christmas?" he asked. "You will come for

Christmas, won't you, Anastasia?"

"I don't know, Ira, I—"

"We could do brunch. Or lunch. Or dinner. You choose. Please say you'll come."

At some point I'd run out of excuses for avoiding Ira and his brood, especially now that they lived in the same town. I hated to hurt his feelings, but the last thing I wanted was to spend Christmas with Ira. Besides, my sons would never forgive me for ruining their holiday if I forced them to spend it with their half-relatives.

For the second time that evening my brain went AWOL. Before I could send out a search party, Sophie said, "Anastasia and her family are spending Christmas with Dad and me. We're having brunch together, then spending the day serving Christmas dinners to the homeless in Plainfield."

Nothing like having your teenage son's girlfriend save your bacon, even if these plans were news to me. Had Sophie made them up on the spot, or had Alex forgotten to mention he'd nominated us for a day of volunteering? Not that I was complaining. What better way to spend Christmas than to remember its true meaning?

Ira studied us, as if trying to ascertain whether Sophie had told the truth. Finally, he said, "That's very...noble of all of you." Then he added, "Why not drop by for some eggnog afterwards? I'm sure you'll be ready to relax at that point."

Relax with Ira and his kids? Being with Ira, Melody, Harmony, and Isaac was the complete antithesis of relaxation.

I suppose I could put off the inevitable only so long, though. At some point I'd have to accept an invitation from Ira, and a cup of eggnog definitely outweighed a meal. With any luck, we could be in and out in under an hour. "That sounds lovely," I told him. "I'll text you when we're on our way." Maybe we'd be too exhausted, and I could use that as an excuse for not showing up. Or if we did go, we could plead fatigue and only stay long enough for a quick house tour.

"Wonderful! I promise, you'll be thrilled you came."

Thrilled? What did he imply by that? And did I really want to know?

~*~

As we hiked back toward Shane's house, he asked, "So what brought you to the neighborhood this evening if not to see Ira's sideshow? You never did say."

I told him about the Peanuts gang, the Minions, and the Grinch, all currently cooling their collapsed tootsies in the trunk and across the backseat of my Jetta.

"We could drive back over there now to return them," said Zack.

"I think I've had enough Ira drama for one night. I'll drop them off before work tomorrow morning. It's on the way, and I'll have an excuse for not staying."

"And if you're lucky, Ira will have already left for the day?"

"That, too." Zack knew me too well, but sometimes life is easier if you take the coward's way out.

I turned to Sophie. "So...about Christmas?"

"What about it?"

"Am I the last to know?"

In the glow of a nearby streetlight, I saw her brows knit together in confusion. "Alex didn't tell you?"

"No."

"I texted him earlier." She withdrew her phone from her jacket pocket. After yanking her mittens off with her teeth, she tapped the screen several times, then handed me the phone. Sure enough, there was a text to Alex about feeding the homeless on Christmas.

"He was helping load all of the unwanted lawn decorations into my car," I said, returning the phone. "He must not have heard his phone ping."

"You'll come, won't you?" she asked.

"Of course." After what Shane had recently done for Alex, there wasn't anything I wouldn't do for him and his daughter. Spending a few hours helping the homeless hardly compared to a full ride at Harvard.

After Karl had drained the boys' college accounts, Alex had resigned himself to attending community college next year. We could no longer afford Rutgers, let alone his Ivy League dream school. Meeting Shane and Sophie changed all that. Karl may have pulled the rug out from under us, but Shane and his private foundation had supplied a cushioned landing after I thwarted a kidnapping and cleared him of a murder rap.

When we arrived back at his house, the benefactor in question said, "I know you turned down Ira, but I make a mean Mexican hot cocoa."

"I'd love some," I said. "I need something to thaw me out."

"I thought that was my job," said Zack.

"There's thawing and then there's *thawing*," I said.

"TMI," said Sophie.

~*~

The next morning, I left the house half an hour early in order to deliver the Grinch and company to their rightful owner. I heard Lucille snoring away as I passed her bedroom. Alex and Nick had already driven to school, and Zack had taken off earlier for a meeting in D.C.

Zack is a world-renowned photojournalist who works for the Smithsonian, the National Geographic Society, and the World Wildlife Fund, among others. Personally, I think the photo gig is a cover for his real work as a government operative for one of the alphabet agencies—FBI, CIA, NSA—take your pick. He claims I'm delusional, but isn't that what every spy would say?

A fresh inch or two of snow covered the world while flurries continued to dance in the air. I cranked the Jetta's engine, turned the heater to full blast, and set about brushing snow from my car.

Ten minutes later I pulled out of my driveway as daybreak filtered through the remnants of the frigid night sky. I took my time, wary of hidden black ice that could result in a fender-bender. Or worse.

I arrived at Ira's house to find his Christmas lights on, half the cartoon characters still dead in the snow, the remainder waving in the breeze, and the reindeer still hauling Santa around the track. At least Ira had had the common sense to turn off the music overnight. Or maybe he'd adjusted the app so Isaac could no longer control the sound feature.

I stepped from my car, leaving the motor running while I fulfilled my task. As I walked toward the house with my first armload of Peanuts characters, I realized not a single interior light was on, at least none I could see. I climbed the steps and deposited Lucy and Linus on the porch floor. Then I peered through one of the windows that looked out onto the porch. The entire downstairs was enveloped in darkness. I listened at the front door for movement within but heard nothing other than the whirring of the fans that kept the lawn decorations inflated and the clickity-clack of the reindeer and sleigh as it made its way around the track.

I hadn't planned to dump and run. Really. However, it didn't appear that anyone was awake yet. Wouldn't it be better to leave everything on the porch and call Ira later to explain? I saw my decision as considerate rather than cowardly. At least that's what I convinced myself as I headed back to the car for another load.

I wrestled the Grinch from the car and half-carried, half-dragged him along the path. The reindeer and I arrived at the intersection of the path and tracks at exactly the same moment. I had no choice but to allow them the right of way. I waited. And waited. And waited. They were definitely taking their time this morning, hardly traveling at prancing speed. Then again, even mechanical reindeer probably grew sluggish after pulling Santa all night.

But I needed to get to work. My fingers and toes were turning to icicles, and I still had quite a few characters to remove from my car. Rather than wait any longer, I dropped the Grinch in front of the tracks and returned to the car to haul out Snoopy and his doghouse.

The last reindeer was crossing the path as I returned, Santa's sleigh following closely behind. As the giant red sleigh pulled in front of me, I realized why the reindeer were struggling to pull their load. Santa had company. Dead company.

THREE

With all the bodies I've encountered over the last year, you'd think I'd become used to seeing dead people. I hadn't, and I seriously doubted I ever would. As the sleigh crossed my path, I let loose a scream guaranteed to wake everyone on Prospect Street, if not all of Westfield.

Strangely enough, no one came running. Were all the surrounding homes soundproofed, or did people no longer care about their neighbors? Perhaps some had glanced out their windows but chose to turn a deaf ear, given where I stood. Too many of them had come to verbal fisticuffs with the property's new homeowner last night—not to mention one person who'd employed an actual fist.

By this time the reindeer and sleigh had rounded the house and were out of sight. Although it traveled at a snail's pace, I hadn't been able to identify the corpse. He—although it could very well be a she—was sprawled facedown across Santa's lap. A blanket of snow covered the body, leaving only a lumpy mound.

Was it Ira? Is that why there was no sign of activity within the house? Were his kids still sleeping, unaware their father was lying dead in Santa's sleigh?

I dropped Snoopy and his doghouse alongside the Grinch, raced back to my car, slammed the trunk, climbed into the driver's seat, and locked the doors. Then I pulled out my phone, called 9-1-1, and waited for the police to arrive.

Within minutes I heard police sirens. Shortly thereafter a squad car pulled up behind me, followed seconds later by an unmarked car. Two officers I didn't know stepped from the squad car while Detective Sam Spader hefted himself out from behind the wheel of his unmarked vehicle. When I exited my car, he took one look at me and shook his head. "Why am I not surprised?"

Detective Spader and I had history, going back to last summer when my mother-in-law became the prime suspect in the strangulation murder of her rehab roommate. Since then, we've interacted on far too many occasions, but I've earned his grudging respect—emphasis on grudging. I doubt any homicide detective likes an amateur upstaging him when it comes to solving a case.

Spader appeared more rumpled and haggard than usual. The dark circles and bags under his eyes made me wonder when he'd last slept. An overabundance of booze, cigarettes, and fast food had taken their toll over the years, and although he'd recently started paying attention to what he put into his body, he had a long way to go to counteract decades of bad health decisions.

Too late it occurred to me that I should have trashed Ira's unwelcome gifts. That way someone else would have discovered the corpse. Then again, that someone else might have been a group of young children on their way to school.

By arriving at Ira's this morning, I'd saved any number of

parents countless years of therapy for their kids and tens of thousands of dollars. Not that I was giving myself a pat on the back. I should probably be in therapy myself to help me come to terms with all the dead bodies I keep discovering. But since therapy sessions cost Benjamins, and I have none to spare, wine would have to suffice.

"So, where's this corpse?" asked Spader, scanning the Christmas-cluttered yard. "Other than the dead characters scattered around the yard."

"Give it a minute," I said. "It's on its way."

If I were anyone else, I'd now be cuffed and in the back of the squad car. Luckily, Detective Spader knew me well enough by now that if I said there was a dead body, he knew there was a dead body, even if he couldn't see it—yet. So instead of hauling my tush to the hoosegow for reporting a phony crime, he merely heaved a long, loud sigh and said, "It's way too early in the morning for games, Mrs. Pollack."

At that moment the reindeer rounded the side of the house and slowly made their way across the front yard. "Here it comes now," I said. "Check out Santa's lap."

Spader and the two uniformed officers strode across the yard to greet Santa. I followed. Spader took one look inside the sleigh, then told the officers, "Fischer, alert CSU to get over here ASAP. Norbert, figure out where the plug is to this thing and pull it."

Spader turned to me next. "Any idea who the deceased is?"

"Not without seeing his face. I'm hoping it's not my half-brother-in-law."

"Tuttnauer's son-in-law?" Spader's eyebrows disappeared under his standard issue knit cop cap. He knew all about Ira and his family ties to Lawrence Tuttnauer, who along with being Ira's ex-father-in-law, was also a murderer, mob money launderer, *and* my mother's ex-husband.

"The only half-brother-in-law I have." At least I hoped Ira was Karl's only half-sibling. Who knew what Isidore had been up to after he walked out on Lucille and before he married Ira's mother? Or even afterwards? Isidore Pollack could have been a serial philanderer for all I knew.

Spader turned his attention to the darkened McMansion. "He lives here?"

I nodded.

"Since when?"

"Moved in over the weekend."

"Did you try ringing the doorbell?"

I hadn't, but Spader didn't need to know that. "It doesn't appear anyone is home."

"Try calling him."

I jogged back to my car and fished my phone out of my purse. The non-dead Ira answered on the second ring. I exhaled my relief as he said, "Good morning, Anastasia. What a pleasant surprise!"

He wouldn't think so in a minute. "Where are you, Ira?"

"I'm taking the kids to school. They're finishing up the semester at their old school. What can I do for you?"

"Hold on a second." I pressed the phone against my coat so Ira couldn't hear me as I relayed the information to the detective.

Spader extended his beefy, calloused palm toward me. "Let me speak with him." He held the phone up to his ear and said, "Mr. Pollack, this is Detective Sam Spader of the Union County Police. I'm afraid there's been an incident at your home. I need you to return immediately."

He paused for a moment, then said, "I'd rather discuss that

when you get here, sir." Another pause. "No, not a fire. We'll wait for you." Spader ended the call before handing the phone back to me.

"I found a series of power strips," Norbert called from the porch. "You want me to wait until the sleigh comes around again before shutting down everything?"

"If we keep the body in the backyard," said Fischer, "we might draw less of a crowd."

"The more the merrier," said Spader. "There was an incident here last night. I want the two of you to start taking names as people begin to gather. Get witness statements. We'll also need to check security footage from surrounding homes."

"I was here last night," I told Spader.

"Again, why am I not surprised?" He whipped out his trusty spiral notepad and with pencil poised, said, "Let's hear it, Mrs. Pollack."

I told him why Zack and I had driven over last night and related what I'd observed of Ira's encounter with his neighbors and the punch that sent everyone scurrying for their homes and cars.

"What brought you back this morning?"

"Last night's rotten timing. I'm not in the habit of kicking a man when he's down."

Spader gestured toward the pile I'd dropped near the tracks. "I suppose that explains Snoopy and the Grinch?"

"Lucy and Linus are already on the porch. The remainder of the Peanuts gang and half a dozen Minions are still in my car."

Spader laughed. "Mrs. Pollack, you're the only person I know who could make such a statement with a straight face."

"I don't suppose I can continue to unload them."

"I'm afraid not. As I'm sure you're aware, this is now an active crime scene."

I was afraid of that. "May I at least leave? I need to get to work."

"I don't see why not. After all I know where to find you. But aren't you dying to know—"

I raised an eyebrow. *"Dying?* Really Detective?"

"Poor choice of words, but aren't you curious to know who our victim is?"

"Absolutely. No one I know is missing, though." At least I hoped that was the case. Wouldn't I have heard? "And as much as I feel for the victim—whoever that might be—I can't afford to lose half a day's pay by hanging around to find out. I'm sure you'll inform me at some point, right?" If nothing else, I'd hear it on the news.

At that moment CSU pulled up to the house. "Looks like we're about to find out," he said. "Stick around, Mrs. Pollack."

Rather than risking frostbite, I opted to sit in my car until Spader called me back to the sleigh. Not knowing how long I'd have to wait, I cranked up the heat and pulled out my phone to shoot off a text to my usually understanding editor-in-chief: *Unavoidably detained. Might be late to staff meeting.*

As I warmed my tootsies, a group of curious onlookers gathered on the snow-covered sidewalk. A screaming woman hadn't roused their curiosity enough for them to venture out into the bitter early morning cold, but a CSU van on their street drew them like vultures to carrion. As the crowd continued to grow, Officers Fischer and Norbert questioned each newcomer.

After about fifteen minutes Spader elbowed his way through the gathering, rapped on my window to draw my attention away from my phone, and beckoned me to follow him back to the sleigh.

Before stepping out of my car, this time I turned off the engine and grabbed my purse. For good measure I locked the door behind me. The last thing I needed was someone hopping into my running Jetta and taking it for a joyride. Not that many Westfield residents would pull such a stunt, but anyone who had committed murder wouldn't think twice about stealing a car.

As Spader shepherded me toward the sleigh, he said, "The crime scene team isn't finished, but they've uncovered enough of the vic to get a look at his face. I want to know if you can ID him. Just don't touch anything."

"This isn't my first rodeo, Detective."

"Consider it a routine disclaimer, Mrs. Pollack." Something then caught his attention over my shoulder, and he muttered under his breath, "Son of a—"

I pivoted to see what had riled him and discovered a news van in the process of parallel parking across the street. "We're going to need backup," he called to Fischer and Norbert.

"On it, Detective," said Fischer.

"How many does this make?" asked Spader as we continued toward the sleigh.

Huh? "How many does what make?"

"Dead bodies. What's your current count, Mrs. Pollack?"

"I'm not keeping score."

"Maybe you should. At the rate you're going, you're probably closing in on Jessica Fletcher's record."

"I hope not." If I never came across another dead body, I'd die happy.

We had arrived at the sleigh. Spader requested the CSU team step aside, then waved me forward. I peered into the sleigh. The snow had been brushed off the body. The man wore a black puffy ski jacket. He lay with the left side of his head cushioned in Santa's lap, the right side visible. Someone had pulled off the ski mask covering his head and face.

"So?" asked Spader. "Any idea who he is?"

"I'm pretty sure it's the guy who slammed into me last night before sucker-punching Ira."

"Only pretty sure?"

I shrugged my shoulders and shook my head. "Sorry. I didn't see him for more than a split second, and never saw his face. All I can tell you for sure is that this man has a similar build, and his clothes match those of the guy last night."

"Assuming this is the guy from last night, you're positive you've never seen him before?"

"Positive. I have no idea who he is. He didn't have any ID on him?"

"None."

"I wish I could be more helpful, Detective."

"That makes two of us, Mrs. Pollack."

"Maybe one of the neighbors can identify him."

"Or your brother-in-law when he shows up."

"*Half*-brother-in-law. And you don't think Ira had anything to do with this guy's murder, do you?"

"Shouldn't I? The victim is most likely the guy who decked him last night. This morning he shows up dead in your *half*-brother-in-law's yard."

"Which is exactly why you should rule Ira out as a suspect. How stupid would he have to be to leave the body on his own property?"

"Point taken. Unless he deliberately left him here because we'd think he'd never do something so stupid."

"Reverse psychology? I hadn't thought of that."

Spader offered me a catbird grin. "Your tax dollars at work, Mrs. Pollack. That's why you pay me the big bucks."

Part of me wanted to ask Spader if I could withhold some of my taxes as compensation for the previous murders I'd solved for him. However, discretion being the better part of valor, I held my tongue and only asked, "Okay if I leave now?"

"You don't want to hang around to help solve this case?"

"As much as I enjoy your company, Detective, I'll leave you to the wintry elements and opt for my warm office."

"Wuss."

"And proud of it." I waved goodbye and added, "Good luck, Detective. May you swiftly solve your case."

As I turned to leave, he stopped me in my tracks by asking, "Even if it means arresting Ira Pollack for murder?"

FOUR

I truly believed that Ira wouldn't hurt a fly, let alone kill another human being, but in the criminal justice system, my opinion meant bupkis. Innocent people are arrested every single day, and often the wheels of justice don't spin very quickly toward their exoneration.

I also had to admit to ulterior motives in championing Ira's innocence. Without a doubt, I knew if Spader arrested him, Ira would plead with me to take his kids. Personally, I'd rather have all the Daughters of the October Revolution permanently move in with me.

"You don't really think...that was all banter a minute ago, wasn't it?"

"I have to follow every lead, Mrs. Pollack. You know that."

"I know. But I also know, even though Ira has his faults and he can be a royal pain in my patootie, the man is not capable of murder."

He cocked his head and stared at me. "Really? You were

singing a different tune only days ago when you called me about Tommy Gravino."

"That was different." Tommy Gravino was a worthless delinquent hired to intimidate me. His goal in life was to become a *made man*. By accident I'd discovered his father and Ira were good friends, having grown up next door to each other.

Given the familial connection between Ira and Lawrence Tuttnauer, I began second-guessing Ira's motives, which led me to freak out and call Spader. "You assured me the Gravinos were upstanding citizens with no connections to organized crime. You claimed Tommy's the black sheep of the family—with a lower-case *f*, not *Family* as in one of the Five Families."

"All true, but I never offered you the same assurance regarding Ira Pollack."

Ominous background music began playing inside my head. "Is there something you're not telling me, Detective?"

"Just that I don't know what will scurry out when I start turning over rocks. You need to prepare yourself for any and all possibilities."

Knowing how much Melody, Harmony, and Isaac disliked me, perhaps they'd prefer to attend boarding school in Switzerland. Ira could certainly afford the tuition, even after hiring the best criminal defense attorneys in the state. Maybe I was needlessly tying myself up in macramé knots. Surely the real killer would crawl out from under one of those overturned rocks.

However, telling myself not to worry was like force-feeding amphetamines down the gullet of my worrywart genes. As a result, I spent the next sixty-five minutes driving to work with one worst-case scenario after another bombarding my brain.

~*~

I work as the crafts editor for *American Woman*, a third-rate monthly women's magazine sold at supermarket checkout lines. We used to be headquartered in Manhattan. Commuting had entailed a short walk to the train station, followed by half an hour on NJ Transit. When Trimedia gobbled up the Reynolds-Alsopp Publishing Company in a hostile takeover a few years ago, the conglomerate moved us to the outskirts of a cornfield in Morris County, New Jersey.

I now spend most days in hour-long or worse, bumper-to-bumper traffic on my daily commute. This morning I'd given myself plenty of extra time to drop the Christmas critters at Ira's house. Of course, I hadn't factored in being waylaid by a snow-covered corpse, not to mention an overturned tractor-trailer on the highway.

By the time I arrived at work, I was two hours late. After dumping my coat, purse, and tote bag in my cubicle, I raced to the conference room, knowing our monthly staff meeting was well underway. When I opened the door and stepped inside, the room grew silent as everyone turned in my direction. "Sorry, I'm late," I mumbled as I took my seat next to Cloris McWerther, our food editor and my best friend.

"You look frazzled," said Naomi Dreyfus, our editor-in-chief. "Everything okay?"

"Things could be better. There was an incident in Westfield this morning."

"Don't tell me you stumbled across another dead body," said Cloris, punctuating her words with a chuckle.

When I didn't immediately answer, her mouth dropped open. "You did, didn't you?" She jumped up and headed for the coffee pot. A moment later she returned, placing a mug of steaming java and a freshly baked croissant in front of me. Cloris believes caffeine and baked goods always help you get through the worst of circumstances. I am a devout disciple.

"Jeez!" said fashion editor Tessa Lisbon. "You're a regular Typhoid Mary."

I clutched the coffee mug with both hands. "I don't go around spreading killer germs."

"Does it matter? People still wind up dead."

What was it about fashion editors? Although not as nasty as Marlys Vandenberg, her predecessor and the first dead body I'd discovered in a year of dead bodies, Tessa was still an arrogant snob. She took great pleasure in continually reminding us that fashion represented the lion's share of our magazine's ad revenues. In other words, we owed our ongoing employment to her.

"Who was it?" asked Jeanie Sims, our decorating editor.

I shook my head. "I don't know. Neither do the police at this point."

"Where did you find him?" asked health editor Janice Kerr.

I had no desire to explain what had led to my early morning discovery. Thankfully, Naomi put a stop to the conversation with a loud clearing of her throat. Had she picked up on my discomfort, or did she merely want to regain control of her staff meeting? The reason didn't matter to me as long as I no longer found myself the center of attention.

"We've already picked the theme and outlined the editorial features for the May issue," said Naomi. "Except for the crafts segment. We're switching things up rather than doing a traditional Mother's Day theme."

"We're not doing Mother's Day?" I asked. "Isn't that a bit risky?"

"We'll still do Mother's Day," she said, "just not in the usual sense. We're going to incorporate some unusual May holidays along with Mother's Day."

Naomi passed me a sheet of paper. "These are the various daily, weekly, and monthly holidays for May. Each editor chose one holiday to incorporate with Mother's Day. You need to choose one."

A quick scan revealed a list of the usual May holidays—May Day, Cinco de Mayo, Mother's Day, and Memorial Day—along with some rather unusual ones. Who knew there was a Lumpy Rug Day? Or a World Naked Gardening Day? Or that the entire month of May was devoted to an ongoing celebration of vinegar?

I studied the sheet of paper in greater detail. With few exceptions, most concerned health or food. There were designated holidays to bring awareness to obscure diseases, people I'd never heard of, and dozens of foods and beverages, ranging from chocolate chips to mimosas. Easy pickings for Cloris and Janice. Our beauty, fashion, and travel editors had fewer options, but I could see where several would work for each of them.

"National Scrapbooking Day would've been the obvious choice," I said, shaking my head.

"If we hadn't featured scrapbooking in a recent issue," agreed Naomi.

Decorating editor Jeanie Sims and I often dovetailed our spreads. I turned to her. "What did you choose?"

"National Photography Month. I'll do something on unique ways to frame and display family photos and memorabilia."

I sighed. "The only other option I see is National Creativity Day. At least it gives me a wide variety of options."

"What about National Lost Sock Memorial Day?" asked

Jeanie. "Aren't there plenty of craft projects you can make with socks?"

I laughed. "As gifts for mothers? How many women do you know who would appreciate a sock monkey for Mother's Day?"

She shrugged. "I suppose only the ones who collect sock monkeys."

"I doubt many of our subscribers fall into that category," said Naomi. "Go with National Creativity Day, Anastasia. Brainstorm with the other editors. Maybe you can come up with an idea that complements one of their features." After I nodded in agreement, she said, "All right, ladies. Let's move on to status reports for the issues already in various stages of production before we break for lunch."

~*~

"So exactly what happened this morning?" asked Cloris as we headed back to our cubicles after the meeting.

I filled her in on everything from finding the Grinch and his buddies camped out in my front yard last night to discovering the dead guy sprawled across Santa's lap this morning.

"You do lead an interesting life," she said.

"Dull and boring are far less stressful."

"I have a couple of chocolate amaretto cupcakes hidden away if you need one later."

"Boozy cupcakes? Why wait?" Along with caffeine and baked goods, chocolate and booze are the other two staples of my diet.

Between the items Cloris constantly receives from food companies, the goodies she bakes for her monthly recipe column, and my lack of both willpower and exercise, I'd long ago resigned myself to accepting my slightly overweight, pear-shaped figure. She, on the other hand, ate whatever she wanted, whenever she wanted, and never added a pound to her size-two figure.

I envied her metabolism. If she weren't my best friend and hadn't once saved my life, I'd probably hate her. Instead, I loved her like the sister I've never had. "I'll grab two cups of coffee. You break out your secret stash."

Five minutes later we were holed away in her cubicle, savoring those alcohol-soaked cupcakes. My taste buds were luxuriating in gastronomic nirvana when my cell phone rang. I glanced at the display and groaned. "Ira."

"You could ignore the call," said Cloris.

"I'd only be putting off the inevitable." I took a final swig of coffee to fortify myself, then answered the phone. "Hello, Ira."

"Anastasia, did you leave the Grinch and Snoopy on my walk and the other Peanuts characters on my porch?"

"That's what you're calling about? Not the dead body in your sleigh?"

"Well, I don't know who he is. The guy was obviously drunk last night. He probably returned, passed out in the sleigh, and froze to death."

"Is that what Detective Spader told you, that he froze to death?"

"No, he said they won't know cause of death until the medical examiner performs an autopsy, but what else could it be?"

"Gee, Ira, I don't know. Maybe murder?"

"You don't think I had anything to do with his death, do you?"

"Of course not, but dozens of people saw him punch you in the face last night. If he didn't die of natural causes, you're the prime suspect."

"I'm not worried. I never touched the guy. I'm the one who landed flat on my back. Now, about those lawn ornaments, I don't understand why you returned some of them."

"My intention was to return *all* of them. That dead body prevented me from completing my task."

"But why?"

I pointed to my phone and mouthed, "Clueless" to Cloris. She rolled her eyes at me.

"Why did finding a dead body on your property keep me from finishing?" I asked.

"No, why would you return them? I thought you and the boys would love my surprise."

"Look, Ira, I really don't want to hurt your feelings, but no more surprises, please."

"I didn't buy them for you. They were from last year's display."

"It's not about the money, Ira."

"Then what?"

"Just promise me you'll ask first next time. About anything. Okay?"

He let loose a long sigh. "All right. If you insist. I suppose I can use them in place of the ones that were destroyed last night, even though the kids insist on a new display each year. However, I really don't understand why you have so much trouble accepting gifts from me. After all, we are family."

He never would understand, and judging from past experience, he'd comply with my request only until he decided to gift me with something else. Still, I had to keep trying. Even the most difficult-to-train dog eventually learns not to pee in the house—at least until he grows old and infirmed. Ira was neither old nor infirmed. "I insist."

~*~

I spent the remainder of the workday answering reader mail,

uploading a new craft project to our website, and waiting for inspiration to strike regarding the May issue. The afternoon mail brought a pile of Christmas cards from vendors and one from Tino Martinelli. "Hey," I called across the hall to Cloris. "Look who sent me a Christmas card."

She stepped into my cubicle and grabbed the card from my hand. "Tino Martinelli? What's he up to?"

Tino and I had crossed paths when Trimedia's former CEO Alfred Gruenwald had hired me to find his mistress's killer. The thirty-something ex-marine had worked as Gruenwald's private right-hand guy. I hadn't seen him since the police made an arrest in the murders of Philomena Campanello and Norma Gene. After scanning the enclosed letter, I said, "He parted ways with Gruenwald shortly after the arrests and took a position with a security firm. Says the pay is good but the work is boring, nothing like our little adventure. He misses me."

Cloris rolled her eyes. "That little adventure could have gotten you killed."

"Don't remind me."

"If you write back to him, tell him to stay out of trouble."

"I think he got that message a while ago. He made a huge mistake and nearly paid dearly for it, but he learned his lesson."

"I hope so. That one lapse of judgment could have ruined his life—not to mention yours."

"But he did the right thing in the end."

"Yeah, all in all, he was a pretty cool dude."

"Not to mention easy on the eyes?"

"That, too."

At five o'clock I powered down my computer, packed up, and set off on my nightly bumper-to-bumper, homeward bound commute. Detective Spader called shortly after I exited Rt. 78 in Scotch Plains. "We've ID'd the deceased," he said. "His name is Dion Leonides. Ring a bell?"

I mulled the name over in my head as I coasted to a stop for a red light. "I don't think so. Should it?"

"Have you seen any local news today?"

"No, why?"

"An arsonist struck a home in Mountainside last night, across Rt. 22 not far from Pollack's home."

"Now that you mention it," I said, "I remember hearing quite a few sirens last night, but only one patrol car showed up at Ira's house after the fight."

"They were on their way to the fire. Emergency crews from several surrounding towns were called in, including Westfield. Luckily, no one was home at the time."

"What does the fire have to do with Dion Leonides?"

"It was his house."

"He torched his own home?"

"I didn't say that."

"But you know it was arson."

"According to the fire marshal."

The light changed, and I continued toward Westfield. "Well, it certainly wasn't Ira. He was being harangued by his neighbors at the time I heard the sirens last night."

"But you and I both know he has connections to men who wouldn't think twice about torching a residence for the right price."

"That's something his ex-father-in-law would do, not Ira. Besides, what would be his motive? Leonides confronted him after the fire started."

"That's what I have to find out. And speaking of Leonides, I got the ME's report." He paused for a moment. "Interested?"

"Of course."

"Dion Leonides was murdered."

FIVE

I suppose, given my track record with dead bodies, it was a long shot to hope the medical examiner's report would indicate Leonides had frozen to death because he'd been too drunk to know he'd face-planted on Santa's lap. "How?" I asked.

"Shot."

"I didn't notice any blood."

"That's because he was killed elsewhere. The body was moved."

"But why to Ira's house?"

"That's the million-dollar question. Along with why the vic attacked Pollack prior to his murder. According to several witnesses who've come forward, he yelled at Pollack before punching him and slashing those Christmas balloons. Did you forget to mention that, Mrs. Pollack? Or are you withholding information to protect your brother-in-law?"

"*Half*-brother-in-law. And no, I'm not. The music was blaring. I don't remember hearing him shout anything. Besides, I would think, Detective, that by now you know me well enough that I'd never do such a thing, no matter how strongly I believed in someone's innocence."

"How I feel about you doesn't matter. I still had to ask. It's my job."

"Fair enough."

"I also have to investigate any connection between Pollack and Leonides."

"Ira already told Harley and Fogarty he didn't recognize the guy who slugged him."

"That wouldn't negate a connection of some sort."

"What do you mean?"

"Even if he didn't know Leonides—and I have no proof that's the case at this point—I'm betting he knows the guy who dumped Leonides in his yard."

"So you no longer believe Ira's using reverse psychology to deflect suspicion from himself and send the police on a wild goose chase?"

"I didn't say that. All options are still on the table."

"Have you talked to Ira?"

"I wanted to speak with you first."

"Why? To see if I know of any connection between them? I already told you I've never heard of the man. So how would I know of any connection between him and Ira? Ask Ira."

"I intend to. I'm on my way to his place now."

"Good. Don't stop turning over those stones, Detective. Ira isn't your killer."

"So you've said. But I doubt the D.A. will take your word alone in ruling out a possible suspect."

"Very funny."

"I'll make you a deal. You keep an open mind, and so will I."

"I'll do my best, Detective."

"As will I. You have a nice evening, Mrs. Pollack."

He hung up before I could wrangle any further information from him. Surely many, if not most of Ira's neighbors, had home security systems with cameras. One of them should have video of the killer depositing Dion Leonides' body in the sleigh on Ira's property, but this early in the investigation his team probably hadn't collected all the recordings, let alone viewed them.

Then again, no matter what video evidence Spader's team uncovered, he'd use his standard line on me: "You know I can't divulge any details of an ongoing investigation." How many times had I heard that since our first meeting?

~*~

Five minutes later I turned onto my street and groaned at the sight of Harriet Kleinhample's circa 1969 orange VW minibus parked in front of my house. I don't know who was trying my patience more lately, my mother-in-law or her devoted sidekick.

Lights were on in the apartment above my garage, but Zack's Boxster was missing from the driveway. I climbed the steps to the apartment and found Alex and Nick inside doing homework. Ralph sat perched on Alex's shoulder. Mephisto had made himself at home on one end of the sofa. "They have the TV turned up so loud we were having trouble concentrating," said Alex. "Even the animals were complaining."

"It's bad enough she stole my bedroom," said Nick. "Now she and her friends are taking over the entire house. It's not fair, Mom."

I ran my hand through my hair and exhaled a sigh of frustration. "How many of them are camped out in the den?"

"Just Grandmother Lucille and Mrs. Kleinhample."

I left the boys to their homework and headed into the house where my eardrums were immediately attacked by an eighties disco beat. I discovered the two commies sprawled on the den sofa, a plate of cheese from my refrigerator and a box of crackers from my pantry wedged between them. An episode of *Dance Moms* filled the television screen.

Not that I ever really liked her, but I liked my mother-in-law a lot more back when she referred to television as the opiate of the masses. Ever since her minor stroke, for some unfathomable reason she's become addicted to reality TV. The woman can't get enough of everything from *Dancing with the Stars* to *Duck Dynasty*.

I spied the unattended remote and swooped in to snatch it off the end table. Then I lowered the volume below earsplitting decibels.

"Hey!" said Harriet, sputtering a mouthful of crackers that I'd later have to vacuum from the carpet and couch cushions.

"How dare you!" said Lucille.

"Your grandsons were trying to study," I said.

"They're not even in the house," said Harriet.

"Because you chased them out with this racket. If you want to watch *my* television in *my* den, you'll be considerate of the other people in this house."

"See what I mean," Lucille said to Harriet. "Absolutely no respect."

Look who's talking! As I stormed from the den, I cursed my dead husband under my breath. What did I ever do to deserve such crappy Karma? Wasn't it bad enough he left me in debt up the wazoo? He had to stick me with the mother-in-law from Hades and her communist horde?

"When's dinner?" Harriet called after me.

My evil alter ego yelled back. "You're eating it." I turned the corner from the hall into the living room and nearly collided with Zack.

"Rough day?" he asked.

"I am not feeding that woman every night. I've reached my limit. She can cook her own dinner in her own apartment and take Lucille with her."

He reached for my hand and led me out of the house and back up to the apartment where the boys still had their noses buried in their books. They glanced up and greeted Zack before returning to their homework.

Ralph squawked at the sight of his favorite person in the entire world. Abandoning Alex, he flew to Zack, landing on his shoulder. Then he nuzzled Zack's cheek until he was rewarded with a sunflower seed.

After we shed our coats, Zack poured two glasses of merlot and handed me one. I collapsed onto the sofa, threw my head back against the cushion, and closed my eyes. He took a seat next to me and asked, "So dare I ask, how was the rest of your day?"

I opened my eyes and downed half the wine before I answered. "Oh, you know, same old, same old. Another day, another murder."

Ralph flapped his wings and squawked. "*How easily murder is discovered! Titus Andronicus. Act Two, Scene Three.*"

My sons' heads shot up from their books and turned to face me, their mouths gaping open. "Not funny," said Alex.

Was he speaking to Ralph or me?

Nick glared at me before returning to his book. Under his breath he grumbled, "So much for promises."

Less than three weeks ago I'd promised him I'd keep my nose—as well as the rest of me—far away from murder and mayhem. As of this morning, I'd now broken that promise twice.

"It's not like I go looking for dead bodies, Nick."

"I'm beginning to wonder. You're not a cat, Mom. You only have one life, and we only have one parent left."

There are few things in life worse than the guilt trips a teenager can lay on a parent. "I'm well aware of that."

Zack's brow furrowed as he studied me. "You're not joking, are you?"

"Afraid not."

"Is it someone we know?" asked Alex, his face filled with worry.

Nick grew pale. "I didn't think about that. It's not, is it?"

Zack held up his hand. "Boys, maybe we should let your mother explain what happened." When they both nodded, Zack turned to me and said, "The floor is yours."

Since we hadn't told the boys what had occurred at Ira's house last night, I first had to explain why I needed to return there this morning. My sons immediately jumped to the wrong conclusion. "Uncle Ira?" asked Alex.

"The guy who decked him came back and killed him?" asked Nick.

"No, Ira's fine."

"Let your mother continue," said Zack.

I drained my entire glass of wine before detailing how I'd discovered the guy who'd attacked Ira face down in Santa's lap. "His name is Dion Leonides, although I didn't know that this morning. He didn't have any ID on him."

"Then how do you know his name?" asked Nick.

"Detective Spader called me on my way home from work. He

didn't say how he learned the man's identity."

"Fingerprints, probably," said Zack.

Of course! Why hadn't I thought of that? I inhaled a deep breath and slowly released it before continuing. "There's more to this mystery than a dead body, though." I turned to Zack. "Remember all those sirens we heard last night that had nothing to do with what was going on at Ira's?"

Zack nodded. "I figured there was an accident on Rt. 22. What about them?"

"Not an accident. At the same time Leonides' fist was connecting with Ira's nose, his house was going up in flames a mile away. Detective Spader said someone torched it."

"Does he think this Leonides fellow set his own house on fire?"

"He didn't say. I suppose that's one possibility if it took time for someone to notice the fire and report it."

"Maybe the guy who killed him torched the house," said Alex.

"There's a third possibility," said Zack.

"What?" asked Alex.

"As odd as it sounds," said Zack, "It could be a horrible coincidence."

"Do you really believe that?" I asked.

"No, but anything is possible. Did Spader offer any other information on Leonides?"

"Only that a few of the neighbors heard him shout something at Ira before he slugged him."

"Like what?"

"He didn't say."

Zack thought for a moment, then shook his head. "I don't remember any one voice standing out over the din of the crowd, but I was focused on keeping you from falling. What about you?"

I shook my head. "Ira and Leonides were at least ten feet from where we stood. Thanks to the deafening Christmas carols, I could barely hear you, Shane, and Sophie."

"Does Spader believe there's a connection between Leonides and Ira?"

"None that he's shared with me, but you know Spader. He never divulges more than he needs to." I recounted my earlier conversation with the detective. "And you heard Ira last night. He claimed he didn't know the guy who attacked him. But it was dark and Leonides wore a ski cap pulled down low on his head. So it's possible Ira wouldn't have recognized him even if he did know him."

"True," said Zack. "None of us picked up on that at the time."

"Not even Harley and Fogarty. Anyway, as absurd as it seems, right now I think Ira is Spader's prime suspect."

Alex's eyes grew wide. "Do you think Uncle Ira would kill someone?"

"Everyone is capable of murder," said Zack.

"Really?" asked Nick.

"If pushed beyond their breaking point? Definitely. Just ask your mother."

"Me? I haven't killed anyone!"

"No, but you nearly killed Lucille and Harriet a few minutes ago."

"I did not!"

"This time," said Zack. He offered me a wink and a knowing grin. "They obviously haven't pushed you far enough yet."

Hopefully, they never will. Orange is not my color. And given my pear-shaped body, horizontal stripes in any color are a definite no-no. I gave myself a mental pat on the back. I had nothing to worry about. Zack's opinion aside, I knew prison garb alone would be enough of a deterrent to keep me on the right side of the law. "Fear not," I said. "I'm strictly passive-aggressive when it comes to Lucille and her minions."

Nick pulled out his phone and glanced at the display. "It's nearly six o'clock. Think the local news will have something about the murder?" Apparently, curiosity about the body I found in Ira's yard had won out over his concerns for my safety. Not that I had any intention of inserting myself into another murder investigation. I would not break my promise to my son a second time. However, given my track record, I mentally crossed all my appendages.

Zack reached for the remote on the coffee table and flipped on the television. A moment later Eyewitness News flashed a banner with the night's top story—*Murder in Westfield*.

One of the news anchors gave a brief intro before turning the story over to an on-scene reporter on the sidewalk in front of Ira's home. Behind her the Christmas extravaganza stood silent and dark—no blasting music, no saluting nutcrackers. Colorful puddles of deflated nylon fabric dotted the snow-covered lawn. Eight metal reindeer stood frozen in time on the train tracks that circled the house. Santa and his sleigh were conspicuously absent from the scene, most likely now residing in the custody of a Union County evidence locker.

The reporter gave a rundown of events, including last night's one-sided boxing match. The network had gotten hold of cell phone video of Leonides punching Ira and flashed it across the screen.

As the reporter continued, a smiling publicity photo of the victim filled the screen. He still looked like a short, stocky bodybuilder, but a jovial rather than menacing one. "The deceased is Dion Leonides, a fifty-two-year-old Mountainside real estate attorney who is also a partner in a home flipping business with his brother Paul Leonides."

The news anchor interrupted with a question. "Darlene, is the man he punched last night a suspect in his murder?"

"Not at this time, Kent, but the police aren't ruling anyone out."

"I understand there are a few bizarre twists to this murder, correct?"

"That's right. First, prior to the murder last night, an arsonist set fire to the victim's house, burning it to the ground." The screen filled with the charred remains of the Mountainside home. "Luckily, no one was home at the time, but two firemen suffered minor injuries."

"Do the police believe the two incidents are connected, Darlene?"

The camera switched back to the reporter. "They haven't said, Kent. Arson investigators are still sifting through the remains of the house, and the police are in the process of interviewing neighbors at both locations, as well as reviewing security footage from nearby homes."

"And the second twist?"

"The body was found by Westfield resident Anastasia Pollack, who some have taken to calling the town's very own Jessica Fletcher."

I groaned as the television screen switched to an image of Detective Spader walking me toward the sleigh.

I shot Zack a sideways glance and caught his frown.

"Here we go again," said Nick.

"Gee, I can't wait for school tomorrow," said Alex. He buried his face in a throw pillow and muttered, "Not!"

I wanted to tell him to blame it all on his father. If Karl hadn't royally screwed us before dropping dead in Las Vegas, Lucille and her commie horde wouldn't have staged the protest rally in Westfield, which ultimately brought Ira into our lives. Instead, as I so often did when it came to my sons and their father, I bit my tongue while the reporter continued to speak. "Over the last year Ms. Pollack, who has no background in law enforcement, has been instrumental in aiding the police in several high-profile cases."

"I understand you were able to speak with the victim's family, Darlene."

"That's right, Kent." The screen filled with a middle-aged man and woman, sitting hand-in-hand on a couch in an upscale living room. Across the bottom of the screen a banner read, *Paul and Olympia Leonides*. "Earlier today I sat down with the victim's brother and sister-in-law at their home in Westfield."

As the camera moved in for a close-up of the couple, I realized the wife looked familiar. "I've seen that woman before," I said.

"Where?" asked Zack.

I wracked my brain. "I'm not sure."

With her free hand the woman silently brushed away a tear streaming down her cheek. Her husband's voice cracked with anger as he spoke. "Our family is devastated. My brother was my best friend. I want his killer caught and brought to justice as swiftly as possible. To that end, I'm offering a twenty-five-thousand-dollar reward to anyone with information leading to his arrest and conviction."

The reporter reappeared on the screen. "Anyone with information regarding either the murder or fire is asked to contact the Union County Police, Westfield Police, or Mountainside Police Departments. This is Darlene Jamison coming to you from Westfield, New Jersey. Back to you in the studio, Kent."

"Thank you, Darlene." The anchor returned to the screen. "We'll stay on top of this unfolding story and provide any updates at eleven. In other news..."

Zack flipped off the broadcast.

"Are we eating dinner tonight?" asked Nick. "I'm starving."

"We're going out," said Zack. "Grab your coats."

I hesitated. "What about Lucille and Harriet?"

"Cheese and crackers, remember? You're not getting cold feet, are you, Ms. Passive-Aggressive?"

"No, but I'm worried they might try to cook something and set the kitchen on fire."

"Just to spite you?"

"I wouldn't put it past them."

"Have they ever used any appliance besides the microwave?"

"No, but there's always a first time."

"Look on the bright side," said Zack. "You have homeowner's insurance. If they start a fire, you get a new kitchen."

Hmm...goodbye cracked linoleum and chipped Formica? Hello hardwoods and granite? Maybe I should tell Lucille from now on she'd need to cook her own meals.

On second thought, that was a monumentally bad idea. She'd probably reduce the entire house to cinders. Not only didn't I have total replacement coverage, I had a sky-high deductible—both thanks to the cost cutting measures I'd instituted to deal with the fallout from Dead Louse of a Spouse.

I heaved a huge internal sigh as I slipped into my coat. Goodbye hardwoods. Goodbye granite. Hello smack-in-the-face reality.

We were about to leave the apartment when my cell phone rang.

SIX

I glanced at the display and decided to let the call go to voicemail. I wasn't eager to speak with Ira under the best of circumstances. On an empty stomach—not to mention after the events of this morning—this call fell into the Worst of Circumstances category.

Being part coward, I waited until we'd arrived at La Famiglia and placed our orders before listening to Ira's message. His voice trembled as he spoke. "Anastasia, I could really use your help. That detective friend of yours thinks I had something to do with the body you found this morning. You can't possibly think I killed him. You know I'd never hurt anyone. Please call me as soon as you get this message."

I handed my phone to Zack. "Have a listen."

He held the phone to his ear. A moment later he passed it back to me. "What do you want to do?"

I glanced at my sons. Both were engrossed in texting or gaming or whatever while we waited for our food. Ordinarily, I had a strict no-devices policy during meals. I'd made an exception this evening when we entered the crowded restaurant, scored the last available table, and were told the kitchen was backed up. "I gave Alex and Nick my word," I whispered.

That was enough to pull them away from their screens. "What's going on?" asked Alex.

Nick simply frowned at me.

"I'm not sure, but Uncle Ira wants to talk to me about Dion Leonides. Would either of you object to that?"

"Just talk?" asked Nick.

"Just talk."

He contemplated my answer before asking, "Nothing more?"

"Absolutely nothing."

"Okay, but we come, too."

I turned to Alex. "Is that okay with you?"

Instead of answering me, he looked across the table to Zack. "Are you okay with it?"

Zack shrugged. "Ira's in a bad place. What if the roles were reversed?"

Alex grimaced. "I suppose when you put it that way...." He nodded. "Okay."

I may have recently been handed a boatload of crappy Karma, but when it came to the men in my life, I'd scored a jackpot. "All right. I'll text Ira that we'll stop by after we finish dinner."

~*~

An hour later we arrived at Ira's house. He'd turned the Christmas display back on but removed the train tracks. The reindeer now stood motionless, interspersed among the inflatable cartoon characters, the four I'd managed to unload this morning replacing four of the slashed ones. The saluting nutcrackers still lined the walkway from the sidewalk to the house, but the music no longer blared at deafening levels. Perhaps this was either out of respect for the murder victim or a concession to his neighbors. Either way, it probably annoyed the heck out of his kids.

Thankfully, no news vans loitered nearby. The last thing I wanted was some reporter shoving a microphone in my face—or worse yet, in my sons' faces.

A small crowd had gathered to check out the display but nowhere near the number of people who'd jammed the sidewalk and street the previous night. I wondered how many of them had come to see the Christmas display as opposed to ghoulish voyeurs drawn to the scene of a crime.

I sensed Ira had been pacing his foyer, anxiously awaiting our arrival, because he swung the front door open and quickly ushered us inside as soon as Zack rang the doorbell. "Thanks for coming," he said. A massive shiner surrounded his left eye, evidence that Ira's attacker had hit him harder than we'd first realized.

He took our coats and led us into the great room—*great* being an understatement. *Enormous*, *gigantic*, or *colossal* were more appropriate adjectives to describe the size of the room. "This isn't the way I expected to invite you to our new home for the first time."

"You've accomplished quite a bit for someone who moved in only a few days ago," I said, scanning the room where a live Christmas tree topped out within inches of the cathedral ceiling. Every square inch of the room, from floor to ceiling, had been decorated for the holidays, not a single horizontal or vertical surface left unadorned.

Ira puffed out his chest. "I hired a decorator. Her team set up everything before we moved in."

Silly me to think Ira had done any of this on his own! "New

furniture?" I asked, not recognizing anything from his former home.

"Yes. Under the circumstances, I thought it best to make a totally fresh start for the kids and me. Everything is new, even the linens and kitchen items."

I forced a smile, wondering if Ira had also rid his home of all reminders of his first wife after she died. If so, that would go a long way toward explaining his ill-tempered children. Imagine losing your mother to illness, only to have your father remove all evidence she had ever existed. I parked that thought in the compassion corner of my brain, ready to access next time one of his kids mouthed off at me.

Ira turned to Alex and Nick. "Why don't you boys head upstairs to the bonus room while I speak with your mother? It's the last room at the end of the hallway."

Alex hesitated. "Are your kids up there?"

"Yes, they'll show you around."

Nick turned to me. "Mom...."

"Everything okay?" asked Ira, turning to me.

"Everything's fine." I pulled my sons aside and whispered, "I'll fill you in on everything afterwards."

"Everything?" asked Alex, the word ringing with his skepticism.

I nodded. They silently consulted each other. Then Alex shrugged and said, "I suppose."

Nick scowled, muttering something unintelligible under his breath before the two of them dragged their feet toward the staircase in the foyer.

"Can I get you anything?" asked Ira as the boys departed.

"We've just eaten," said Zack.

"What did you want to discuss?" I asked. "The boys have homework to finish this evening." I didn't know if that were true or not, but it gave me an excuse for moving this impromptu gathering along.

Ira waved toward a seating arrangement in the middle of the room. "Please, sit."

Once we did, he leaned forward. "I want to hire you, Anastasia."

"What for?"

"To prove my innocence. I didn't kill that man."

"I'm not a lawyer, Ira."

"No, but you've helped catch several killers."

"Anastasia is out of the sleuthing business," said Zack. "She promised Alex and Nick she'd leave the detective work to the professionals."

"But we're family!" said Ira, panic coloring both his words and his face. "We're supposed to help each other."

Zack speared Ira with his official don't-mess-with-me glare, the one he probably employs while engaged in the undercover operations he claims are a figment of my imagination. "Not when it involves jeopardizing Anastasia's life."

And with that, the alpha males began their dance. Ira shot back a look that needed no interpretation, his words pure ice. "Maybe you should let Anastasia speak for herself."

He then turned back to me, softening his demeanor to that of a desperate puppy in need of a warm hug and asked, "Will you help me, please?"

I shook my head. "I'm sorry, Ira. I nearly lost my own life recently. I can't put my children through that again."

He jumped up and began pacing in front of the fireplace,

waving his arms frenetically. "What about *my* life? I didn't kill that man. I can't go to prison. What about my kids?"

I quickly launched a prayer into the universe that it wouldn't come to that. I knew in my heart of hearts I wouldn't allow Ira's kids to land in foster care. However, I also knew I'd wind up in a padded cell if I had to step in as a substitute parent to Isaac and the twins. "Did Detective Spader lead you to believe he intends to arrest you?"

"No, but what if he does?"

"Is there any evidence that points to you?"

"Besides the body left on my property?"

"The body of a man who assaulted you last night," said Zack as a reminder.

Ira glared at him as he shook his head. "I haven't forgotten, but I also have no idea why he attacked me, and I made that perfectly clear to the detective."

"What did he shout at you?" I asked.

"The detective?" Confusion settled across Ira's face.

"Leonides," said Zack.

"Nothing."

"Detective Spader told Anastasia that several witnesses claimed he yelled something before he punched you."

Ira's brows knit together. "I don't remember him saying anything before he hit me. What about either of you?"

"No," I said.

"Why would someone lie about that?" asked Ira.

"They may not be lying," I said.

"But you just said you didn't hear anything."

"We weren't close enough," I said. "And the music was extremely loud."

"You also might not remember due to the shock of the attack," added Zack.

Ira returned to the sofa, collapsed onto the cushion, and buried his head in his hands. "None of this makes any sense." He looked up and cast pleading eyes at me. "All I know is I didn't kill him. Anastasia, you have to believe me."

"I do believe you."

He turned to Zack. "And you?"

"If what you claim is true, you have nothing to worry about."

Ira sneered. "Easy for you to say. You're not the one who was questioned by the police for several hours. What if they can't come up with any other suspects?"

"If there's no evidence that points to you," said Zack, "it won't matter."

"Says the man no one is trying to pin a murder on."

I stood, ready to end this unpleasant get-together. "Ira, Detective Spader is a competent investigator. He's not out to railroad you."

"Really? Didn't he recently arrest your friend Shane Lambert for a murder he didn't commit?"

Okay, score one point for the Person of Interest. "That was different. Someone tried to frame him."

"And what if someone is trying to frame me? Why else would a body be left on my property?"

I couldn't answer that. It did seem quite random unless it was deliberate. "Are you certain you didn't know Dion Leonides? You've never crossed paths with him?"

"Never."

"You haven't sold him a car?"

Ira ran his hands through his hair. "Are you kidding? I own

half a dozen dealerships around the state. We sell dozens of cars each week. I don't meet every buyer. I hardly meet any of them."

"So, it's possible he purchased a car from one of your dealerships."

Ira jumped up and began pacing again. "I suppose so. I'd have to check the sales records, but I don't see what that has to do with anything."

I glanced at Zack and shook my head. "Anastasia is looking for some sort of connection between the two of you. If he bought a car from one of your dealerships and was dissatisfied—"

"And I'm telling you, there is no connection," said Ira, raising his voice several decibels. "But even if he did buy a car from one of my dealerships, why would he attack me? We offer a hundred percent satisfaction guarantee. There are lemon laws in this state. I may not interact with most of our customers, but if someone had a problem with a car, I'd know about it. We'd either fix the problem or allow the customer to return the vehicle. I can assure you, we never had a problem with anyone named Dion Leonides."

"What about problems with anyone else?" I asked. "Employees? Vendors? People you interact with outside of work?"

Ira offered me a broad smile. "You know me, Anastasia. I get along with everyone."

"Including your neighbors?" asked Zack.

Ira shot him a dagger-filled scowl. "I had no idea I was moving into a neighborhood of Ebenezer Scrooges. Do you seriously believe one of them is trying to frame me for murder over a Christmas display?"

"Not necessarily," I said. "But if someone had a beef with Leonides and witnessed him punch you, he could have seized on the opportunity to misdirect the investigation."

Ira parked himself on the coffee table across from where I sat and grabbed my hands in his. "See, that's why I need your help, Anastasia. You think outside the box. That detective isn't going to consider something like that, not when he's already made up his mind about me."

"I can assure you Detective Spader is looking at all possible angles, Ira, including Lawrence."

Ira released my hands. His mouth dropped open, and he shook his head. "No, Lawrence would never hurt me. He likes me." He grew pensive for a moment before adding, "But what if someone wants to harm Lawrence by framing me?" He snapped his fingers. "That has to be it!"

In the world of organized crime, there were far more sinister ways to harm a man like Lawrence Tuttnauer than by framing his ex-son-in-law for murder. Ira's high opinion of himself aside, it was far more likely that a psychopath like Lawrence would orchestrate a hit and frame Ira simply to amuse himself.

However, since I needed to extricate myself from this situation as easily and quickly as possible, I said, "That's an interesting theory, Ira. How about if I mention it to Detective Spader for you?"

He grabbed my hands again and squeezed. "Would you? I know he'll listen to you." Then he stood, pulling me up with him and grabbed me into a suffocating bear hug. "Thank you, Anastasia! I knew you wouldn't let me down."

~*~

On the ride home I conveyed the conversation to Alex and Nick. "So that's all you're doing?" asked Nick, "Mentioning a theory to Detective Spader?"

"Not even that," I said. "Lawrence is in solitary confinement for a month. There's no way he's connected to Dion Leonides' murder. I was merely humoring Ira."

"Uncle Ira doesn't know about Lawrence?" asked Alex.

"Apparently not." But that didn't surprise me. I doubt my own mother knew of her ex-husband's latest escapade. I certainly hadn't told her he'd been caught with a contraband cell phone that he'd used to hire a wannabe Mafia thug to intimidate me. She already carried around enough guilt regarding her last marriage.

I decided to change the subject. "Were Ira's kids civil to you tonight?"

"They totally ignored us," said Nick. "Never even said hi."

"The twins were glued to their phones and Isaac to his video game," added Alex. "They didn't so much as look up when we entered the room."

That didn't surprise me, given Ira's lack of parenting skills. Someone needed to knock some sense into that man before his spoiling did irreparable damage to those kids—if it hadn't already. However, talking sense into Ira was like trying to convince a leopard to switch from spots to plaid.

"So what did you do?" asked Zack.

"Shot pool," said Alex.

"Uncle Ira has a bodacious table," said Nick. "And four pinball machines."

Of course, he does.

~*~

We arrived home to find Harriet's orange VW minibus missing. If the gods were smiling down on me, I'd find Harriet had taken Lucille with her for a commie sleepover. However, the gods rarely smile in my direction lately, and tonight turned out to be yet another example of them turning their backs on me.

We entered the house to find the curmudgeonly communist had locked herself in the bathroom she shares with the boys. At least the shrill sounds of *My Big Fat Gypsy Wedding* weren't emanating from the den. With any luck, Lucille would call it a night after her extremely lengthy nightly ablutions. A daughter-in-law stressed to her limits can only hope.

I suggested Zack and I wait it out in the apartment. After our trip to Ira's, I needed his strong shoulder for resting my head and a bottle of wine for mellowing purposes. I knew he wouldn't be happy when I told him I wanted to surf the Internet to learn more about Dion Leonides.

SEVEN

Zack laughed.

Not the reaction I'd anticipated. "What's so funny?"

"I knew you wouldn't be able to resist getting involved." He pulled a bottle from the fridge and another from the wine rack on the kitchen counter. Holding up both, he asked, "Red, white, or something stronger?"

"White. And I'm not getting involved. I promised Alex and Nick."

"I see."

He didn't. "I'm simply curious. What harm could a little Googling do?"

"Assuming a little Googling doesn't lead to a little snooping? Nothing."

"Exactly."

He uncorked the bottle of pinot grigio. "Only I'm not convinced you'll restrict your curiosity to the Internet."

"Just watch me, ye of little faith."

"Oh, I plan to." He filled two glasses, then walked over to the sofa and handed one to me. "Like a hawk."

"No need. My latest brush with death was my last."

"It better have been. You're not sticking me with Lucille and your mother."

I paused just as I was about to take a sip of the wine. "Are you saying if something happened to me, you'd take care of the boys?"

"And Ralph."

"Of course. You couldn't live without Ralph." Or Ralph without Zack. I doubt there had ever been such a bond between man and parrot.

He wrapped his free arm around my shoulders. "More importantly, I couldn't live without you."

"Good to know. However, I can't help but notice you didn't mention Mephisto."

"The jury's still out on him."

Zack drained his glass and rose to his feet. He walked over to his desk, grabbed his laptop, and returned to the sofa. "Let's see what we can find out about Mr. Leonides."

He proceeded to type the victim's name into the search bar and hit the Enter key. In less than three seconds numerous links filled the screen. "That was easy," I said. The late Dion Leonides was on the Internet. Then again, who wasn't these days?

Zack clicked on the first link. Up popped the landing page of Parthenon Construction, the home-flipping business Leonides, a real estate attorney, had owned with his realtor brother Paul and his architect sister-in-law Octavia.

An animated, toga-clad man, with a hammer in one hand and a fistful of nails in the other, executed a series of back flips across the screen while a sing-song voiceover said, "Parthenon

Construction, you'll flip for our flips." The acrobatic toga guy then flipped into the black hole of cyberspace, replaced by the website's menu buttons, including one that linked to Paul's real estate business and another to Dion's law firm.

According to the company history, Aristotle Leonides had opened Parthenon Construction shortly after emigrating to the U.S. from Greece in the nineteen-fifties. Fifteen years ago he shifted his business away from general construction to take advantage of the booming house-flipping craze that had hit New Jersey. His sons and Paul's wife had joined him. When Aristotle died last year, Dion and Paul jointly inherited the business.

"An attorney, a realtor, and an architect walk into a construction company—"

Zack raised an eyebrow. "Are you making a joke?"

"No, I'm serious. Think about it: the guy who knows about construction died a year ago. Who's been doing the actual work on these flips?"

"I'm guessing the same crew they've employed all along. They probably hired a general contractor to take their father's place. Why does it matter?"

"Maybe the changes to the business are tied to Dion's murder."

Once again Zack raised an eyebrow. "Because this is New Jersey?"

I shrugged. "Hey, if it walks like a duck and smells like a duck..." Construction was one of many businesses the mob had infiltrated over the decades, but I'd never heard of them targeting residential construction. Commercial construction offered far more revenue streams in the way of graft and extortion.

Zack clicked on the button labeled "Meet our Flipping Family."

I stared at the images that filled the screen. I immediately recognized Dion, Paul, and Octavia—as well as the fourth and newest member of the company, general contractor Jesse Konopka. "It's not a duck," I said.

"What makes you so certain?"

"I know Jesse Konopka. He lives around the corner. His wife and I were in a book club together before Karl died." Not until that moment did I realize how much I missed getting together once a month for stimulating conversation with the Lit Chicks, as we called ourselves.

Although it didn't rank in the Top Ten, it was yet one more change Karl's death had precipitated in my life. Maybe it was time to remedy that—if only I could somehow carve out the time to read a book once a month.

Zack topped off my wine and poured another glass for himself. "I'm confused. Exactly what makes him incapable of murder? That he lives around the corner or that you and his wife belonged to the same book club?"

I sighed. "Point taken." I certainly hoped Jesse Konopka was incapable of murder. He seemed like a great guy. Then again, once upon a time I thought my dead husband was a great guy—before I learned he tried to kill his own mother.

After reading through the website, Zack clicked on a few other links. We learned that Dion Leonides had studied law at Seton Hall, worked for a firm in Manhattan before leaving to join his father's company, and had an ex-wife and two kids living in Pound Ridge, New York. His wife, also an attorney, had remarried several years ago. Dion had remained single.

He posted infrequently on social media but from what we could see, nothing controversial that might cause someone to want him dead. Most of his posts were the same before-and-after photos of homes that also appeared on the company website. We also found no evidence of prior arrests or lawsuits filed against him or Parthenon Construction. Dion Leonides was pretty much a nothing burger who seemed to keep to himself when he wasn't working. So why had he attacked Ira? And why had someone killed him and left his body in Ira's Christmas sleigh?

"Maybe this is all about drugs," I said. "What if he was high on something the other night when he slugged Ira?"

"I don't suppose Spader mentioned the results of a toxicology report."

"Of course not."

"Even so, let's assume you're right. That might explain his attack on Ira, but who killed him?"

"Maybe it was a drug deal gone bad later that night."

"And the dealer just happened to dump his body in Ira's yard?"

"That does sound highly unlikely."

"You think?"

I stuck my tongue out at him. Sarcasm was my go-to response, not his.

"I hope you're planning to use that," he said, a glint in his eye and a challenge in his voice.

~*~

Before Trimedia took over Reynolds-Alsopp Publishing, we received generous holiday bonuses, never stockbroker-sized sums but always enough to cover my Christmas shopping list. Now, depending when Christmas falls, our bonus consists of a limited amount of time off. With Christmas on a Sunday this year, the corporate bean counters had magnanimously decided to give us half of Thursday and all of Friday.

As editorial director, Naomi didn't have the power to tell us not to come to work on Thursday, but she snubbed her nose at corporate by inviting her entire staff to a morning-long holiday brunch in our conference room. She even snuck in bottles of chilled champagne to make mimosas and vodka for those who preferred Bloody Marys.

Of course, we were sworn to secrecy regarding both the brunch and the alcohol. The head honchos expected us peons to work until noon, and work sober, which precipitated Naomi's only other rule: no shoptalk allowed during brunch.

Luckily, no one from corporate ever bothered to set foot on our floor. If they wanted to speak with us, we were summoned upstairs. The one exception being former owner and Naomi's significant other, Hugo Reynolds-Alsopp, but the other mucky-mucks never paid any attention to Hugo's comings and goings. He had no real power, only a meaningless title.

Rumor had it, Hugo was secretly orchestrating a buyback, but Naomi would neither confirm nor deny that anything was in the works. However, since hope continues to spring eternal, we all kept our fingers crossed. If Hugo regained control of the company, we might even find ourselves back in Manhattan instead of stuck in the middle of a cornfield in Morris County. I'd go back to an easy train commute instead of dealing with daily bumper-to-bumper traffic.

As Cloris and I grazed the spread of gourmet offerings Naomi had assembled for our enjoyment, she asked, "So how are things in Murderville, Sherlock?"

I scooped a spoonful of crab salad onto my plate. "Not funny."

"Well, at least this time the corpse wasn't someone you know."

I continued heaping delicacies onto my plate, adding some

ceviche, a deviled egg, a mini quiche, and a stuffed mushroom. "But it involves someone I know, and he thinks Detective Spader is determined to pin the murder of Dion Leonides on him."

"That sucks, but does Ira really have anything to worry about?"

"Probably not. Ira's a worrywart, but after Cynthia's murder and Lawrence's arrest, I suppose no one can blame him for exhibiting a certain amount of paranoia."

After grabbing mimosas, we made our way to the conference table. Once we'd settled into two cattycorner chairs, Cloris resumed her interrogation, "What's your theory on the murder?"

I took a sip of my mimosa before answering. "I don't have one, at least not yet. All I know is that if Ira were capable of murder—which I don't believe he is—he certainly wouldn't be dumb enough to leave the corpse in plain view on his property."

"And Spader thinks otherwise?"

"He's floated a reverse psychology theory."

"With which I take it you don't agree. Do you believe someone's setting Ira up?"

"That's one possibility."

"Lawrence?"

If only it were that simple. "Definitely not."

"How can you be so sure?"

I explained how, given his current solitary domicile, Ira's ex-father-in-law would have no means of orchestrating such a plot.

"Unless he set the wheels in motion prior to landing in solitary."

"To what end?"

She executed an eye roll that suggested I'd lost all the sleuthing genes I'd ever possessed. "Making your life a living hell comes to mind. The man does hate you."

"That makes no sense."

"Really? I think it makes perfect sense. Lawrence sets Ira up for a murder rap, and you get stuck with his kids—a fate worse than death."

"Highly unlikely."

She raised an eyebrow. "Which part? Lawrence setting up Ira? Or you getting stuck with his kids? And don't lie to me. I know you. Saint Anastasia would not turn her back on Ira's brats."

"Fine. You're right about the kids, but Lawrence likes Ira, at least according to Ira."

"Maybe, but I'm betting Lawrence doesn't like Ira as much as he hates you. After all, you're the reason he's serving life in prison."

"Then why wouldn't he simply take out a hit on Ira? Or me, for that matter? That's his standard M.O."

"Are you kidding? Killing you wouldn't be any fun. He'd want to make you suffer for as long as possible."

"All the more reason to take out a hit on Ira. Besides, all the evidence against Ira is circumstantial." Lawrence had to know that barring the most incompetent defense attorneys ever to set foot in a courtroom, Ira would never go to prison for Dion Leonides' murder. He also knew Ira had the funds to hire the best criminal defense attorneys in the country.

"Because, as you said, Lawrence likes Ira. He doesn't want to kill him, just get him locked up long enough to torture you."

"Interesting theory, Watson."

"I think so."

I shook my head. "I'm not buying it."

"Fine. Here's another one. How about someone from Cynthia's past?"

I allowed this to percolate in my brain for a minute as I

consumed a mini-quiche. I knew nothing about Cynthia's life pre-Ira and little about her relationship with her husband throughout their brief marriage. I'd only met her once prior to her murder. "Possibly. What if she was cheating on Ira with someone in addition to Pablo the Pool Boy?"

"Or more than one someone." Cloris grabbed a mini quiche off her plate and popped it into her mouth. As she chewed, I could almost see the wheels turning in her brain. "Perhaps she dumped a previous lover when she fell in love with Ira's enormous bank account."

"You're suggesting this fictitious former paramour has been nursing a grudge against Ira for several years, waiting for the right opportunity to seek revenge?"

She shrugged. "Why not? What if Dion Leonides was an unlucky convenient target, someone the killer didn't even know?"

"Because anyone would have served the killer's purpose?"

"Exactly."

"But why? Cynthia wasn't that great a catch. She had no money of her own."

"She stood to inherit her father's ill-gotten gains, didn't she? What if the guy was connected? He may have met Cynthia through Lawrence. She rejects him for Ira, and he loses his future life on Easy Street. Maybe he even planned to knock Lawrence off at some point to get his hands on the money sooner than waiting for Lawrence to die a natural death."

"You've been spending too much time with me." I thought it more likely that someone had it in for Leonides. And that brought me back to Jesse Konopka. I pushed my chair back and stood. "Don't let anyone clear my plate. I'll be back shortly."

Once back in my cubicle, I placed a call to Robyn Konopka.

"What a lovely surprise," she said after answering her phone. "When you didn't come back to book club after a few months, we weren't sure what to think. You never returned any of our calls after the funeral."

"It's been a tough year," I said.

"Then the rumors are true?"

"Depends on the rumor, but probably." I'd tried my best to keep people from finding out what Karl had done to us, but my mother, unable to contain her anger at Dead Louse of a Spouse, had blabbed his sins to half the population of New Jersey. They in turn told the remaining half of the population. Or so it seemed.

"Life is looking up, though," I said. "That's why I'm calling. I thought it was time I rejoined Lit Chicks. Are the meetings still at your home the first Wednesday of each month?"

"They are, but I'm going to have to cancel January's meeting. Jesse had an accident at a job site three days ago. He's in the hospital recovering from surgery."

"I'm sorry to hear that. What happened?"

"He's not exactly sure because he suffered a concussion. You wouldn't believe the size of the goose egg on the back of his head!

"How did he manage that?"

"He thinks he may have tripped and fallen through an opening where they hadn't finished installing the plywood subfloor."

"He fell an entire floor?"

"Twelve feet. Even now I grow cold and clammy thinking about it. They were using the basement to store materials. We think he first bounced off a pile of lumber before landing on his back on the concrete floor. Then some of the lumber gave way and toppled over on him. He was probably out for at least twenty minutes before someone found him."

"He was alone at the time?"

"Yes, he'd gone in early to open up for one of the subcontractors." She sighed. "I keep telling myself it could have been much worse. He's banged up pretty badly, has a broken leg, and several broken bones in his hand. He may need some additional surgery, but at least he's alive, and the doctors say he should make a full recovery."

"Is there anything I can do?"

"That's so sweet of you, Anastasia, but I know you have your own problems. Why don't you plan on coming to the February meeting? We're reading Shelley Noble's newest historical mystery. If I have to postpone, I'll call you."

"I'll do that. But before you hang up, is Jesse at Overlook?"

"Yes, why?"

"I'm working half a day today and drive right past the hospital on my way home. I can stop in to say hello."

"Would you? With everyone at work during the day, he only gets visitors in the evenings. He hasn't complained, but I can tell he's going stir crazy."

"I'm happy to."

After hanging up from Robyn, I considered the murder timeline and heaved a huge sigh of relief. Jesse Konopka couldn't have killed Dion Leonides. At the time of the murder he was either on an operating table or in a hospital bed with his leg and hand encased in casts.

Of course, that still left not a single viable suspect to draw suspicion away from Ira. Since Jesse Konopka worked for the victim, perhaps he could offer up a name or two of someone who might have had it in for his boss.

Apparently, the same thought had occurred to Detective

Spader because when I arrived at the hospital two hours later, he nearly collided with me as he exited Jesse Konopka's hospital room.

EIGHT

"What the hell are you doing here, Mrs. Pollack?" Surprise can take many forms—from pleasantly delighted to downright incensed. Spader's tone put him squarely in the incensed-and-then-some category. He grabbed my arm and marched me away from the hospital room as the door whooshed closed behind him.

Halfway down the corridor he stopped in front of a bank of elevators, turned to face me, and said, "I don't appreciate you nosing around my investigation, Mrs. Pollack."

I focused on his beefy right hand, still grasping my upper arm. Then I raised my gaze to his face, smiled, and in a calm voice and as sweetly as possible, said, "And I don't appreciate being manhandled, Detective." I saw no point in sounding confrontational, but I wanted to make it clear he'd definitely overstepped his bounds. After all, I certainly wasn't a suspect in his investigation.

Shock transformed his features. Realizing the inappropriateness of his actions, he quickly dropped his hand, took a step away from me, and mumbled, "Sorry."

When I nodded my acceptance of his apology, he segued back into cop mode and asked, "Care to explain why you're here?"

"I'm visiting a friend."

"Jesse Konopka is a friend of yours? Funny how you failed to mention that, given he works for my murder victim."

"Really?" I mustered all my minimal acting skills to register my own shock. Then I sent up a swift plea to the God of Prevarication, hoping Spader would buy into my innocent act. "Jesse works for Leonides? Talk about a coincidence!"

He eyed me skeptically. "You telling me you didn't know that?"

"If I'd known, I certainly would have told you, Detective."

Spader smirked. "He's a friend, but you didn't know what he does for a living?"

"I know him through his wife. We're in a book club together. I was aware Jesse is a general contractor, but I had no idea he worked for Leonides."

"I didn't fall off a turnip truck this morning, Mrs. Pollack."

So much for the God of Prevarication cutting me a break. I held up the box of chocolates I'd purchased in the hospital gift shop. "When I spoke with Robyn this morning, she told me about Jesse's accident. She said he's going stir crazy laid up here. Since I drive right past the hospital on my way home from work, I thought he might appreciate a visit from someone who didn't want to stick a needle in him."

"And you expect me to buy that this is all a coincidence?"

I shrugged. "I don't know what else it could be."

"Uh-huh." He wasn't buying it. Assuming a pose of intimidation that had probably worked on countless suspects over the years, he crossed his arms over his expansive barrel chest and stared down at me from his considerable height advantage.

Since redirecting the conversation might ease me out of an awkward situation, I asked, "Why are you here, Detective? Jesse can't possibly be a suspect, given the timing of his accident and the murder."

He studied me for a moment. I'd known Detective Sam Spader long enough to pick up on a few of his tells, and one of them—the way he tilted his head to the left and quirked the right side of his mouth upward—now told me he was in the process of debating whether or not to divulge any new information to me.

"I had some questions regarding Parthenon."

"Parthenon?" Sometimes the best course of action is to keep playing dumb. Spader didn't have to know Zack and I spent last night in a threesome with Google, learning everything we could about Leonides and his business.

"The company owned by the Leonides brothers."

"You think one of their employees killed Dion?"

"Not necessarily."

"But that's one of those stones you're turning over?"

"Exactly."

"Did you learn anything?"

He huffed out an annoyed gust of air. "Mrs. Pollack, you know I—"

"Can't divulge information about an ongoing investigation."

"Precisely."

Only he had, time and time again, but only whenever it suited him. I refrained from stating the obvious rather than push my luck by reminding him of that fact. "Understood."

I executed a verbal pivot in another direction. "I don't suppose you've uncovered anything that rules Ira out as a suspect at this point."

Instead of answering me, he asked, "Have you heard any news today?"

This time there was no need for me to play dumb. I really should download one of those local news apps. However, every time I remember, I'm away from home, and I've heard too many horror stories regarding hackers targeting people who use public wi-fi. "No, what happened?"

"Sometime this morning a fire broke out at a house on Fair Ridge."

"Fair Ridge?" I thought for a moment, trying to place the street.

"It's parallel to Prospect."

"Yes, of course." A wooded expanse of public green space separated the two streets.

"The home on Fair Ridge is owned by Paul Leonides, Dion's brother. It's about a football field's distance from your brother-in-law's house."

This time I didn't bother to correct him regarding my relationship to Ira. The theme from *Twilight Zone* had begun to play in my head. "I hope you're going to tell me the fire was sparked by a faulty space heater and not an arsonist."

"I wish I could."

A bowling ball settled in my stomach. "Was anyone hurt?"

Spader shook his head. "Luckily the smoke alarm woke Leonides and his wife. They escaped without injury."

"And their home?"

"Sustained minimal damage."

"So it seems someone has it in for the Leonides brothers."

"It appears that may be the case." Spader didn't have to state the obvious. Another circumstantial nail had been hammered into Ira's coffin.

The elevator opened, discharging several people. Spader stepped forward. I followed. He stopped and turned to face me. "Aren't you forgetting something?"

"Am I?"

He pointed to the box of chocolates. "The reason you're here?"

Busted! I stepped back and waved to him. "Of course. Have a nice day, Detective."

He tipped an imaginary hat as he stepped inside and pushed the button. As the doors swept closed, he said, "Stay out of trouble, Mrs. Pollack."

~*~

Did the man think I go looking for trouble? I'd like nothing better than to turn back the clock to a time when I didn't have an intimate relationship with dead bodies and the murderers responsible for them. Then again, if I returned to that time, Dead Louse of a Spouse would still be alive and continuing to perpetrate financial malfeasance against his family. And if Karl were still alive, I wouldn't have Zack in my life. Dead bodies and debt notwithstanding, I was much better off now. The universe certainly works in weird ways.

I headed back to Jesse Konopka's room and knocked on the door.

"Come in."

After pasting a smile on my face, I pushed open the door and stepped inside the room. "Hey, Jesse!"

He winced as he tried to paste a smile on a face covered in bruises, bandages, and abrasions. "Anastasia Pollack. This is a surprise."

Jesse Konopka normally possessed an *aw shucks* grin and attitude that reminded me of Jimmy Carter. His shock of blond hair, large lips, and twinkling eyes reinforced the resemblance to the point that I once asked Robyn if her husband and the former president were related. They aren't.

I crossed the room to his bed, handed him the box of chocolates, and quickly explained how I'd learned about his accident. "Robyn said you're climbing the walls."

"That's an understatement. I haven't spent this much time on my back since the day I clambered out of my crib."

He tapped the candy box with his good hand. "Thanks for the chocolates. Would you mind opening the box?"

He lifted his left hand, completely encased in a cast that ran from the tips of his fingers halfway to his elbow. Much of the white plaster had been decorated in brightly colored flowers, stars, rainbows, and unicorns. Similar artwork covered the cast on his right leg. Both color-coordinated with the various hued wounds to his face and head. "As you can see, I'm currently useless when it comes to doing just about anything for myself."

"Looks like your daughters had a blast, though."

He chuckled. "Nine-year-old twin budding Picassos. They're not going to be happy when the doctor cuts the casts off."

"You'll have to save a few chunks. Mount them in a memory box."

"A memory of my own stupidity and clumsiness? No thanks."

I removed the cellophane wrapper, opened the lid, and placed the box on the tray table next to his bed. He chose a dark chocolate nut cluster. After popping it into his mouth, he said, "This sure beats hospital Jell-o. Help yourself."

He didn't have to ask twice. I'd never met a chocolate I didn't love, unless it contained peanut butter. I'm one of the few people on the planet who can't stand the stuff. I chose a raspberry cream enrobed in milk chocolate and savored the mouthful of pleasure.

When Jesse had finished devouring his nut cluster, he said, "So why are you really here, Anastasia?"

"Am I that transparent?"

"Given that you pretty much dropped out of my wife's life for nearly a year, then suddenly call her today, and pay me a visit a few hours later...."

"Too much of a coincidence?"

"I'd say so. Besides, I overheard the detective ask what you're doing here. The two of you obviously know each other."

Timing is everything. Mine sucks. "Your boss's body was left in my half-brother-in-law's front yard."

He nodded. "When the detective told me his name, I figured there might be some relation. I asked."

"And he confirmed it?"

Jesse nodded again. "I really wasn't surprised when you walked into the room. Robyn mentioned you might stop by. Adding two plus two doesn't take an advanced degree in mathematics, even if I do have one."

This was news to me. "And yet you work in construction?"

He shrugged his shoulder, and his face immediately clouded over in pain. "Shouldn't have done that," he said through gritted teeth.

"Should I get the nurse?"

"No, it's residual pain from a dislocated shoulder. I really should have zigged instead of zagged the other day. It's subsiding."

He took a breath before continuing. "Anyway, as I was about

to say, I like working with my hands. If I'd had my way, I would have gone to trade school instead of college. My parents insisted otherwise. Claimed carpentry was a waste of my talents. So I did what they wanted and taught calculus for a few years, hating every minute of it."

"I can relate. Successful teachers have a passion for teaching. I didn't."

"Neither did I. Now I love what I do. And although my parents don't believe it, you'd be surprised how much math I use on a daily basis."

"Measure twice, cut once?"

"And so much more."

Since Jesse knew the real reason for my visit, I changed the subject. "Would you mind telling me what Detective Spader asked you?"

He reached for another chocolate, popped it in his mouth, and spoke around it. "Primarily checking to see if I had an alibi for the night of the murder."

"Which you obviously do."

He lifted his plastered arm and pointed it in the direction of his plastered leg. "Kind of hard to kill someone when you've only got one working arm and leg. And I certainly didn't hobble out of here early this morning to set Paul's house on fire. Once the detective realized I wasn't his man, he asked for the names and contact information for my crew, then left, bumping into you on his way out."

"Do you think someone on your crew had a beef with Dion?"

He shook his head. "I'd know if they did."

"How well do you know them?"

"They've been with me for years."

"I'm confused. Didn't you only recently start working for Parthenon, after Dion and Paul's father died this past year?"

"I did, but when the Leonides brothers offered me the position, I told them I'd only take it if I could bring along my entire crew. My guys are loyal and trustworthy. I wasn't about to strand them in an unemployment line."

"What happened to the other crew? Were they all fired?" If so, that could be a motive for someone to seek revenge on both brothers.

Jesse grabbed a third chocolate. "I was told the company had plenty of connections and Octavia—Paul's wife—would contact other local construction companies to make sure they all found jobs."

"Did they?"

"I assume so."

"But you don't know for sure?"

"How could I? I never met any of them. My primary concern was my own crew, but I didn't want to be responsible for another group of men losing their jobs. I took Dion and Paul at their word." He paused for a moment before stating the obvious. "But if they lied to me, one of those men could have killed Dion and tried to kill Paul."

NINE

I left Jesse's room confident that Detective Spader now had a long list of possible suspects and would most likely soon drop his suspicions regarding Ira. Jesse might not think any of his crew had issues with Dion and Paul, but just as the wife is often the last to know, the same could be said for the employer/employee relationship. How many times over the past few years had a disgruntled employee settled a score by bringing a gun to work?

Ex-employees often have even more motive to seek revenge. No doubt Detective Spader had gotten hold of Parthenon's employee records and was in the process of tracking down all the men Dion and Paul had laid off when they hired Jesse.

As I drove away from the hospital, another thought niggled at my brain. Given that any of Parthenon's former or current employees were much more likely suspects than Ira, why did Dion attack Ira Tuesday night?

I drummed my fingers on the steering wheel, mulling the question around in my brain as I waited for a light to turn green.

None of it made any sense. Dion lived a mile away and across a major highway from Ira. The lights, noise, and traffic from the Christmas display wouldn't impact him. How would he even know about Ira's extravaganza?

The only logical conclusion was that either Ira was lying about not knowing Dion, or someone else had attacked Ira, possibly someone Ira knew but refused to name. And if that were the case, why?

That brought me to Lawrence. Was it possible my mother's ex-husband had set something in motion prior to landing in solitary confinement? Ira had nothing to do with Lawrence's arrest and conviction, but Lawrence wouldn't be the first member of a crime syndicate to continue his operations from behind prison walls, even if he had no chance of parole. What if he'd pressured Ira to do something for him and Ira had refused? Knowing Lawrence, he wouldn't take no for an answer. Had he sent Ira a message in the form of an underling's fist?

Too bad none of us heard what the attacker had yelled at Ira before punching him in the face. Contrary to his denial, I suspected Ira clearly remembered what was said but was too scared to tell Spader. If so, that would mean there was no connection between the attack on him and Dion's murder. But if that were the case, why would the killer dump Dion's body in Ira's front yard?

Such randomness stretched coincidence beyond credibility. Maybe it was time for me to have a talk with Ira, just the two of us this time.

Ira had never come right out and admitted it, but I was certain he had a crush on me and harbored a fantasy about the two of us walking hand-in-hand into the setting sun of a happily-ever-after.

Zack or no Zack, that was never going to happen. I'd sooner join a convent.

However, Ira saw Zack as an obstacle to his conquest of my heart. He didn't have to voice his feelings; his attitude toward Zack spoke volumes. He very well may have known the reason for his attack but decided not to divulge it last night in front of Zack.

Of course, that still didn't explain why he hadn't told Detective Spader, unless he was too scared to do so—which sent my brain whiplashing back to Lawrence. Either way, I was convinced Ira held the key to at least one part of this mystery.

Christmas was only three days away, and I had planned to spend the afternoon doing some last-minute shopping. Zack and I had agreed not to exchange gifts, but I didn't feel right going empty-handed to Shane and Sophie's for brunch or to Ira's later in the afternoon, especially since I suspected both would have gifts for us.

Besides Christmas presents, etiquette also dictated I bring Ira a housewarming gift. It didn't matter that he already owned ten times more than any one person could possibly need in three lifetimes. As the former social secretary of the Daughters of the American Revolution, Mama would insist I follow Emily Post protocol.

However, since murder trumped shopping, and the stores were open late tonight, I put my afternoon plans on hold. Instead, I pulled into the nearest empty parking space and called Ira. "Sorry to disturb you," I said when he answered.

"You could never disturb me, Anastasia. I always enjoy hearing from you. What's up?"

"Do you have any free time today?"

"For you, I'll make time."

As it turned out, Ira was at his dealership in Springfield, all of five minutes from my current location. "Perfect. I'll see you shortly," I said and ended the call.

Minutes later, as I drove into a spot in the customer parking lot, I glimpsed Ira standing at the glass wall that ran the length of the showroom. Hands in pockets, his expression, both anxious and eager at the same time, reminded me of a little boy hoping that against all odds Santa had come through with the puppy his parents had nixed.

As I approached the showroom, he vacated his observation post and met me at the double-doors, swinging one open for me to enter. I stepped across the threshold and was immediately enveloped in a bear hug. "What a wonderful surprise," he said.

The overly affectionate embrace lasted far too long. When I was finally able to extricate myself, I noticed several of his employees and a few customers with their heads turned in our direction. Oblivious to their stares, Ira looped his arm across my shoulders and led me across the floor.

The showroom looked more like the lobby of a high-end Manhattan hotel than a car dealership, except for the half dozen luxury vehicles on display in the massive room. Ira never did anything halfway. Everything sparkled, from the crystal chandeliers dripping from the ceiling to the polished chrome, glass, and black leather furnishings scattered in groupings around the room. Rows of glass-walled sales office cubicles lined two walls. A sweeping staircase, leading to the mezzanine, ran the length of the third wall.

"Can I offer you anything?" he asked, waving toward the alcove under the staircase where a complimentary spread of coffee, tea, bagels and donuts filled the surface of a polished ebony credenza.

Alongside the credenza a wine fridge held a variety of soft drinks, juices, and bottled water.

"No, thank you."

"I can have something brought in if you prefer."

"I've already eaten, Ira." His crestfallen demeanor caused me to add, "We had our annual holiday brunch at work today. I ate so much that I might even skip dinner tonight."

That seemed to appease him. His smile returned as he led me up the staircase and into his office. Containing a door and privacy blinds covering the showroom-facing glass wall, Ira's office afforded him an amount of privacy his sales force lacked.

"Let me take your coat," he said. After I slipped out of it, he hung it on a hook on the back of his office door. Then instead of directing me toward one of the two visitor chairs facing his desk, he ushered me toward a black leather sectional that filled one corner of the room.

This didn't bother me at first. After all, as Ira so often pointed out, we were family. Besides, I wasn't here for a business meeting. I took a seat at the nearest end of the couch and placed my purse on the cushion beside me. Ira immediately moved the purse to the glass-topped coffee table and sat close enough that our hips nearly touched, trapping me between him and the arm of the sofa. Could he be more obvious?

He turned sideways, knocking knees with me, grasped my hand, and said, "What can I do for you, Anastasia? Do you need something? Name it, and it's yours."

Ira saw the world and everyone in it through the lens of a bank account. In his world money could solve every problem known to mankind. I pulled my hand away. "How about the truth, Ira?"

"I..." His jaw flapped open. "What do you mean? The truth

about what?"

"The guy who attacked you Tuesday night."

He shifted a few inches away from me. "I told you all I know."

"I don't believe you, Ira, and I don't think Detective Spader does, either. Someone had to have heard what that guy said to you. Do you think Spader isn't going to find out?"

That caused the color to drain from his face, making his bruises and contusions even more prominent. "What did he say to you?"

Instead of answering, I pressed on. "What are you hiding?"

"N...nothing."

Mama claimed she always knew when I was lying because I couldn't keep a straight face, which is why I never play poker. With Ira, his entire body gave him away. "Try again. Is Lawrence somehow behind this? Has he threatened you?"

Ira's entire body shuddered a huge sigh. "It's not Lawrence."

"Then who? And why?"

He stood, hugged his arms to his chest, and began pacing the office. "Two weeks ago I was supposed to attend an all-day dealers' meeting in the city. At the last minute I had to cancel because Isaac got into trouble at school."

"What kind of trouble?"

"His teacher caught him cheating on a test."

When he didn't continue immediately, I prodded. "And?"

"According to his teacher, she marched him down to the principal's office where he cursed them both out." His voice grew agitated. "I had no idea he even knew such language. He certainly never heard those words from me."

"What did the school do?"

"He was given an in-school suspension through Christmas break."

That seemed like a rather severe punishment for a nine-year-old, especially if he hadn't become physically violent—unless this was just the latest instance in a pattern of troubling behavior at school. Given what I'd observed of Isaac, I had to assume it was. "Was this the first time Isaac's gotten into trouble at school?" I asked.

Ira shook his head. "He's bullied a few kids, picked some fights. But all boys misbehave from time to time, right? I'm sure in the past you've been called to school over something Nick or Alex did."

His eyes pleaded with a confirmation I refused to corroborate. "No, I can't say I have."

He stopped pacing and offered me a sheepish grin. "Probably because they got lucky and were never caught. Anyway, it's a good thing Isaac is switching schools in January."

What was wrong with this man? Could he not see that a new home with new furniture in a new town was no substitute for proper parenting? If he didn't do something about his kids soon, all three of them would eventually wind up in serious trouble.

However, now wasn't the time for a parenting discussion. I'd come for answers. "What does this have to do with your attacker?"

"I was getting to that. I needed to go over a few things with the manager of this dealership, so after I left the school, I drove up here."

He paused, glancing up at the ceiling as if searching for divine intervention. Then he hung his head and mumbled, "I didn't bother to call ahead to let him know I was on my way. When I unlocked my office door, I found him and one of my customer service reps naked and...." He pointed to the sectional. "Well, I'm sure you get the idea."

Eww! I got the idea all right, enough so that I jumped up and stepped away from the scene of the crime, hoping someone had taken a disinfectant wipe to the sectional after the coitus interruptus. "What does that have to do with Tuesday night?"

"I'm getting to that. I fired them on the spot."

"As you should have."

Ira collapsed into the chair behind his desk and lowered his head into his hands. "At some point afterwards my manager's wife found out what happened. She kicked him out and has filed for divorce and full custody of their kids."

"He's the guy who punched you?"

Ira raised his head and nodded.

"Why keep that a secret?"

He stared straight at me. "Don't you think he's suffering enough? I don't want him arrested."

I had no sympathy for any man who cheats on his wife. As far as I was concerned, the creep who attacked Ira got exactly what he deserved, but women often see adultery—not to mention other unacceptable male conduct—differently than men. They tend to employ a boys-will-be-boys standard defense for questionable behavior. Hadn't Ira just used a version of it to explain away Isaac's actions?

I tried to get through to him another way. "That man could have killed you, Ira. He stabbed the lawn balloons with a knife. What if he'd stabbed you?"

"But he didn't."

How often had I used the same logic over the past year? Hearing similar words from someone else forced me to confront my own stupidity. I shook my head. "You have to tell Detective Spader."

"I can't."

"You're impeding an investigation."

"How? What difference does it make who punched me?"

"It makes a huge difference. Resources are being misdirected because the police are operating under the assumption that the person who attacked you is their murder victim."

"So?"

So? I walked over to the opposite side of the desk, planted my palms on the surface, and leaned over until we were nearly nose-to-nose. "A killer is on the loose, Ira. One man is already dead. Another survived an arson fire. What if the killer strikes a third time?"

Ira couldn't look me in the eye. He directed a blank stare over my shoulder to a spot across the room. I needed to bring him down out of whichever mind cloud he'd retreated into. I dropped into the chair behind me and softened my tone. "Look, maybe telling Detective Spader won't make a difference in his investigation. But maybe it will. Do you really want to take that chance?"

He turned his attention back to me and released a long, slow sigh that reminded me of those deflating lawn balloons. "I suppose you're right."

I stood and walked back to the coffee table to retrieve my phone from my purse. "So you'll contact Detective Spader?"

Panic consumed his features as he zeroed in on the phone in my hand. "Now?"

"No time like the present." I pulled up Spader's number and initiated the call.

TEN

Spader answered with a variation of his usual greeting to me. "Mrs. Pollack, staying out of trouble, I hope?"

"Trying my best, Detective."

"What can I do for you?"

"It's what I can do for you. I'm with my half-brother-in-law. He has some information regarding your case." Before handing the phone to Ira, I tapped the speaker icon. After all, I'd gotten Ira to confess he knew his assailant. Shouldn't that entitle me to listen in on both ends of his conversation with Spader?

The seconds ticked by as Ira stared at the phone in his hand.

"Mrs. Pollack?" asked Spader. "You there? What's going on? I don't have all day."

I poked Ira out of his stupor. "Tell the detective what you told me."

After a few stammered false starts, Ira finally came clean. Then he cringed as Spader reamed him out for withholding information about an ongoing case. Spader finished by hurling the ultimate cop threat. "Do it again, and you'll find yourself behind bars, understood?"

Ira nodded.

"He can't hear you nod," I said and pointed to the phone.

Ira's voice quaked as he forced out a weak confirmation. "Yes, sir. Understood."

"One last question, Mr. Pollack. What's your former sales manager's name?"

Ira hesitated.

"A name, Pollack!"

"Showalter. Chuck Showalter."

"Put your sister-in-law back on the phone."

Ira handed me the phone, and I disabled the speaker. "Yes, detective?"

"Thanks. I owe you one." He hung up before I could respond.

I turned to find that Ira had collapsed onto the sofa. His body nearly doubled in half, he sat with his head buried in his hands and shaking from head to toe, as if he were in shock. I suppose in a way he was, not from an accident but a mental shock that manifested as tremors. "I hope I did the right thing," he half-whispered.

I settled beside him and reached over to place a hand on his shoulder but kept half a cushion's space between us. I needed to calm him down but didn't want him collapsing into my arms. He might never let go. "You did."

He lifted his head and turned to me. "One mistake shouldn't define the remainder of a man's life."

Was he speaking about himself or his former sales manager? As far as I was concerned, Ira had made more than one whopper of a mistake in his life—chief among them, his dubious parenting skills. Marrying Cynthia the Gold Digger came in at a close second. Both had already wreaked serious havoc in his life.

Since I had no desire to open up the can of worms that constituted either of the former, I opted for the latter. "The man was cheating on his wife, Ira. I doubt it was the first time, and it probably wouldn't have been the last if she hadn't found out. You don't owe him anything."

"Still...."

"Still what?" I found it incredulous that Ira's need to be liked by everyone extended to sleazeballs. "He should be grateful you're not pressing charges."

He sighed. "I suppose."

I shook my head and stood. "Eventually Spader would have found out your assailant wasn't Dion Leonides, whether you told him or not. And then he may have locked you up to teach you a lesson. Are you really willing to go to jail to protect an adulterer?"

"No, you're right."

"I know I am." With that, I grabbed my coat.

"You're leaving? I thought maybe we could get a drink. I could sure use one right now."

I raised an eyebrow. "Don't you have to pick your kids up soon?"

"Right." He shook his head. "What was I thinking?"

He wasn't, as usual. But since I'm not the sort of person who pours salt in someone's wounds, I bit back the words straining to force their way out of my mouth. Instead, I donned my coat, said goodbye, and slipped out of the office before he thought to rise from the sofa to embrace me.

Hopefully, he didn't have a bottle of whiskey stashed in a desk drawer. Or if he did, he had the common sense not to indulge in a solo pity party.

On my way home I stopped at a gourmet food shop to purchase two breakfast gift baskets. At least that had been my intention when I entered the shop. Sticker shock forced me into a quick about-face and out the door.

Once back in my car, I drove to the supermarket where I purchased the components to assemble two baskets myself. I spent half the money for twice the amount of food, even though I bought gourmet brands instead of the generic store labels.

As I glanced at the total displayed on the cash register, I wondered if I should go into the gift basket business. Those folks had to be clearing a tidy profit, given they were able to buy their components wholesale. If I operated the business from my home and advertised online, I wouldn't have the overhead of a retail location. Of course, I'd have to figure out how to do without sleep. But since I still had plenty of Karl's debts hanging over my head, I parked the idea in a corner of my brain to access at a later date. Sleep was overrated anyway.

I arrived home to find Mama camped in my living room.

~*~

My mother was not used to living on her own, having spent her entire life with my grandparents until the day she married my father. After Dad drowned while scuba diving in the Yucatan on their twenty-fifth anniversary, Mama moved in with Karl and me.

As it turned out, Mama needs a man like a fish needs water. Her widowhood didn't last long. Unfortunately, four months into Mama's second marriage, Husband Number Two was gored to death by a bull while racing through the streets of Pamplona.

A pattern began to emerge with Husband Number Three, who died from an allergic reaction to shellfish shortly after their first anniversary. Number Four never made it past their honeymoon.

He plunged to his death at the Grand Canyon. Within days of Karl's death, Mama lost Husband Number Five. That relationship only lasted six months, after an ill-fated attempt to kiss the Blarney Stone resulted in a cerebral aneurysm.

Once Nick was born, whenever Mama camped out between husbands, he and Alex were forced to share a bedroom. By the time Husband Number Five slipped his earthly coil, Lucille was permanently ensconced in Nick's bedroom. That resulted in the former social secretary of the Daughters of the American Revolution and the self-appointed leader of the Daughters of the October Revolution becoming reluctant roomies, which in turn triggered World War Three within the walls of Casa Pollack.

Last summer after Ira walked into our lives, he took it upon himself to play Cupid between Mama and his widowed father-in-law. Within days of Lawrence and Mama meeting, they were going at it like teenagers with raging hormones. One day I had the misfortune of arriving home early to find them in the middle of an afternoon delight—an image I will unfortunately take to my grave.

When Mama and Lawrence wed a short time later, Flora Sudberry Periwinkle Ramirez Scoffield Goldberg O'Keefe became Flora Sudberry Periwinkle Ramirez Scoffield Goldberg O'Keefe Tuttnauer. However, unlike Husbands Two through Five, Lawrence had money, having sold his commercial laundry upon retiring. Or so he said. We later learned he never laundered garments; he laundered money—for the mob.

Ira, never one to do anything small, had given Mama and Lawrence a townhouse as a wedding gift. Because he hadn't gotten around to signing over the deed prior to Lawrence's arrest, the government couldn't seize the place when they scooped up

Lawrence's other assets.

However, although she now had her own home, Mama often spent more time in mine than her own, habitually dropping in shortly before mealtime because mastering kitchen skills had never been high on her list of priorities. If my father hadn't enjoyed cooking, we either would have starved to death or died of ptomaine poisoning.

My mother didn't even give me a chance to drop my packages and remove my coat before she jumped to her feet and began peppering me with questions. "What's this I hear about you finding a dead body in Ira's front yard? And why did I have to hear it on *Eyewitness News* while I was eating my lunch? I nearly choked on my tuna sandwich! Is this Lawrence's doing?"

I placed my grocery sacks on the foyer floor and hung up my coat as I tackled Mama's last question first. "I don't know."

"Well, I do."

I spun around to face her. "What do you mean? Have you spoken with him?"

"Of course not! I wouldn't give that man the time of day after the way he deceived me."

I grabbed the groceries and headed for the kitchen, Mama following close on my heels. "Not to mention orchestrating several murders?"

"That, too."

I dropped the sacks onto the kitchen counter. "Coffee?"

"Of course." She started rifling through my groceries. "Do you have anything to go with the coffee? Some cake or pastry? I could use something sweet."

I grabbed a jar of jam from her hand and returned it to the bag. "These aren't for me. Check the pantry. There should be some cookies, assuming Lucille hasn't scarfed them all down."

Mama poked her nose into the pantry as I started a pot of coffee. "Speaking of the commie heathen," she said, retrieving half a package of chocolate chip cookies, "where is she?"

I shrugged. "Don't know, don't care." I secretly think Mama missed getting under Lucille's skin. It didn't seem to matter to her that in doing so, she also got under my skin—which is why, as much as I resented Ira trying to buy his way into our lives, I didn't say a word about the extravagant wedding present or that he now paid her condo fees, taxes, and utilities. In addition, I suspected he also paid for her Uber account and possibly even her credit cards at this point.

Mama had a Blanche duBois way about her, always relying on the kindness of friends, relatives, and strangers—especially male friends, relatives, and strangers, who were always eager to accommodate her. She bore such a striking resemblance to a younger Ellen Burstyn that people often asked if she was the actress's daughter, and with the face and body of a much younger woman, she knew how to use those assets to her advantage.

I moved the conversation back to her ex-husband. "What makes you so certain Lawrence is involved in the murder of Dion Leonides if you haven't spoken with him?"

She settled into a kitchen chair, removed a cookie from the package and took a bite. Mama wasn't the sort to talk around a mouthful of food. It wasn't ladylike. After she'd swallowed the morsel and patted her lips with a napkin, she answered me. "Because I know Lawrence. Prison isn't going to keep him from exacting his revenge on this family."

She sighed. "And here I thought having five husbands drop dead on me was the worst luck I could possibly have! Nothing compares to learning your husband is in the mob."

"Back up, Mama. What do you mean about exacting revenge on us?"

"I should think it's obvious. Have you told that detective friend of yours to check into all of Lawrence's associates? I know he's got them doing his dirty work for him."

"What makes you say that? Is there something you're not telling me, Mama?"

She hesitated for a moment. "I suppose I should call him."

I poured two cups of coffee and brought them to the table, taking the seat across from her. "Call Lawrence?"

"No, the detective. Really, Anastasia, focus!"

"I've spoken with Detective Spader, Mama. You don't need to call him."

"Good. What did he say?"

I knew of only one way to keep her from meddling. "Lawrence hasn't been ruled out as a suspect, Mama."

She slammed her hand on the table. "I knew it!"

"Only because this early in the investigation, the police are looking at everyone with a connection to Ira. They haven't ruled out anyone—including Ira and Lawrence."

"Ira? Why Ira?"

"Because the body was found on his property."

"Well, that's just ridiculous. Why would Ira kill someone and leave the body in his yard?"

"He wouldn't, but the police have to follow procedure."

"They're wasting their time. It's obviously Lawrence."

"There are more credible suspects." Mama may have made up her mind, but from what Jesse Konopka had told me, Parthenon's former employees pushed Lawrence way down on the list.

"Like who?"

"Detective Spader hasn't shared any names with me." Which was a completely truthful answer, but I decided we were in need of a quick subject change before her questioning necessitated fibbing on my part. "Are you staying for dinner, or do you have other plans?" Given her history, by now Mama should be in full hubby hunting mode. I expected any day she'd sashay into my house on the arm of my next stepfather.

"Depends. What are you making?"

Did it matter? Even if I served cornflakes, Mama would stay unless she had a better offer. "Baked tilapia."

"I'll stay."

~*~

Lucille, with Harriet in tow, walked into the house as Mama, Zack, the boys, and I were finishing dinner. I had defrosted and baked six tilapia fillets, setting one aside with some brown rice and broccoli for my mother-in-law. "Your dinner is in the microwave," I told Lucille as she and Harriet dropped their coats on the sofa.

Hearing the return of his mistress, Mephisto padded into the living room from where he'd been camped out in the den. He stopped in front of Lucille. As she stooped to cuddle him, he bared his teeth and growled at her. She straightened and jumped back.

"What have you done to my dog?" she demanded. Her eyes narrowed at those of us seated around the dining room table as Devil Dog retreated back down the hall.

"Us?" asked Nick. "You're the one who's abandoned him lately. He's just letting you know how he feels."

Lucille ignored Nick and hurled a verbal jab at me. "If my son were still alive, he'd never allow such insolence."

"Speaking the truth isn't insolence," said Mama.

Lucille spun around to face Mama. "No one asked you for your two cents."

"Well, I'm giving it anyway," said Mama, "and it's worth a heck of a lot more than two cents." She punctuated her words by sticking her tongue out at Lucille.

"Very mature," said her nemesis. "I'd expect no less from the likes of you."

Lucille and Harriet then turned their backs on us and strode into the kitchen. I braced myself for the explosion I knew would follow. They didn't disappoint. A moment later the two women stormed into the dining room. "Anastasia, there's only one dinner in the microwave," said Lucille.

"That's right. Yours."

"What about Harriet?"

"You're welcome to share your dinner with your friend."

Lucille banged her cane on the floor, her voice climbing several decibels. "She's my guest! You will treat her accordingly."

"I am. She's a freeloader, and thanks to your son, I can't afford her constantly mooching meals."

"How dare you blame Karl for your selfishness!"

"And what does that make her?" asked Harriet, pointing a gnarled finger at Mama.

I kept my voice calm and soft. "My mother. And unlike you, she was invited."

Harriet's face contorted into a look of pure hatred. I ignored her and directed my comments back to my mother-in-law. "If you want Harriet to join us for meals every night, you can kick in more money for weekly groceries. Otherwise Harriet can eat her own food in her own apartment. I will no longer allow you and your friends to take advantage of me."

Mama clapped her hands. "Brava, dear. It's about time you stopped letting that parasite and her cronies walk all over you."

I turned to frown at her and caught Alex gesturing to Nick with a wave of his thumb toward the kitchen. The boys rose and began clearing the remains of dinner, stepping around their grandmother and Harriet to carry the empty dishes into the kitchen.

Instead of responding to Mama, Lucille zeroed in on Zack. "This is all your doing, isn't it?"

Ralph, who had perched silently on the breakfront up until now, squawked once and said, "...'twere a concealment, worse than a theft, no less than a traducement, to hide your doings....Coriolanus. Act One, Scene Nine." Then he flapped his wings and flew across the room. After settling on Zack's shoulder, he nuzzled his cheek until Zack rewarded him with a sunflower seed.

Zack finally answered Lucille. "Are you insinuating Karl stood by and allowed you to take advantage of Anastasia before she met me?"

Her jaw flapped open. She sputtered once or twice before she finally said, "How dare you!" Then she stormed into the living room and grabbed her coat. "Come, Harriet."

"Leaving so soon?" asked Mama as they marched toward the front door.

I shook my head and muttered, "Not helpful, Mama."

Lucille stopped short, turned, and glared at all of us but said nothing before pivoting and continuing into the foyer. A moment later the front door slammed.

"Is it safe to come out?" Nick called from the kitchen.

Before I could respond to him, the phone rang. Alex answered, then stepped into the dining room, his hand over the receiver. "It's

Uncle Ira. He sounds really upset."

I shook my head and sighed. "Any chance we can implement a One Family Drama Per Dinner policy at Casa Pollack?"

"With your family?" asked Zack. "Doubtful."

I hate it when he's right. I sighed as I held my hand out for Alex to pass me the phone. "Hello, Ira."

Between gulping sobs, he said, "Anastasia, you...you have to hel...help m...me.

"What's wrong? Did your sales manager come after you again? Are you hurt?"

"N...no, it's Isaac. I don't know wha...what to do!"

"What about Isaac?"

"He...he's missing."

ELEVEN

"Missing?" I asked. "What do you mean? Wasn't he at school when you went to pick him up?"

"N...not school. Here."

"Okay, Ira. Take a deep breath, calm down, and tell me what happened."

I heard him inhale a ragged breath, then the whoosh of air when he forcefully released it. He repeated this a second, then a third time. Finally, he attempted to speak again. With each word, his voice grew steadier and stronger until anger supplanted fear and uncertainty, and he shouted, "Someone's kidnapped him!"

"What! Are you sure?"

"Of course, I'm sure. What else could it be? He wouldn't run off."

Knowing Isaac, I had my doubts. The kid had anger issues and a short fuse. Several viable scenarios sprang to mind, but instead of suggesting any of them, I asked, "Have you called the police?"

"They're on their way." His voice segued into pleading mode.

"Would you come, too, Anastasia? Please?"

I didn't believe for a moment that a kidnapper had grabbed Isaac. The boy probably had gotten into a snit about something and stormed out of the house, but I couldn't know for sure, especially after learning about Chuck Showalter this afternoon.

Then there was Ira's wealth. Kids of rich people are often the targets of kidnappers. At any moment Ira might receive a phone call demanding ransom for the return of his son. Under the circumstances, how could I ignore his plea? "I'm on my way."

"What's going on?" asked Zack after I ended the call.

"Isaac is missing."

"I'll go with you."

"Me, too," said my mother.

"That's not necessary, Mama."

"Of course, it is. If you're all going off to search for the boy, someone needs to stay at the house with the twins."

"She has a point," said Zack.

~*~

A police cruiser was parked in front of Ira's house when we pulled up. As we approached the door, we heard shouting coming from inside. I recognized Ira's voice, but the other voice was that of a woman, shrill and consumed with what sounded like righteous rage.

Zack rang the doorbell. Ira's voice grew silent, but the woman continued to scream. "This is not my fault! I didn't sign up for this!"

The door swung open. We stepped inside to find a short, squat woman of about fifty shoving her arms into a coat. She continued to yell at Ira as Officers Harley and Fogarty looked on. "Your children are monsters," she said, wagging her finger at Ira. "You need a prison warden, not a housekeeper. I quit!"

Ira's jaw dropped. "You can't quit!"

"Oh yeah? Watch me!"

She elbowed her way past Zack, Mama, and me and stormed out of the house.

Ira stepped across the threshold onto the porch and called after her as she raced down the steps and along the path toward the sidewalk, "Carmella, come back! Please!"

"No way!"

"I'll double your salary."

She paused mid-stride and spun around. "Not even if you tripled it." Then she marched down the sidewalk. We watched as she got into an older model sub-compact car parked at the curb of the house next door and drove off.

Ira stepped back inside, hung his head, and asked of no one in particular, "Now what am I going to do?"

Melody—or Harmony—slammed the door behind him and said, "Good riddance!"

Her sister added, "We don't need a babysitter. We can take care of ourselves."

"Has Isaac returned?" I asked.

Ira shook his head. "Maybe she's in on it." He turned to Harley and Fogarty. "Why else would she turn down a higher salary? She could have set the whole thing up. She probably has accomplices. Maybe she's in cahoots with Showalter."

Zack whispered in my ear, "Who's Showalter?"

I hadn't had a chance to tell him about my visit with Ira earlier in the day. "I'll tell you later," I whispered in reply.

"Mr. Pollack, there's no indication your son was kidnapped," said Harley.

123

"You don't know that," said Ira.

"What exactly happened?" Zack asked, directing his question to the two officers.

"From what we can gather," said Harley, "the kid mouthed off at the housekeeper when she told him he couldn't eat candy and play video games before dinner. He ran up to his room and slammed the door. That's the last anyone saw of him."

"His bedroom window is open," added Fogarty. "Looks like he climbed out onto the porch roof, shimmied down the column, and ran off."

"Without his coat?" asked Ira. "When it's freezing outside? My son's smarter than that."

I wasn't so sure. "So what are you suggesting, Ira? That someone was hiding in his room?"

"Nothing else makes sense."

"There's no evidence of a struggle," said Harley.

"The kidnapper must have drugged him," said Ira.

"Does he have his phone with him?" I asked. "Have you tried calling him?"

"Calls go straight to voicemail, and the Find My Phone feature isn't working. He wouldn't turn that off."

He would if he didn't want his father to know where he'd gone.

"How long since anyone last saw him?" Zack asked.

"As best we can figure," said Harley, "nearly three hours. No one realized he was gone until he was called to come down for dinner."

I turned to Ira. "Where were you?"

"After I picked the kids up at school and brought them home, I ran back over to the Springfield dealership. I arrived home around six-thirty." He turned on Harley and Fogarty. "Why are you two still here? Why aren't you trying to track down whoever took my son?"

"We've issued an APB to all units, sir," said Harley. "Every cop in town is on the lookout for your son."

"Which does no good if a kidnapper stashed him somewhere!"

Fogarty shook his head and rolled his eyes. His partner said, "We're going to leave now and help look for him, Mr. Pollack. You stay here in case the kidnapper calls."

"So you do believe he was kidnapped! I knew it! We need to call the FBI."

"We'll handle it," said Fogarty.

I turned to my mother. "Mama, why don't you stay here with Ira while Zack and I help in the search?"

"Of course, dear."

Zack and I followed Harley and Fogarty outside. Once on the sidewalk, Zack said, "He's probably wandering around town."

"That was our thought," said Fogarty.

"So you have no plans to call in the Feds?" I asked, already knowing the answer.

"Sometimes it's best to humor irrational people," said Harley.

"There is an extremely slim possibility Ira is correct," I said, filling them in on the incident with the sales manager.

"That was the guy who punched Pollack out the other night?" asked Fogarty. "Does Detective Spader know?"

"He does, as of this afternoon. He's probably tracked him down and questioned him by now."

"We'll contact Spader. Meanwhile, let us know if you find the kid before we do."

"Will do," said Zack.

Once we were back in the car, Zack asked, "When were you

going to tell me about Showalter?"

"As soon as we had a moment alone. I didn't want to say anything in front of Mama. You know how she is."

"True." Zack turned over the engine and pulled away from the curb. "So any idea where the kid is?"

"I think so. Head into town."

~*~

"Okay, now where?" asked Zack once we arrived at the edge of the business district.

"Knowing Isaac and his obsession with video games, my guess is he's at the arcade."

Zack turned left on Broad St. and found a parking space across the street and half a block down from the entertainment center. With only three days until Christmas, the business district was filled with last-minute shoppers scurrying in and out of the retail stores that lined both sides of Broad St. As we walked the short distance to the arcade, a gust of wind blew at our backs. Within seconds a light flurry of snow began to whip around us.

We ducked into the arcade and scanned the darkened interior, searching for Isaac. Colorful lights from the various games flashed all around us. Strobe lights pulsated from the ceiling keeping time with the piped in hip-hop blaring from wall-mounted speakers. A cacophony of other sounds assaulted my eardrums—everything from bells and whistles to weapons explosions and the roar of monstrous aliens coming from dozens of games competing with the shouts and laughter of a multitude of teens and pre-teens filling the place.

When Alex and Nick were younger, Chuck E. Cheese was the birthday party venue of choice for boys under the age of ten. As I stood in a room that made Chuck E. Cheese look like a Buddhist meditation garden, I decided that given a choice between Chinese water torture and spending ten minutes in this arcade, water torture would win hands down. "Do you see him?" I shouted.

Zack shouted back. "Not yet." He reached for my hand, and we began walking up and down the aisles.

We found Isaac at the back of the room, sitting at a console in front of a large screen where zombies and space aliens battled for world domination. The collar and cuffs of a long-sleeve shirt poked out from under a sweatshirt. Two fleece-lined zippered hoodies lay in a heap on the floor alongside his seat. At least he'd had enough common sense to grab some warm clothes from his closet before climbing out his bedroom window.

He wore a contraption on his head that I assumed was some sort of virtual reality apparatus. "Isaac!"

He ignored me. I shouted louder. "Isaac!" Nothing. Finally, I tapped his shoulder.

He jerked his body away from my hand. "Wait your turn!"

I grabbed the headgear and yanked it off his face. That finally got his attention.

"Hey! Give that back!" He reached for my arm and tried to grab the goggles from my hand.

Zack clamped his fingers over Isaac's wrist and yanked him from his seat. "Time to leave, kid."

"You're not my father. I don't have to do what you say." He swung his leg and kicked Zack in the shin.

Big mistake. The nine-year-old was no match for Zack. Before Isaac could strike again, Zack picked him up, pinning his arms to his sides. I scooped up the hoodies. Unless Zack sat on Isaac while I forced his arms into the sweatshirts, we stood little chance of getting him dressed. I opted against creating an even bigger scene, not that anyone was paying attention to us. Snow or no snow, Isaac wouldn't freeze during the short time it would take to haul him half a block.

Carrying Isaac under one arm, Zack headed toward the exit. I followed behind, steering clear of Isaac's flailing legs.

Isaac directed a string of expletives at Zack. When that proved futile, he screamed, "Help! I'm being kidnapped!" but no one batted an eye in our direction—most likely because Isaac's words were drowned out by the migraine-inducing noise bombarding us from every direction.

Even the teenager manning the cash register at the entrance seemed unfazed at the sight of our unusual departure. He simply waved and mouthed, "Merry Christmas" as we passed him. Apparently, Isaac was not the first kid to be extricated from the place in this manner.

Once outside I pulled out my phone and first contacted Officer Harley to call off the cavalry. Then I phoned Ira.

"He's okay?" he asked.

"He's fine, Ira. Just pissed that we dragged him out of the arcade." Before hanging up, I told him I'd contacted the police.

As we approached my Jetta, Isaac continued to squirm, attempting to break free of Zack's grip. An elderly couple, laden with shopping bags, came toward us from the opposite direction. "Uh-oh," said the man, "looks like someone landed on Santa's Naughty List."

Isaac hurled the F-bomb at him.

The couple's eyes widened, their jaws dropped. The woman shook her head and said, "This is what comes from permissive parenting."

As they continued on their way, I called after them, "I totally agree. Thankfully, he's not our kid."

Zack unlocked the car and dropped Isaac into the backseat. "Put your seatbelt on."

"Make me!"

"You really want to go there, kid?" He reached into his back pocket and whipped out a pair of handcuffs. Isaac's eyes bugged out. A moment later he'd belted himself in.

"You came prepared," I said as Zack closed the door.

"Boy Scout motto."

Why was I surprised that my boyfriend, who claims he's not a spy even though he owns a badass handgun and is always running off to Third World countries, also possesses a pair of handcuffs?

"You want to read him the riot act before we take him home?" he asked.

"Definitely."

Zack engaged the childproof locks once we settled into the car, just in case Isaac got any bright ideas and tried to bolt. He started the engine and cranked up the heater but didn't pull out of the parking spot.

Zack and I turned around to face Isaac. He sat with his arms crossed over his chest, a belligerent expression on his face. "Do you have any idea how worried your father is?" I asked. "He thought you were kidnapped."

"I was kidnapped. By you." He pulled his phone out of his pants pocket and powered it up.

Zack reached over the seat and grabbed it out of his hand. "Wrong answer."

"Give me back my phone!"

"Still wrong answer."

Isaac glared first at Zack, then me. "I don't know what you

want me to say. No one lets me do anything. I'm sick of following everyone's rules. Do this. Do that. Stupid teachers. Stupid housekeepers." He crossed his arms back over his chest. "Stupid you! Just leave me alone."

"Let's get him home," I said to Zack. "He's Ira's problem, not ours."

Zack pulled out of the parking space and drove back to Ira's house. "We should have let the cops pick him up," he said. "Maybe a stint in juvie would straighten him out."

"What are you two talking about?" asked Isaac. "What's juvie?"

"Juvenile Detention," I said. "It's prison for troublemaker kids like you."

"You're making that up," said Isaac. "There's no such place. You're just trying to scare me."

"Perhaps a field trip is in order," said Zack. He glanced up into the rearview mirror. "What's the matter, Isaac? You look nervous."

I twisted in my seat. Isaac's lower lip trembled. His eyes filled with tears. "I want to go home. I want my dad."

Three minutes later we pulled into Ira's driveway. Isaac breathed a huge sigh of relief when he realized he was home. As soon as Zack disengaged the childproof locks, Isaac swung open the door and made a mad dash for the house.

We followed behind Isaac and found him in the great room, clinging to Ira's waist. Ira's relief at having his son home safe and sound was evident on his face. Isaac took one look at Zack and inched behind his father.

Mama sat on the sectional. The twins were nowhere in sight. "Mama," I said, "I'm sure Isaac is hungry. Why don't you take him into the kitchen and make him a sandwich?"

She rose and held out her hand to Isaac. "Come on, young man. Let's see what we can rustle up for you."

Isaac refused to budge. "Go on," said Ira. "Aren't you hungry?" Isaac gave Zack and me a wary look before he allowed Mama to take his hand and lead him into the kitchen.

"How can I ever thank you?" said Ira.

"Is there someplace private we can talk?" I asked.

"Of course." Ira led Zack and me to a small den situated behind French doors off the dining room. Once inside, he closed the doors. A gray microfiber sofa and loveseat with overstuffed pillows filled one corner of the room. Zack and I settled into the sofa, Ira dropped onto the loveseat, perching on the edge of a cushion.

"I know what you're going to say," he said. "He's out of control. They all are. They don't listen to me. They don't listen to anyone."

"Because you've spoiled them," I said. "Kids need boundaries."

"But it's been so hard on them, first with their mother's illness and death, then everything that happened with Cynthia."

"You're not doing your kids any favor," said Zack. "You're making things worse."

Ira's eyes flashed anger. "You've never had kids. You have no idea what it's like, what we've been through."

"Maybe not," said Zack, "but I know what's going to happen if your parenting skills don't improve." He proceeded to tell Ira what had transpired at the arcade and afterwards. "You've got a budding juvenile delinquent on your hands, Ira. This is serious."

Ira turned to me. "Is that how you feel?"

"I do."

He placed his elbows on his knees and lowered his head into his hands. "I don't know what to do. Cynthia had wanted to send all three kids off to boarding school. Maybe that would be best." He lifted his head and looked at Zack and sighed. "I'm sorry. You're right. I'm a failure as a father."

"That's not what we're saying," I said, "but you need help before it's too late."

"Do you have any idea how many nannies and housekeepers we've gone through? No one hangs around for very long."

I couldn't blame them. Isaac and the twins would present a challenge to Mary Poppins. Then again, so would their father. But at least Ira finally admitted he had a problem. Recognition brought him a giant leap toward resolution. "Have you considered a family therapist?"

"More than one. Therapy only works if everyone agrees to participate, and my kids are stubborn. They sat stone-faced at each session. Short of calling in the Marines, what more can I do?"

Marines? Talk about an ah-ha moment! Suddenly I knew just the person to straighten out Ira and his kids, assuming he was up for the challenge.

TWELVE

"You're kidding," said Zack when I told him my idea after we dropped Mama at her condo. "Tino Martinelli? The guy involved in the murder of your ex-CEO's mistress?"

"You make it sound like he had something to do with her death. He didn't."

"Yet he made some questionable decisions in conjunction with that death, decisions that could have landed him in prison."

"Granted, but in the end he came clean, stepped up, and helped catch a killer who was about to strike for a third time. Besides, he's a former Marine. How perfect is that?"

Zack scrubbed at his way-past-five-o'clock shadow. "I don't know."

"He's got a good heart. That's what got him in trouble in the first place. He acted out of some misguided sense of family loyalty."

"So do Mafia hit men. That doesn't excuse them."

Score one point for Zack.

"Marines are supposed to be rational thinkers," he continued. "They're trained to use reason and logic and keep emotion out of the equation."

"There were extenuating circumstances. Besides, no one is perfect."

"What makes you think he'd even be interested?"

"I received a Christmas card from him today. He's working security for some tech company and bored out of his mind. I think he'd jump at the challenge to straighten out three delinquents-in-training."

Zack slowed for a traffic light and turned to face me. "You really think this is a good idea?"

"Tino wouldn't hurt a fly. And he'd do anything for me."

"I'm not sure how I feel about that."

I playfully swatted his arm. "In a brotherly way."

He shook his head and sighed. "Since I've never met the guy, I have to bow to your judgment, but you need to let Ira know what happened with Martinelli a few months ago."

"I will."

~*~

First thing the next morning, after the boys left for school, I phoned Tino. He answered with an excited, "Mrs. P.!"

"Hey, Tino, it was good to get your note."

"I miss our adventures. Life is downright boring lately. You haven't replaced me, have you?"

"Never! You'll be first on my list the next time I go undercover as a reality TV producer."

He chuckled. "We had some fun with that, didn't we?"

"Putting aside we were interviewing possible killers?"

"Well, yeah, there was that. Still, it was kind of an adrenaline rush, right?"

Personally, I could use a little less adrenaline in my life. Then again, I wasn't an ex-Marine. They probably required a certain number of cc's per day to survive. "I'm off work until after New Year's. Any chance you're free for coffee or lunch today?"

"You miss me?"

"Absolutely! And I also have a proposition for you if you're interested."

"Why, Mrs. P., you cougar, you!"

"Not that kind of proposition!"

He laughed again. "Only kidding. But if you ever change your mind—"

"Tino!"

"Just pulling your leg, Mrs. P. Anyway, I'm off until after New Year's, and I'd love to meet for lunch. You've certainly piqued my curiosity. I can't wait to hear about this proposition of yours."

We made arrangements to meet at a diner on Route 22 at noon. When I ended the call, Zack said, "I'd feel more comfortable going with you."

"I thought you had a meeting with your publisher." Zack had been working on a new book of photographs based on his recent trips to commune with lemurs in Madagascar.

"I can reschedule."

"What are you afraid will happen?"

He paused from wiping down the kitchen counter, turned to face me, and said, "Nothing, I hope."

"You worry too much."

"Says the woman who nearly got herself killed recently."

"Tino wouldn't kill me; he'd kill *for me*."

Zack raised an eyebrow. "Something you're not telling me?"

"It's just an expression." However, perhaps not the best choice of one, given Zack's wariness of the ex-Marine in question.

He stared at me for a moment before turning his attention back to clean-up duty. "Keep it that way."

I tapped him on the shoulder. When he spun back around to face me, I looped my arms over his shoulders and locked lips with him to show my appreciation for his concern.

Unfortunately, the amorous moment was abruptly interrupted by one of my mother-in-law's trademark harrumphs. I opened my eyes to find her standing in the kitchen doorway. She speared me with a glare and a scowl before taking a seat at the kitchen table. "At least my dear son didn't live to see the kind of woman he really married."

I placed her breakfast in front of her. "And what kind of woman would that be, Lucille?"

"A hussy."

A great retort danced on the tip of my tongue, but I decided against letting it loose. Instead I poured her a cup of coffee before Zack and I left the kitchen.

We were halfway to the living room when she called out, "Anastasia, my eggs are ice cold!"

"You know where the microwave is," Zack called over his shoulder.

"No one's talking to you," she said.

I circled back to the kitchen, placed my hands on the table, and leaned forward until inches separated my nose from hers. "This isn't a diner, and I'm not a short-order cook. If you want your breakfast prepared for you, show up in the kitchen on time. Otherwise, prepare your own meals."

Her jaw dropped, and she began to sputter, but I didn't hang around. I stormed out of the kitchen and didn't stop until I entered my bedroom, slamming the door behind me.

A moment later the door opened a few inches, and Zack stuck his head inside. "Is it safe to come in, or are you going to throw a lamp or something?"

I dropped onto the bed. "At you, no. At her? Possibly."

He pulled me to my feet and held me until my anger subsided. "Maybe I should start buying lottery tickets," I said.

"I can think of better ways to throw away money."

"Maybe so, but if I won, the first thing I'd do is pay to put her in assisted living. It would be worth every penny."

He reached into his pocket, pulled out his wallet, removed a dollar, and handed it to me. "The first ticket is on me."

I couldn't help but laugh.

~*~

Once Lucille had wolfed down her breakfast, she hobbled into the den and parked herself in front of the television to watch *Judge Judy*. Zack left for the train station, and I caught up on laundry and various other household chores normally relegated to weekends. Then I made a supermarket run.

When I returned, I found my mother-in-law hadn't moved, other than to pick up the remote to switch the channel to an episode of *Sister Wives*. I knew this because she'd turned the volume up to such deafening decibels that I could hear every word all the way on the other side of the house as I put away groceries.

At eleven-forty I escaped the ear-splitting onslaught of reality TV and drove off to meet Tino. Ten minutes later I arrived at the diner and spied him in a booth along the windows.

I was used to seeing Tino in sunglasses, dark suits, white shirts, and conservative ties. The guy looked like the quintessential Secret

Service agent—if Secret Service agents could afford twelve-hundred-dollar Bulgari shades and bespoke suits. Today he wore jeans and a Giants sweatshirt, looking like a defensive end on a day off. As I approached, he rose, met me halfway down the aisle, and wrapped me in a bear hug that sucked the air from my lungs.

"Sure is good to see you, Mrs. P.," he said once he released me. I slid into the booth, and Tino wedged himself into the side opposite me. He offered me a wide grin that took up the entire lower half of his face, his eyes twinkling. "So, about this proposition...."

Two menus were already at the table. I grabbed the one in front of my place setting, smiled back at him, and said, "How about if we order first?"

He sighed and raised his own menu. "If you insist."

Once the waitress had arrived to take our orders, I got down to business. "You inferred you're unhappy at your new job."

He shrugged. "It's okay, and the pay is good."

"But?"

"There's little challenge." He ran his hand over his buzz cut. "I'm not unhappy so much as bored with the tedium of it. I spend most of my days sitting in front of a bank of computer screens looking for cyber incursions into one specific company that few hackers seem interested in breeching."

"That's a good thing, right?"

"I suppose. Makes for a long day, though."

"Have you found any?"

He puffed out his chest. "Of course. I'm good at what I do, but it's like playing the same video game day in and day out for years. Once you've saved the village from the zombie apocalypse a hundred times over, you can do it with your eyes closed and one hand behind your back. There are only so many ways the zombies can attack the village. It's not like I'm monitoring the electric grid or working for Homeland Security."

"Is that what you want?"

He thought for a moment. "Maybe. I've put some feelers out. I want to do something where I'm making a difference."

"How do you feel about kids, Tino?"

His eyes bugged out. "Wow! I never saw that one coming."

I chuckled. "Threw you for a loop, did I?"

"I figured you were mixed up in some new murder investigation."

"Well...now that you mention it—"

He slapped the table, rattling the silverware." I knew it!"

"There has been a murder, but the police are handling it."

He raised an eyebrow. "Like they did the last one?"

"Different cops. This murder occurred in my town."

"What's your connection?"

"The killer dumped the body on my half-brother-in-law's property."

"*Half*-brother-in-law?"

"Long story."

"And I suppose he's Suspect Numero Uno?"

"Possibly, but that's not what I want to discuss with you."

Tino's brows knit together. "The plot thickens."

Before I could say anything further, the waitress appeared with our coffees. I added cream to mine and took a sip prior to continuing. "This is a convoluted, multi-part tale. It's best I start from the beginning, filling you in on the back-story first."

He leaned back and crossed his arms over his chest. "I'm all ears, Mrs. P."

For the next ten minutes I explained how I'd come to meet Ira and his kids, how my mother had married his second wife's father, and how Lawrence now resided in federal lock-up for a host of crimes, including his own daughter's murder.

"You lead a very interesting life, Mrs. P. You should write a book."

Maybe I should. I could certainly use the royalties to pay down some of my still staggering debt.

By this time our food had arrived. I continued my tale. "Ira and his kids recently moved to Westfield," I said.

Tino took a huge bite of his cheeseburger and talked around the mouthful. "Let me guess, to be closer to you?"

I answered with a grimace.

"The guy's got a crush on you, Mrs. P."

"Tell me something I don't know."

"You want me to set him straight?"

I nearly choked on my corned beef special. "No! At least not in the way I think you're suggesting."

He shrugged, then dipped a French fry into a pool of ketchup and popped it into his mouth. "Then what?"

I continued with the events leading up to finding the body in Santa's sleigh and segued into the problems with the twins and Isaac, finishing with what had occurred last night. "Those kids need someone to whip them into shape before they all wind up locked up. Or worse."

Tino raised both eyebrows. "And you think I'm the person to do that?"

"Absolutely."

"I don't know, Mrs. P. I—"

"You said you were looking for a challenge."

He scrubbed at his jaw and shook his head. "*A manny?* This is so not what I had in mind."

"What greater challenge than something you'd never thought to consider?"

"In a million years."

"But if you succeed, you'd have the satisfaction of knowing you'd turned three miscreants into model citizens."

"There is that."

"Then you'll think about it?"

He stared at me for a long moment before nodding. "Ira and his kids are lucky they have someone as caring as you in their lives. Most people would just turn their backs and walk away."

Now it was my turn to shrug. "It's either my best trait or my worst flaw. I haven't figured out which yet."

"Does Ira know about me?"

I shook my head. "I wanted to see if you were interested before I said anything."

"I think it would be a good idea if I met him and his kids first. I need to know what I'm getting myself into."

"Then you might be interested?"

"We'll see."

"You doing anything for dinner tonight?"

"Depends. How good a cook are you, Mrs. P.?"

"Not as good as my boyfriend. How does six-thirty sound?"

"Text me your address. I'll bring dessert."

"We'll need enough for ten."

"Ten?" He counted on his fingers, stopping at seven. "You have three kids?"

"Two."

He held up his fingers and wiggled them, minus one thumb.

"That makes nine by my count."

"Plus my communist mother-in-law." I frowned. "Unfortunately, I'm stuck with her."

"Sounds like you need me to whip her into shape, too."

I laughed. "Tino, I doubt even you could accomplish a miracle of such magnitude."

~*~

Before leaving the diner, I called Ira to invite him and his brood to dinner. "What's the occasion?"

"Does there have to be one?"

"No, but I'm surprised. You never want to get together on weeknights."

Or any other night, really, but I refrained from spouting the mean comment. My motives were pure. Ira needed help, and I had the solution. "I'm off until after New Year's."

"In that case, we'd love to come."

We being more of a "royal we", even though Ira might think he spoke for his kids as well. I could bank on the twins and Isaac not sharing their father's enthusiasm over spending the evening at Casa Pollack.

Tino made the universal time-out sign with his hands. "Hold on a second, Ira." I muted my phone.

"Tell him you have a friend interested in a new car. Ask him if he has time to meet with me this afternoon."

I relayed the message and received an affirmative response from Ira. "Two o'clock at his Flemington dealership."

Tino nodded.

"You really need a new car?" I asked after ending the call.

He shrugged. "Maybe."

"I can trust you, right?"

"Have I ever let you down, Mrs. P.?"

~*~

Since nothing in my pantry or fridge would serve a dinner party of ten, Ira's acceptance necessitated the second trip of the day to the supermarket. I loaded up on the components for spaghetti and turkey meatballs, a tossed salad, and garlic bread. Not a gourmet meal by any stretch but who doesn't like spaghetti and meatballs? I frowned at the items in my cart. With my luck? Melody, Harmony, and Isaac, that's who.

~*~

I pulled into my driveway to find Robyn Konopka standing at my front door.

THIRTEEN

Robyn turned and waved to me as I parked the Jetta. I grabbed my purse and bag of groceries and joined her at the front door. "This is a surprise," I said.

She bit down on her lower lip, her expression conveying either worry or nervousness. I wasn't sure which. Perhaps both. "I hope you don't mind the unannounced visit. I took a chance you'd be home."

"Is everything all right?"

Robyn was a petite woman who looked lost, swallowed up in an overly puffy powder blue parka that fell below her knees. She shook her head as she fought to get the words out. "I don't know...I'm probably acting paranoid...I'd heard you were involved with helping the police in a few investigations...so I thought...maybe...."

Becoming Westfield's very own Jessica Fletcher didn't fill me with warm fuzzies. People talk. There was little I could do about my newfound reputation other than ignore it or embrace it. I'd prefer the former. However, the more people talked, the less I could ignore the moniker and the problems that came with it—like people trying to kill me. Of course, my inability to turn my back on a friend in need or an injustice that needed righting didn't help.

I placed my hand on Robyn's arm. "Is it Jesse? Has something more happened?" Lately the news was full of scary reports about hospitals becoming breeding grounds for antibiotic-resistant superbugs. A patient could go in for a broken leg and wind up with MRSA.

Her eyes glistened with unshed tears, and she blinked several times to stave off an imminent flow. "I'm not sure."

She wasn't sure if her husband was all right? What an odd answer, not to mention somewhat ominous. "Come inside. Let's talk."

I unlocked the door and swung it open. Blessed silence greeted us. Not so much as a whisper of battling housewives, gypsy brides, foreign fiancés, or polygamists emanated from the television in the den. Casa Pollack appeared devoid of Lucille and any of her commie cotillion.

I took Robyn's coat, hung it in the closet along with mine, and ushered her toward the kitchen. "Sit down. I'll make a pot of coffee."

She grabbed a seat at the table and said nothing while I started the coffee. I then placed the perishables in the fridge and brought milk and sugar to the table. Once the coffee had finished dripping, I poured two cups and joined her. "So what's going on?"

She bypassed the milk and sugar to take a slow sip of the black coffee before speaking. "Like I said, it's probably nothing, but the more I think about it, the more something doesn't seem right about Jesse's accident, especially with that goose egg on the back of his head."

"In what way?"

"He's not clumsy. Never has been. And if he tripped, wouldn't he have fallen face down?"

"Accidents do happen, and didn't you mention his fall was broken by a pile of lumber?"

She nodded. "That's what the doctors surmise. Jesse doesn't remember anything."

"Depending on the angle in which he struck the lumber, his body probably twisted as he fell toward the floor."

"I guess that makes sense. But this seems so out of character."

"How?"

She heaved a deep sigh. "I don't know."

"Has Jesse mentioned anything unusual happening at any of the job sites?"

She thought for a moment. "Not really. He did say something about a delivery the other day, that the materials were a lesser quality than what he'd ordered."

"That's never happened before?"

"Sure, it has. Like everyone, suppliers make mistakes. They take care of it."

"And this time?"

"He did what he always does. He sent the shipment back and arranged for delivery of the materials he'd ordered."

"So, what's the problem?"

She shrugged. "Nothing, I suppose. Not with that. But he's just not clumsy."

"Then you're not suggesting someone caused Jesse's injuries over a clerical error?"

She grasped the mug with both hands and stared into it as she forced a laugh. "Of course not. The idea sounds beyond silly. Mix-ups happen occasionally."

"In every business."

Robyn shook her head. "Yes, and accidents. My husband isn't Superman. Even he makes mistakes. What was I thinking?" She took one last sip of coffee, then pushed away from her and stood. "I'm sorry I wasted your time, Anastasia. You must have a million things to do with Christmas only two days away."

I rose, walked over to her, and wrapped her in a hug. "Nonsense. Don't give it another thought. It's good to see you, even under these circumstances. Stress can cause you to go a bit bonkers. Believe me, I know."

"I suppose you do."

I walked her to the foyer and retrieved her coat. "You'll feel much better once Jesse is home and recovering."

Robyn embraced me before leaving. "Thanks. I feel so much better. Amazing what a cup of coffee with an old friend can do to put things in perspective."

I smiled. "Anytime."

But as I watched her walk down the street, my own suspicions gnawed at the corners of my brain. Robyn hadn't brought up Dion's murder, perhaps because she didn't connect it to Jesse's accident. Not wanting to upset her further, I had deliberately refrained from mentioning the murder. In my mind, though, I began connecting dots.

What if the Leonides brothers hadn't fulfilled their promise to find new jobs for all their former employees? What if one or more disgruntled ex-employees had killed Dion and attacked Jesse? If so, Paul Leonides, and possibly his wife, were also in the killer's crosshairs.

~*~

After Robyn left, I walked Devil Dog, released Ralph from the confines of his cage, and began dinner prep. Zack returned from Manhattan while I was two-wrists-deep in an enormous bowl of ground turkey. He leaned in and kissed me, careful to stay clear of the mess that covered my apron and the counter where I worked. *Mess* being the operative word; I'm not exactly the world's tidiest cook, but it's the results that count, right?

"Are we feeding an army tonight?" he asked, deep frown lines etching into his forehead and around his mouth as he stared at the massive amount of ground turkey.

"Only a platoon." I told him about my lunch with Tino and what we'd decided.

"Good. I'm looking forward to meeting this guy who's captured your heart."

"You're lucky I'm incapable of swatting you at the moment."

"Promises, promises." He scanned the kitchen. "Give me a minute to change my clothes, and I'll create some order out of this chaos."

"Promises, promises."

I began rolling the seasoned ground turkey into small meatballs and placing them on a baking tray. Zack returned before I'd fashioned two-dozen. He proceeded to put away the various ingredients I'd used for the recipe and dump dirty utensils and dishes into the sink.

"How was your meeting?" I asked as I continued to scoop and roll raw meat.

"Lemurs are the new penguins. Or at least, that's what my publisher is hoping."

Last summer Zack had gone on assignment to photograph lemurs in Madagascar—or so he claimed. Whatever else he'd been up to in Madagascar, for whichever alphabet agency employed him, he did return with scores of lemur portraits. Proof, he claimed, that he wasn't a spy.

But wouldn't any spy worth his salt have an ironclad cover profession? Zack's was as a world-renowned photojournalist. At least that was my theory, and no matter how much he protested otherwise, he'd as yet failed to disabuse me of that notion. And then there was the badass gun and handcuffs.

"Never going to happen," I said. "Not that I don't want your book to do well."

"But?"

"I've seen *March of the Penguins*. Lemurs are interesting. I'll give you that. And your photos of them are gorgeous."

"I'm still waiting for the *but*."

"But penguins are downright adorable. When it comes to cute, lemurs are no match for penguins."

He placed his hand over his heart. "I had no idea I fell in love with a woman who harbors lemur prejudices."

"If you don't tell the lemurs, they'll never find out."

Zack removed a large frying pan from a lower cabinet and set it on the stove. "I'll cook the meatballs while you prepare the salad and garlic bread."

"I was hoping you'd say that." I finished forming the meatballs, washed the raw meat from my hands, and placed the mixing bowl in the dishwasher. "By the way, I have more news. Robyn Konopka stopped by this afternoon." I told Zack about our conversation and my thoughts concerning Parthenon's former employees.

"I'm sure Detective Spader is looking into the alibis of all the workers who lost their jobs."

"Agreed. He wouldn't be much of a detective if he ignored all those possible suspects."

"Just so long as you don't take it upon yourself to start asking questions of those men, Ms. Fletcher."

"Who me? Wouldn't think of it." Besides, I had no way of learning their names, short of asking Paul or Octavia Leonides, which most likely would get back to Detective Spader. I didn't mention that to Zack, though. No point poking the bear.

Anyway, my only interest in the case had involved making sure Ira wasn't charged in Dion's murder. Since Chuck Showalter and not Dion Leonides had attacked Ira Tuesday night, and since Spader now knew there were many more likely suspects, I had no reason to stick my nose where it didn't belong. Except that still didn't explain why Dion's body ended up in Ira's sleigh. Coincidence? There had to be more to it than that.

~*~

Mama walked into the house at five-thirty. "I thought I'd join you for dinner this evening, dear."

Oops! That made eleven for dinner. Since Mama was a semi-regular, why had I forgotten to include her in the dessert count I gave Tino?

Twenty minutes later Lucille hobbled in with Harriet close on her heels. "I've invited Harriet to stay for dinner."

FOURTEEN

Lucille had thrown down the gauntlet. "I expect you to be civil to her," she continued.

Or what? This was my home, not hers. A less kind daughter-in-law would have tossed her out on her polyester pantsuited tush a long time ago. I had tolerated more than enough from Lucille Pollack since Karl had moved her in with us. I refused to become her doormat. Nor would I pick up that gauntlet and give her the fight she seemed itching to start. The situation called for a bit of psychology.

I eyed Harriet, standing with her arms crossed over her puffed-out chest, daring me to refuse her a seat at my dinner table. Then I turned to Lucille. "Harriet is quite welcome to stay for dinner tonight, but if you want to make her a regular addition at mealtime, one of you will have to kick in an additional twenty-five dollars a week to pay for her food."

Lucille's mouth hardened into a thin line, but she said nothing, so I continued. "By the way, we're having company this evening."

"I can see that," she said, sneering at Mama. "Has she paid for her dinner?"

I ignored her question. "The company is in addition to my mother. Ira and his children are joining us tonight."

Lucille whipped her gaze away from Mama and redirected the sneer at me. "You're a fool, Anastasia. That imposter is taking advantage of you."

"In what way?"

"In every way."

I had not asked Ira to present DNA evidence of his relationship to Dead Louse of a Spouse. I hadn't needed to. One look at him told me he'd emerged from the same genetic soup as my husband.

Ira had also never asked for anything from me other than to be acknowledged as part of my family. Although his overwhelming generosity bordered on smothering and was difficult for me to accept, it never came with any strings attached. Not only had Ira never taken advantage of me, I knew he never would. Ira's greatest flaw was his neediness, and needy people don't take. They give— in excess and often *ad nauseum*, as in Ira's case—in order to garner acceptance and friendship.

"You don't have to stay," said Mama.

"I will not subject either myself or my friend to that man and his brats," said Lucille. She turned to Harriet. "Come, Harriet. We're dining out this evening."

"Good riddance," said Mama to their departing backs.

My thoughts exactly, but I wouldn't voice them, especially within earshot of my mother. She didn't need any additional encouragement in her ongoing battle with Lucille.

That brought the dinner count back to ten, and without

Lucille, it lowered the anticipated ulcer-producing meal from a seismic level down to a few shaky tremors. I'd take my victories, no matter how small, wherever I could get them.

As soon as the front door slammed behind Lucille and Harriet, Zack emerged from the kitchen, a contented Ralph perched on his shoulder. "Well done," he said, wrapping an arm around my shoulders and planting a kiss on my cheek.

"You could have given my daughter support," said Mama, wagging her finger at him. "Instead of hiding like a coward with that filthy bird."

"Did you need my help?" Zack asked me.

"Did it sound like I needed your help?"

"Not in the least." He turned to Mama. "Flora, if you haven't realized by now, your daughter is quite capable of fighting most of her own battles and smart enough to know when to ask for assistance."

Was I? Sometimes I wondered, given the predicaments I'd found myself in lately, but Zack's words of support filled me with warm fuzzies.

Mama shook her head at both of us and emitted a huge sigh. "Chivalry is definitely dead."

Alex and Nick bounded into the house a few minutes later. After they both greeted us, I said, "I need you guys to pull the leaves out for the dining room table, bring the chairs in from the kitchen, and set the table."

"All four chairs?" asked Nick.

"All four."

"We're having ten people for dinner?" asked Alex. "Who?"

"An old friend from work, plus Ira and his kids."

Alex dug into his pocket, removed his phone, and glanced at

the display. "Look at that. Sophie just invited me to dinner."

"Ask her if I can come, too," said Nick.

I whipped the phone out of Alex's hand and checked the blank screen. "Nice try, kiddo."

He shrugged. "Hey, you can't blame me for trying, Mom. Why do Uncle Ira and his kids have to come? And why would you subject your work friend to them?"

"I'll tell you later tonight after they leave."

"Sounds intriguing," said Nick. He turned to Zack. "Kind of spy-like, huh?"

Zack winked at him. "It's an extremely clandestine operation."

Tino arrived shortly before six-thirty. He'd traded his jeans and Giants sweatshirt from earlier in the day for a pair of sharply pressed charcoal tweed slacks. A gray pinstripe oxford shirt peaked out from the crew neckline and wrists of a black cashmere sweater. The guy had impeccable taste and wore everything as if he had stepped out of a Barney's window display.

Tino brought with him a twelve-layer chocolate fudge cake that would easily serve twenty—or nine other people and me. He'd apparently paid close attention to my eating habits during his short stint as my bodyguard during my investigation into the murder of *Bling!* editor Philomena Campanello.

To my amazement, he and Zack hit it off immediately, bonding over their Y-chromosomal shared desire to keep me out of trouble, as well as an appreciation for fine French wine, courtesy of Zack's extensive collection.

While we waited for the remaining dinner guests, the adults polished off a bottle of Bordeaux. Tino appeared mesmerized by Ralph. "Does he talk?"

"Only to quote Shakespeare," I said.

Tino snorted. "You're pulling my leg, right? You can't expect me to believe a bird knows Shakespeare."

Ralph answered for me. *"Believe then, if you please, that I can do strange things,"* he squawked. *"As You Like It.* Act Five, Scene Two."

Tino's head swiveled back and forth from me to Ralph to Zack to the boys. "Okay, which one of you is a ventriloquist?"

Tino was going to take some convincing of Ralph's talents. Meanwhile he also charmed my sons, who both completely forgot about trying to escape the impending dinner with their bratty half-cousins.

However, aside from a few pleasantries, he steered clear of Mama and her batting eyelashes. "Is that the commie?" he asked me at one point when she left to powder her nose.

"No, the commie stormed out in a huff before you arrived. That's my mother. Romanoff blood courses through her veins, making her the commie's arch nemesis."

"You've lost me."

"Czar Nicholas? Russian Revolution?"

Tino shrugged. "If you say so."

"My mother's maternal grandmother was a Romanoff. Whether she belongs to the royal line or not is up for debate."

Tino remained puzzled.

"Not up on your early twentieth-century European history?"

"I guess not. Anyway, don't take this the wrong way, Mrs. P, but is it my imagination, or is she coming on to me?"

"She's on the hunt for Husband Number Seven," said Zack.

From his perch on Zack's shoulder, Ralph said, *"Her love is not the hare that I do hunt." As You Like It.* Act Four, Scene Three."

Tino's jaw dropped, and his eyes grew wide. I wasn't sure

whether this was from realizing Ralph spoke for himself or Zack's comment about Mama's search for her next husband until he said, "She's nearly old enough to be my grandmother!"

"According to Mama, age is just a number, but you're wise to keep a wide berth."

"Duly noted. I like you, Mrs. P., but royalty or no royalty, I'm not interested in becoming your stepfather."

"Nor would I want you to, Tino."

"Good. I'm glad we got that cleared up."

At seven forty-five Ira and his brood were still no-shows. The salad sat on the table and the meatballs simmered in sauce on the stove, but I didn't dare cook the spaghetti or garlic bread until they arrived.

I was about to text Ira when my phone chimed an incoming text from him: Sorry for the delay. On our way now.

Before heading to the kitchen to pre-heat the oven and turn the burner on to boil water for the spaghetti, I suggested, "Best put Ralph in his cage."

Ralph squawked his displeasure.

Zack reached into his shirt pocket and handed him a sunflower seed. "Don't think of it as banishment, pal. Consider it protection against the spawns of Satan."

When Ira and his brood arrived less than ten minutes later, the reason for their delay became crystal clear. He practically had to drag the twins and Isaac into the house. "This does not bode well for the evening," I muttered to Zack.

"Hey, it was your idea."

"And one I'm now seriously regretting."

~*~

Within seconds of being served dinner, Isaac and the twins lived up to their less-than-stellar reputations. As usual, they brought their phones to the table and proceeded to bury their noses in them as I filled their plates. "Put your phones away," I said.

As usual, they ignored me. I pulled their plates back to my side of the table. Once everyone else was served, we began to eat. When Isaac and the twins realized they wouldn't get any dinner until they'd put down their phones, they finally placed them on the table.

"Face down," I said.

"Huh?" said Isaac.

"Your phones. Place them face down."

If looks could kill, I'd now be a corpse, but after a few extremely tense seconds ticked by, all three finally complied, and I returned their plates.

After shooting me an evil eye that rivaled any I'd ever received from Lucille, Isaac took one bite of his turkey meatball and spit the mouthful onto his plate. "Yuck! What is this?"

"Not meatballs," said Melody—or Harmony—also disgorging her half-masticated mouthful onto her plate. "Probably some vegan crap."

I'll admit, I'm nowhere near the gourmet chef Zack is, but prior to this evening, no one had ever spit out my cooking—not even Alex and Nick when I'd shoveled strained peas into their adorable infant mouths.

The other twin sniffed at the meatball on her fork, scrunched her face, and said, "Gross!" before flinging the utensil across the table where it landed in the salad bowl.

I suppose I should be grateful she hadn't first put the meatball in her mouth, but at the moment I was struggling to keep from committing an act that would land me behind bars for the remainder of my life. Good thing common sense—not to mention Zack's firm hand on my thigh—forced me to conclude that retaliation wasn't worth prison time.

Not satisfied with his initial act of defiance, Isaac twirled a large mound of spaghetti onto his fork and catapulted it into the air. It spiraled in a wide arc, landing on Mama's overpriced salon dye job. She gasped and jumped up, toppling her chair backwards. Red sauce dripped down her forehead and onto her cheeks as she attempted to detangle strands of spaghetti and fork prongs from her hair. "Don't just sit there," she screamed at Ira. "Do something!"

Ira stood and reached tentatively toward Mama's hair. She smacked his hand away. "Not me. I can take care of myself." She swept her arm in the air toward his kids. "Grow some balls and do something about those monsters of yours."

You go, Mama!

When Ira turned to face his children, Isaac added insult to injury by laughing as Mama spun on her Ferragamos and raced from the room. He then smirked at his father, Zack, and me, as if daring us to make the first move.

Zack squeezed my thigh and gave a nearly imperceptible shake of his head, then a nod in Ira's direction. I took this to mean we should wait to see how Ira reacted. But Ira said nothing as he returned to his seat and lifted his water glass to his lips. Only a slight trembling in his jaw and the white-knuckled grip on the glass betrayed his emotions as he nodded toward Tino.

That's when the Marines rushed in—or at least one former Marine. Before our eyes teddy bear Tino transformed into avenging angel Tino. Without saying a word, he reached across the table and removed Ira's kid's plates.

"See?" said Isaac. "Even he won't eat this slop."

Tino didn't react to Isaac's comment as he deposited the plates in the kitchen. When he returned to the dining room, he pointed to Isaac, Melody, and Harmony. In drill sergeant tones he barked orders. "You three, up. Now!"

Isaac crossed his arms over his chest. "You can't tell us what to do."

Tino gave Isaac the most menacing smile I'd ever witnessed. And I've seen some menacing smiles in my time, having tangled with a few really bad dudes over the past year. "Is that so?" he asked, his voice an eerily calm singsong of dripping venom that sent shivers up my spine.

Apparently, Tino's voice had a similar effect on not only Isaac but also his sisters. To my amazement, all three kids grabbed their phones and stood. Shaking with fear, they glanced over at their father and whimpered for him to come to their rescue, but Ira remained impassive.

"Leave the phones," said Tino.

When they didn't immediately place the phones back on the table, Tino forced them from their grips and pocketed them.

"You can't do that!" said one of the girls.

"I just did," said Tino. He pointed toward the living room. "Now, march."

The three of them made one last pleading attempt for their father's intercession, but to their shock Ira said, "Do as you're told."

Melody's—or Harmony's—eyes nearly bulged out of her head. "You're taking his side?"

Ira raised his arm and pointed toward the living room.

"I don't believe this!" said the other twin.

All three then glared at Tino before finally complying with his order. Ira, Zack, the boys, and I watched as Tino herded them down the hall toward the bedrooms and den. A moment later we heard a door slam.

"You worked with that guy?" asked Nick. "What did he do at the magazine?"

"Whatever he was asked to do," I said.

Nick turned to Alex. "Maybe we've got this all wrong. Maybe it's Mom who's really the spy."

Zack stifled a laugh.

"Do you think they'll be all right?" asked Ira, finally releasing his two-fisted grip on the glass.

"Tino wouldn't harm a fly," I said.

"Too bad Uncle Ira's kids aren't flies," said Alex.

Ira chewed on his lower lip. "When I met with him earlier in the day, he assured me he wouldn't lay a hand on them. I hope he meant it."

"He did," I assured him.

"I take it you've already made up your mind to hire Tino?" asked Zack.

Ira hung his head. "You and Anastasia have made me realize my parental shortcomings. It's obvious I need more help than I can get from a housekeeper." He laughed. "House*keeper*? Like I can keep one. I'm willing to try anything at this point. Still...." He cast a hesitant glance in the direction of the hallway that led to the bedrooms as Mama rounded the corner from the bathroom.

"It's called tough love," she said, now free of the spaghetti in her hair and red sauce on her face. She placed the fork on the table and took her seat. "And if you hadn't spoiled them so much, they wouldn't need this type of intervention now."

After that pronouncement, she turned her attention to her plate and began eating. Zack and I exchanged surprised looks. Sometimes my mother truly amazes me—in a good way.

Twenty minutes later we had finished our dinner, but Tino and the three delinquents had still not returned. Alex and Nick began clearing the table and loading the dishwasher. When Nick reached for Tino's plate, I said, "Cover that with waxed paper and place it in the microwave."

"What about the others?" asked Alex. "They're sitting on the kitchen table."

"Leave them for now." I had a feeling I knew what Tino had planned.

Sure enough, ten minutes later he marched the kids back into the dining room where their father, Mama, Zack, and I still sat. "Go ahead," said Tino.

One by one each of Ira's kids offered up an apology. I wouldn't go so far as to describe them as heartfelt, but they were spoken without an ounce of belligerence, and for Ira's kids, that's one giant leap for parent-kind.

"Your dinners are on the kitchen table," Tino told them. "I expect every last morsel eaten."

"Yes, sir," they mumbled in unison.

"What was that? I can't hear you."

"Yes, sir!" they repeated like good little cadets.

"That's better."

"Yours is in the microwave," I told Tino as the children headed into the kitchen.

"Thanks, Mrs. P." A moment later I heard the microwave whirring.

"Our dinners need to be heated up," said one of the twins from the kitchen.

"You should have eaten them when they were served to you," said Tino.

"But you're heating yours," said Isaac.

"Yes, I am," said Tino. "You have a problem with that?"

"No, sir."

Tino carried his plate into the dining room, joined us at the table, and began eating. "Delicious meatballs, Mrs. P," he said between mouthfuls.

Ira glanced toward the kitchen where the only sounds were from Nick and Alex continuing the cleanup. Not so much as a peep or a conspiratorial whisper could be heard from Isaac, Melody, and Harmony. "How did you do it?" he asked Tino. "What did you say to them?"

Tino winked. "Trade secret."

A few minutes later all three children appeared at the doorway, empty plates in their hands. "Excuse me, sir," said one of the twins. "We've finished dinner. May we be excused?"

"You may," said Tino. "Place your dishes in the dishwasher. Then return to the den and continue working on your assignments."

"Assignments?" asked Ira.

"All part of the program," said Tino. He clapped his hands together. "Now let's have some of that chocolate cake."

"Chocolate cake?" asked Isaac.

"Do you think you deserve any dessert?" asked Tino.

Isaac hung his head, shuffled his feet, and whined, "But I love chocolate cake."

Tino lifted an eyebrow. "Excuse me?"

Isaac raised both his head and his voice. "No, sir, I don't."

"Don't what?"

"Don't deserve any dessert, sir."

"And why is that?"

"Because of the way I behaved at dinner, sir."

"Indeed. Actions have consequences, young man."

"Yes, sir. May we be excused, sir?"

When Tino nodded, Isaac and the twins pivoted and marched toward the den.

Alex and Nick returned to the dining room, Alex carrying the cake and Nick holding plates, forks, and a cake cutter. "Mephisto is sleeping under the coffee table in the den," said Nick. "Want me to get him?"

I deferred to Tino. "They've already been instructed not to bother the dog," he said.

To my knowledge, Ira's kids had never followed instructions given by anyone, but then again, they'd never before come up against Tino Martinelli. From what I'd seen so far, they'd met their match and conceded. "He should be all right," I told Nick.

"I started a pot of coffee," said Alex. "It's almost ready."

"You have very thoughtful sons, Anastasia," said Ira, his voice wistful."

I glanced at Tino. "I think you're on your way toward having equally thoughtful children, Ira."

He turned to Tino. "When can you start?"

"Tomorrow too soon?"

"You don't need to give two-week's notice?"

"I do, but they'll escort me from the building the moment I hand in my resignation. No one wants to run the risk of an exiting employee planting a virus in the systems or walking off with proprietary information."

Ira nodded. "What about Christmas?"

"What about it?"

"I assume you'll take some time off to be with family?"

"I have no family."

I glanced at Tino, and he held my gaze for a moment. He'd never mentioned anything about his adoptive parents or any extended family. Perhaps they were no longer alive. However, his biological mother was still very much alive, although currently a guest of the state for the next twenty years to life. I hardly blamed him for distancing himself from her after the way she'd used him as a means to a devious end.

"Then it's settled." Ira beamed at Tino. "Welcome to the family."

As I sliced the cake and passed around plates, I wondered if I'd made a huge mistake by setting these wheels in motion. Not that I worried about Tino. He could take care of himself. But the ex-Marine wouldn't hang around forever. Once he whipped those kids into shape, he'd leave. Ira was the wild card in this family drama. Would Tino also be able to whip him into shape? Probably. Would it last once Tino moved on? The jury was out on that one.

The manny in question shoved a large forkful of chocolate cake into his mouth and said, "Now, Mrs. P., since we're on our way to solving one of your problems, let's tackle the other one. I'm itching to know more about this dead body and what you've learned so far."

FIFTEEN

Mama's fork froze halfway to her mouth as her eyes narrowed and her jaw clenched. She pivoted her head, first toward Tino, then me, then back to Tino. "Anastasia, you're not getting involved in that murder investigation, are you?"

Too late I realized I should have warned Tino not to mention Dion's murder in front of my mother, given recent history and her suspicions that Lawrence had a hand in his death.

She speared me with the sort of look I hadn't received from her since tenth grade when she'd forbidden me to join a student walkout in protest of *hands-on* behavior by an extremely popular football coach. Since his hands hadn't made contact with any of my body parts—private or otherwise—Mama saw no reason for me to get involved. I ignored her, figuring she'd never learn of my involvement. Unfortunately, as with Dion's murder, an *Eyewitness News* cameraman zeroed in on me, and my face was splashed across the evening news.

"No, Mama."

"Really?" She leaned forward, slammed her fork onto her plate, and rolled her eyes. What was I thinking? Mama always knew when I was being less than truthful with her. Now was no exception. "Then perhaps you'd explain why we're talking about this dead body you found in Ira's yard. Or have you discovered a second murder victim?"

"*We're* not talking about any dead body, Mama. And no, there hasn't been another murder." At least none that we know of—yet. I was still concerned for the safety of Paul Leonides and his wife, given it appeared likely Dion's killer could be an out-of-work former employee.

Mama narrowed her eyes at me. "Is that so?" She poked her fork in Tino's direction. "Then why did this young man ask you if you've learned anything more about the dead body?"

Ira cleared his throat. "Uhm, Flora...."

Mama turned her attention to him. "Yes?"

When Ira hesitated, she said, "It's Lawrence, isn't it? Why are you all pussyfooting around the truth? Don't try to protect me by withholding information."

Ira continued to stammer. "I...we don't know if it's Lawrence...I mean...the detective hasn't...there are other...."

She crossed her arms over her chest, huffed out her displeasure and said, "Spit it out, Ira. I want all the details. Every single one, not the thirty-second *Eyewitness News* sound bite."

"There isn't much more to tell at this point," he said, "other than what's been on the news."

She rolled her eyes at him. "Do you all think I'm stupid?"

He shook his head. "No, of course not. Anastasia discovered the body Wednesday morning when she came to drop something off on her way to work."

"Where were you?" Mama apparently wasn't about to settle for the Cliff Notes version, either.

"I'd already taken the kids to school."

"And you didn't notice a dead body in your yard when you left the house?"

He shrugged. "It was still dark. Besides, he was in the sleigh, and it had snowed that night."

Mama continued with her Torquemada-style inquisition. "And what was your connection to poor Dion? Why would the killer leave his body in your yard of all places?"

Ira's jaw dropped. "I don't know, Flora. I never met the man."

I studied my mother. All of a sudden she'd segued from *the dead body* to being on a first name basis with the deceased. *Poor Dion?*

Déjà vu smacked me in the face. From the time her ex-fiancé Louis Beaumont had met an untimely death—stabbed in the heart with one of my knitting needles—she'd referred to him as *Poor Lou*. Something was definitely going on with her besides her concern about me getting involved in another investigation. "Mama, what are *you* not telling us?"

"Me?" She reached for her napkin and began twisting it into a tight coil. "Why would you think I know anything?"

"Because you do, don't you?" asked Zack, eyeing her fidgeting fingers.

Mama cowered as all of us zeroed in on her and waited for her to answer. Her entire body sagged as she sank back into her chair. Her chin trembled, and her eyes filled with tears.

"Mama?"

A lone tear tracked down her cheek. "I knew Dion Leonides."

"How?" Although I really didn't have to ask. I'd already tapped into my inner Jessica Fletcher and figured that one out for myself.

Mama sniffled once before saying, "We were dating."

My suspicions confirmed, I quickly did a bit of mental arithmetic. Mama had nearly fifteen years on the unfortunate Dion Leonides. I doubted he'd known her true age. With each passing birthday she shaved a few years from her chronological age, rather than adding one. At some point I fully expected she'd begin introducing me as her not-too-younger sister. She certainly had the well-preserved looks to get away with the deception.

Nick's eyes grew wide. "You dated the dead guy?"

Mama dabbed at the corner of her eyes with the strangled napkin. "He was very much alive the last time we were together."

Knowing Mama, I was certain that sentence was loaded with double meaning. Before she could elaborate, I spared my sons the embarrassment of hearing any of her sexual exploits by asking, "Where did you meet him?"

"At a YMCA singles mixer."

"When?"

"A few weeks ago."

"Why didn't you mention this yesterday?" I asked.

She untwisted the napkin and blew her nose before answering. "I told you Lawrence was involved. Isn't it obvious he put a hit out on Dion?"

"Lawrence is locked up in solitary," said Zack.

Mama turned on him. "You think that would stop a man like Lawrence Tuttnauer? Don't be so naïve."

"Zack naïve?" asked Nick, sputtering with laughter. "Grandma, he's a badass spy!"

Alex elbowed his brother in the ribs. "Shh! Don't give away his secrets."

Zack shook his head and scowled at both boys. "Not the time or place to joke, guys."

Nick shrugged. "Whatever. Mom doesn't think it's a joke."

"What's he talking about?" asked Mama, pivoting her attention back to me.

I glared at my son, and he clammed up.

"Nothing, Flora," said Zack. "I'm not a spy."

She waved the thought away as if swatting at a gnat. "Of course, you're not. That's ridiculous."

Ira brought the conversation back to her ex-husband and his ex-father-in-law. "How would Lawrence even know you were dating? If he's in solitary, he has no way of communicating with the outside world."

"Not necessarily," said Tino. "All it takes is paying off a corrupt guard or two."

Not helpful. I seriously considered kicking him under the table to keep him from espousing any further comments, no matter how probable. Too bad my legs weren't long enough.

Mama nodded at Tino. "I'm sure he has. For all I know he's even bugged my phone. I certainly wouldn't put it past him." She pulled her mouth into a thin line and shook her head. "I'm so stupid. Why did I never think of that? He could have someone listening in on this conversation right now."

"I can check your phone for you," said Tino.

"How can you do that?" she asked.

"I'm in cyber-security."

"I thought you worked with my daughter."

"Used to."

Mama turned to me. "Explain to me why a crafts editor needs to work with a cyber-security expert."

"Tino worked for corporate, Mama. He wasn't on the *American Woman* staff."

She mulled that over for a moment before nodding. "I suppose these days even women's magazines need to guard against hackers stealing their subscribers' personal information."

"Hackers are targeting all sorts of companies," I said. Mama didn't need to know Tino had had nothing to do with cyber-security at Trimedia."

She turned her attention back to Tino. "Thank you, young man. I'd appreciate that." Then she batted her eyelashes and graced him with one of her come hither smiles.

Warning! Cougar on the prowl.

Tino squirmed in his seat. Wide-eyed and out of Mama's line of sight, he silently mouthed to me, "Did she just put the moves on me again?"

Oh yeah.

One moment Mama's bemoaning Dion's death. The next moment she's trolling for his replacement, totally forgetting that she's convinced her ex-husband has murdered her latest boyfriend and could very well set his sights on her next one. The mama cougar known as Flora Sudberry Periwinkle Ramirez Scoffield Goldberg O'Keefe Tuttenauer would never change her spots.

"Not only that," she continued, "now that I think of it, he's probably had his flunkies following me, maybe even since before we were married." She glanced toward the window. "I'll bet there's someone lurking outside right now with orders to eliminate anyone I date." Mama lowered her head into her hands. "Poor Dion. He's dead because of me."

Given Lawrence Tuttnauer's record, I had to admit that nothing Mama suggested seemed beyond the realm of possibilities.

Besides, hadn't I already raised suspicions concerning Lawrence's possible involvement in Dion's murder?

Forget solitary. Tino was right. At most, solitary confinement put a minor hiccup in Lawrence's plans, one he'd easily overcome. If Lawrence knew Mama was dating Dion, he could kill two birds with one stone—eliminate one of Mama's suitors *and* scare the caca out of me.

If so, Paul and Octavia Leonides didn't have to fear for their lives. We did. Because at some point Lawrence might not be satisfied with only knocking off Mama's prospective beaus.

~*~

I spent the next half-hour calming down my mother and convincing her Lawrence hadn't orchestrated Dion's murder, even if the needle of my Suspicion-O-Meter had once again veered closer in his direction. Then I hinted none-too-subtly that Ira should round up the Brat Pack and head home. Given this new wrinkle, I needed to place a call to Detective Spader and the sooner, the better, especially if Lawrence had one of his henchmen following my mother.

"No rush," he said, clueless as ever. "Tomorrow isn't a school day."

"But I'm sure you probably have last minute wrapping and other Christmas chores left to do," I said.

"No, not really."

"But we do," said Zack.

"Oh." Ira's features deflated. He trained his gaze on Tino. "I'll see you tomorrow?"

"Bright and early."

Ira nodded. Then with all the enthusiasm of a dead man walking, he said, "I suppose we should get going, then."

"We'll see you Sunday," I said. That perked him up. Then I added, "Would you mind dropping Mama off so she doesn't have to call for an Uber?" For all I knew, Lawrence might have his underlings posing as Uber drivers.

"Of course, Anastasia. Anything for you."

Ira grabbed everyone's coats from the closet, passing Mama hers. As he headed for the den, Tino sauntered toward the front door. When he passed me, he whispered, "Big time crush."

Zack draped an arm over my shoulders and whispered back, "No secret there. Lucky for me it's not reciprocal."

A moment later Melody, Harmony, and Isaac dashed toward the front door, only to find Tino, feet spread, arms crossed, blocking their escape. "Aren't you forgetting something?" he asked them.

At first it appeared all three had inherited their father's clueless gene. "Dad said it was time to leave," whimpered one of the twins.

Tino knit his brows together and peered down his nose at them. "And?"

The children glanced toward their father for help. "What do you say to your Aunt Anastasia?" asked Ira.

"Oh," said Melody—or Harmony. "That. Thank you?"

"Yeah, thank you," parroted the other twin.

"Ditto," said Isaac, shuffling his feet.

But Tino continued to glare at them, his massive Marine bulk blocking the door. "Anything else?"

"The assignments?" asked one of the girls.

"We left them in the den," said Isaac.

"Is that what you were supposed to do with them?"

The three raced back down the hall and returned a moment later, each grasping several sheets of lined notebook paper, which they held out toward Tino.

He continued to stand with his arms crossed over his chest. "Aren't you going to take them?" asked one of the twins, waving her papers at him.

"Are they for me?"

"You made us write them," said Isaac.

"For?"

"Oh," said the other twin. She collected the papers from her brother and sister and walked over to me. "These are for you," she said holding them out to me.

I accepted them from her. "Thank you."

When Tino cleared his throat, she glanced over her shoulder at him, then turned back to me and added, "You're welcome, Aunt Anastasia."

"That's better," said Tino, stepping away from the door. "Now you may leave. I'll see you tomorrow."

"What!" cried Isaac. "Tomorrow?" Shocked settled over all three kids.

"How come?" asked one of his sisters.

"Tomorrow is Christmas Eve," said the other. "Why would we see you tomorrow?"

I didn't think it possible, but Tino's face grew even sterner as he answered her. "Because I'm your new nanny."

"No way!" She turned to her father. "You can't do this to us, Dad. He's so mean!"

The other twin grabbed her father's arm and tugged at it. "We'll be good, Dad. We promise!"

"Please, Dad!" said Isaac, latching on to Ira's other arm. "We'll apologize to Carmella!"

Ira stood firm, not saying a word to his children. Instead he drew a deep breath and nodded to Tino. The new manny swung open the front door and gave the children one final order for the evening. "Get in the car."

Ira's kids made one last silent plea to their father, but he ignored them. Finally, they hung their heads, mumbled, "Yes, sir," and marched out single file.

Mama followed them. As she passed Tino, she said, "Good luck. You're going to need it with those three."

Tino smiled at her. "Luck has nothing to do with it, ma'am."

Ira brought up the rear. He extended his right hand to Tino and said, "This has been one of the most difficult things I've ever had to do."

Tino clasped Ira's hand and gave it a firm shake. "You did good, man."

After Tino closed the door behind Ira, Nick said, "Holy moly! Remind me never to mess with you, dude." He made himself comfortable on the living room carpet, leaning his back against the ottoman and sticking his long legs toward the center of the room. "Did you drug those brats or hypnotize them?"

Tino winked at him. "Sorry, that information is classified."

"Maybe *he's* a spy," said Alex, sprawling alongside his brother.

"Speaking of spies...." Tino turned to Zack. "Are you?"

Zack huffed. "Only in Anastasia's extremely fertile imagination."

"Which is what all spies would say," said Tino, parroting my constant rebuttal of Zack's denials.

Zack threw up his arms. "I can't win. How about some wine?" He headed toward the kitchen. A moment later we heard the back door slam.

"Was it something I said?" asked Tino.

I settled onto the sofa. "He'll be back. We keep all the alcohol locked in the apartment above the garage where my mother-in-law can't get her hands on it. She's never met a bottle of wine she couldn't polish off in a nanosecond."

Tino took a seat in one of the armchairs in front of the bay window. "You have an extremely interesting family, Mrs. P."

"That's one word for it."

While we waited for Zack to return, I leafed through the assignment Tino had given Ira's kids. Each child had written one hundred times: *I apologize for my bad behavior. I promise to treat my family and others with respect at all times or suffer the consequences.*

I glanced up from the pages. "Suffer the consequences? What kind of consequences?"

Tino shrugged. "I left that up to their imaginations."

"I'm going with Nick on this one," said Alex. "You definitely drugged or hypnotized them. Maybe both."

Zack returned a few minutes later with a bottle of pinot noir, three glasses, and two small cans of Coke for the boys. He took a seat next to me and poured the wine, passing a glass to Tino and one to me. Then he stood, raised his glass and said, "I have an announcement to make."

I raised an eyebrow, wondering what he was up to. "An official announcement?"

"Definitely."

"Concerning what?"

"Speculation. I officially give up. Yes, I'm a spy."

SIXTEEN

"Dude!" said Nick.

"For the CIA," Zack continued.

"Whoa!" added Alex.

"And the NSA, the FBI, MI-5, MI-6, Mossad, Opus Dei, *and* the Loyal Order of the Mousse."

"All of them?" asked Nick.

Alex yanked at the hem of his brother's jeans. "He's pulling our legs, Doofus."

I shot him the most skeptical look I could muster while keeping laughter at bay. "Loyal Order of the Mousse?"

Zack nodded. With complete seriousness he said, "Chocolate Division."

"So that's m-o-u-s-s-e? A *French* spy organization?"

"*Bien sûr.*"

Two could play this game. "*Merde.*"

Zack reclaimed his seat next to me and patted my thigh. "*Touché, madame!*"

Deciding the time had come for a redirection of the conversation, I passed him the assignment papers. "On another subject...."

Zack quickly leafed through the sheets, then placed them on the coffee table and asked Tino, "Exactly what did you say to them? I've never seen such a rapid behavioral about-face in anyone, least of all kids."

"Especially those kids," I said.

Tino chuckled. "I happened to mention I was Special Forces, which made an immediate impact on young Isaac. The kid is obsessed with video games."

"We know," said Zack. "I carried him out kicking and screaming from the arcade last night."

"So they did what you said because Isaac thinks you're like the dudes in *Close Combat* and *Call of Duty*?" asked Nick.

Tino grinned. "I didn't see any reason to point out the difference between fantasy and reality. Once I had him in the palm of my hand, he convinced his sisters they'd better do as I said."

"You sure you don't have a degree in child psychology?" I asked.

"Computer technology." He then added, "By the way, I'm really sorry about bringing up the murder, Mrs. P., I had no idea it would unleash a can of worms."

"My fault. I should have said something to you ahead of time."

"Your mom going to be okay?"

Zack laughed. "Did you not notice Flora was already trolling for her next husband?"

"Yeah, that sort of creeped me out. Give me Ira's little monsters over that woman any day." Color immediately suffused Tino's cheeks. He quickly added, "No offense, Mrs. P."

"None taken, Tino. Mama is an acquired taste. I am concerned, though. I think Detective Spader had pretty much eliminated Lawrence as a suspect and is concentrating on Parthenon's ex-employees. Now I'm not so sure."

"You should call him about what we learned this evening," said Zack.

"Agreed."

However, at that moment my phone rang. I glanced at the display. "Cue the *Twilight Zone* theme," I said. "It's Spader." I already suspected the detective never slept. Now I had to add ESP to his list of superpowers.

"Put the call on speaker," said Zack.

I nodded as I answered. "Good evening, Detective."

"Mrs. Pollack, I'm sitting here going over Dion Leonides' phone and text records, and you'll never guess who he was dating."

"My mother."

Seething anger shoved aside the forced calm I had initially detected in his voice as he began shouting at me. "How the—? You didn't think I'd—? Why the hell would you not—?"

I suspected Spader's blood pressure now hovered dangerously close to stroke territory, and I certainly didn't want to cause the detective's premature demise. "Because I only just found out. I was about to call you."

"I see."

"No, I don't think you do, Detective. My mother suspects Lawrence is having her followed and gave orders to eliminate anyone she started dating."

"Why would he do that? They're no longer married."

"Because he's a control freak and royally pissed that she ended the marriage after his arrest." Not that I blamed Mama. I'd have been more concerned if she'd pulled a Tammy Wynette and decided to stand by her man. "If he can't have her, he's going to make damn sure no one else will."

Spader huffed out a gale wind of frustration. "I swear your family is going to be the death of me."

Contrary to his accusation, my money—not that I had any—was on a lifetime of booze, cigarettes, and fast food doing him in. Although Spader had recently cut back on all three vices and shed a few pounds, he still had a long way to go in his recent quest to live a healthier lifestyle. Of course, I kept those thoughts to myself and instead said, "Now is that fair?"

"You tell me. Exactly how old is your mother?"

"Pushing sixty-seven."

"And she was dating a fifty-two-year-old guy?"

"You wouldn't question the age difference if the sexes were reversed, Detective."

He heaved a frustrated sigh. "I suppose, but this is too coincidental for my blood."

"And mine. After speaking with Jesse Konopka, I was leaning toward a disgruntled ex-employee. Did you check to see if Paul and Dion lived up to their promise of finding employment for all the laid-off Parthenon construction workers?"

"Working on it. We're having trouble tracking down some of the guys on the list Mrs. Leonides provided us."

"That sounds suspicious."

"Not necessarily, but we won't know for sure until we speak with all of them. Keep in mind, this isn't my only case. I've also got two homicides in Plainfield and one in Linden I'm investigating. And on top of that, we're short-staffed right now. Several of my guys are laid up with a stomach bug."

"I understand, but what about my mother? If her suspicions are correct, I'm worried about her safety." What if Lawrence decided to eliminate Mama instead of her dates? After all, the man had put out a contract on his own daughter. He wouldn't think twice about hiring one of his henchmen to eliminate an ex-wife.

Spader sighed again. I noticed he sighed a lot lately whenever we spoke, but at least he was no longer screaming at me. Or hurling accusations. "I'll see if I can free up a patrol officer to shadow her for a few days, but I can't promise anything."

"Thank you. Does that mean you agree one of Lawrence's goons may be stalking her?"

"With your family, anything is possible. Meanwhile, I want to hear from you immediately—not a day, an hour, or a minute after the fact—if your Jessica Fletcher radar kicks in or you learn something else. Anything at all, no matter how insignificant it might seem to you. Understood?"

"I've got your number on speed-dial, Detective."

When I disconnected from the call, Tino said, "Maybe I can track down those former employees."

"How?" I asked.

Tino winked. "I work in cyber-security, remember?"

"But come tomorrow you're Ira's manny."

Tino shrugged. "You think only women can multitask?"

I did, but given the estrogen to testosterone ratio presently filling my living room, I held my tongue.

"Besides," Tino continued, "My employer doesn't know I plan to leave. I'm on vacation through the end of the year."

"So you'd bring Isaac and the twins into your office tomorrow?" asked Nick. "Good luck with that."

"No need," said Tino. "Ever hear of cloud computing? Lend

me a computer, and we can hunt down those ex-employees right now."

"Wouldn't Detective Spader have already tried that?" asked Alex.

"Probably not," said Zack. "He'd hand the task over to his computer people."

"Who, in addition to the detective's caseload," said Tino, "would be investigating all major crimes in the county, not just homicides." He ticked off a list on his fingers. "Embezzlement. Money laundering. Kidnapping. Drug trafficking. Arson. You name it. I bet I can track down the whereabouts of those former employees way before the cyber-cops."

"But we don't even know their names," said Nick.

"Not a problem," said Tino. "Give me a few minutes."

"So, you can find out who they are *and* where they are?" asked Alex.

Tino puffed out his chest and cocked his head. "We wouldn't be having this conversation if I couldn't."

"This I've got to see." Alex jumped up. As he raced toward his bedroom, he called over his shoulder, "You can use my laptop."

"You're not going to do anything illegal, are you?" I asked Tino.

"Like what?" answered Mr. All-Innocence.

My skepticism trumped the guileless look plastered across his face. What an actor! He knew that I knew he'd tap danced around the law at least once before when his heart had overruled his head. He'd gotten away with a slap on the wrist only because he'd agreed to cooperate with law enforcement to bring down a killer. But Tino had acted on his own then. This time was different. "Like hacking into private servers? I don't want the FBI bashing down our door in the middle of the night and hauling us off to some undisclosed location."

"Would I do that to you, Mrs. P?"

I hoped not.

"Not to worry," he continued. "You can trust me."

I turned to Zack. "You're very quiet. What do you think about this?"

"Ideally, I'd prefer the police handled the investigation, but Flora's life could be in danger. We need to know one way or another if Lawrence is behind the Leonides murder."

An involuntary shiver coursed up my spine. "Even if he's not, he still may have someone tailing Mama."

Then, as if that weren't bad enough, an even darker thought edged its way into my brain. "What if he's got people following all of us?" Tommy Gravino may no longer pose a threat to me, but that didn't mean Lawrence hadn't replaced him with a more deadly thug.

Had I fallen into a false sense of security lately? I glanced at Nick, anxiously awaiting whatever computer magic Tino had up his sleeve. How safe were my sons? Would Lawrence stoop that low?

Zack squeezed my hand. "Let's take this one step at a time." Then he asked Tino, "You plan to log into your work computer and spoof the IP address?"

Tino nodded. "And use proxy servers to route the connection through secure servers that won't log or record the connection details."

I rolled my eyes. "In English, please."

Zack translated. "Basically it means you have absolutely nothing to worry about."

Tino nodded in agreement.

"What about a VPN?" asked Zack.

"That, too."

I'd obviously stepped into an alternate universe. "What's a VPN?"

"Virtual Private Network," said Tino. "It encrypts the network traffic for an extra layer of security."

I turned to Mr. I'm-Not-a-Spy and asked, "How do you know all this?"

"Mom," said Nick, rolling his eyes at me, "even I've heard of proxy servers and VPNs."

I shook my head. Processing all the new information and technology constantly bombarding me was an exhausting and never-ending task. The world was changing faster than I could keep up with it, leaving me wading through a pool of outdated and useless cyber-debris. Then again, the horse and buggy crowd probably felt the same way about the horseless carriage crowd when they spoke of pistons and carburetors.

Alex returned and handed his laptop to Tino. The boys crowded around either side of Tino's chair. Zack stood and crossed the living room in a few long strides, taking up a position behind the chair in order to observe over Tino's shoulder.

I remained seated on the sofa knowing whatever information flashed across the computer screen might as well be written in Swahili or Cantonese for all the sense it would make to me. My twentieth century brain processed names and locations far better than it comprehended twenty-first century computer jargon.

I poured myself another glass of wine and waited for the results of Tino's cyber-sleuthing. I'd only taken a few sips when he said, "I've accessed the Parthenon payroll records."

"We need the names of the men who are no longer on the current payroll," I said. "The ones the Leonides brothers laid off when they hired Jesse Konopka after their father's death."

Tino spent another minute or so clicking away at the keyboard before saying, "Got it. Twelve men."

That was probably the easy part. He'd only had to hack into Parthenon's computer to access the names of the former employees. "Now what? How will you figure out if they're all working at new construction companies?"

He glanced up from the laptop and winked at me. "Have some faith, Mrs. P. All I have to do is cross-reference the names with those listed in other databases."

"What other databases?"

Tino closed the laptop screen and stood. "Maybe I should do this in private."

"Why?" asked Nick.

"Because he doesn't want any of us to know where he's going to snoop next," said Alex.

"Proprietary information," said Tino.

"I don't like the sound of that," I said.

"Relax, Mrs. P."

And exactly how was I supposed to do that? "Tell me you're not going to hack into any government computers."

"Okay," said Tino. "I'm not going to hack into any government computers."

I wished I could believe him. I glanced at Zack. From the tightness in his jaw, I didn't think he believed Tino, either, but instead of saying anything, he stared after Tino as he exited the living room and hooked a right down the hallway, presumably heading for the den.

"He's hacking into a government database, isn't he?" I asked Zack.

"Looks that way." He returned to the sofa and took a seat next to me.

"Which one?"

"Social Security, probably. Maybe the IRS. He'll look for recent withholding payments made to each of the men."

I gulped. "You still okay with this?"

"Not really."

"What do we do?"

"Keep reminding ourselves that Flora's life could be in jeopardy. Tino's motives are pure."

"As they were last time. It doesn't negate the criminality of his actions."

He wrapped his arm around my shoulders. "If it's any consolation, he definitely knows how to hide his cyber-fingerprints. There's no way anything can be traced back to Alex's computer."

That wasn't my only worry, though. I turned to my sons. "Both of you are sworn to secrecy about this, understand? You tell no one. Not even Sophie."

"Got it," said Alex.

"Nick?"

"Understood, Mom. Tell no one."

Fifteen minutes later Tino returned to the living room. "I've got good news and bad news. Which do you want first?"

SEVENTEEN

"I'm not sure I'm up for any more bad news," I said. "Let's have the good news first." Maybe it would temper the bad news to come.

"It looks like Parthenon lived up to its promise and found jobs for most of those guys."

"Most?" asked Zack.

"Eight of the twelve."

"That doesn't prove Parthenon secured new positions for the men," I said. "They may have gotten their new jobs without Parthenon's help. What about the other four men?"

"That's the bad news."

I swigged the last bit of wine in my glass, then sighed as I waved my hand at Tino to continue. "Lay it on me."

He returned to the chair he'd earlier vacated and opened the laptop. Referring to notes he'd apparently made, he said, "Of the four men who are still unemployed, one moved to Florida before the murder, one is cooling his heels in lockup on an unrelated charge, one is collecting unemployment, and one is in the wind."

"Meaning you weren't able to track him down?" asked Alex.

"He's off the grid," said Tino. "He could be anywhere. I tried the phone number I found for him. It's been disconnected, and the address Parthenon had for him was a post office box."

Tino and I had been down that road before while investigating Philomena Campanello's murder and discovered an unrelated crime, a massive embezzling operation involving payroll checks, bogus employees, and post office box addresses.

"That sounds suspicious," said Nick.

"Not necessarily," said Zack. "What's his name?"

Tino referred to the computer screen. "Mateo Garza."

"He could be undocumented," said Zack.

Tino shook his head. "If so, he's not on any immigration list. I checked all the Homeland Security databases."

"I didn't hear that," I said. Tino's snooping into government databases sent visions of all of us wearing matching orange jumpsuits ricocheting through my brain. "Was he the only employee with a post office box for an address?"

"Yeah. The only other P.O. box listed was for some credit union where they'd established a line of credit."

"What about the other men?" I asked. "What are their names?"

"The guy who moved to Florida is Gonzalo Sandoval. The one collecting unemployment is Darnell Johnson, and the one sitting in a cell is Weldon Smith."

"What's he in for?" asked Zack.

"Drugs. He was caught selling Fentanyl."

"When?" I asked.

"Before the murder."

"So if Dion's murder is connected to the layoffs," I said, "we have two possible suspects, Mateo Garza and Darnell Johnson."

"Johnson we can talk to," said Tino. "Garza could be anywhere in or out of the country at this point."

"Which makes him the prime suspect," I said, "especially if we rule out Johnson after speaking with him."

"We?" asked Zack, leveling a pointed look at me.

"Well, we can't exactly hand the names over to Spader. What am I supposed to tell him when he asks where I got them? I've got a friend who hacked into government computers?"

"Mom...." Nick's voice sounded both a plea and a warning. "You promised."

"I know, Nick." Once again, I was squeezed between the proverbial rock and hard place. I needed to make sure Lawrence wasn't targeting my mother or anyone else in my family, but to do that I again had to break my promise to Nick by inserting myself into a situation where only the police should tread.

I turned to Zack. "You have a gun."

"Which you're not getting."

"I don't want it. I want you with it." I turned to Tino. "What about you?"

"What about me?"

"You own a gun?"

"I'm an ex-Marine, Mrs. P. Of course, I own a gun. More than one."

I turned back to Nick and explained why it was imperative we spoke with Darnell Johnson. "It's for your grandmother, Nick, and you and your brother. We need to know if Lawrence is behind Dion's murder because we all may be at risk."

He chewed on his lower lip for a minute before responding. "I suppose that makes sense." Then he turned to Zack and Tino.

"You better keep her safe."

"She'll be very safe," said Zack. "Because she's not coming with us."

My mouth dropped open. "Don't you dare play the chauvinist card with me, Zachary Barnes! We're talking about my family."

"Which is why you need to stay far away from any potential killer. Your sons need you. Your mother needs you. And I need you."

"And what if Johnson has an alibi and it turns out Lawrence orchestrated the hit?"

Zack grimaced. "Let's first rule Johnson in or out. Then we'll worry about Lawrence."

I conceded. Reluctantly. "When do you plan to speak with him?"

"How about tomorrow?" asked Tino.

"Tomorrow is Christmas Eve," I reminded him. "Besides, you have a prior commitment."

"I'm not working for Ira twenty-four seven," he said. "We can catch Johnson first thing in the morning."

"Unless he's out doing last minute holiday shopping or flying off to visit family," I said.

"What are the chances of that?" asked Tino. "The guy is unemployed. He's probably sitting at home in his underwear, nursing a six-pack."

I raised an eyebrow. "First thing in the morning? No wonder he's unemployed."

Tino offered me a shrug accompanied by a sheepish grin. "Hey, it's a guy thing. Breakfast of champions. Anyway, all we can do is try."

"There is no try," said Nick.

"Do or do not," added Alex, completing the famous Yoda quote from *The Empire Strikes Back*, although inverted.

Do or do not. Precisely. I needed to do something besides sit on my hands. "How about if we compromise?" I asked.

Zack eyed me suspiciously. "In what way?"

"I go with the two of you but wait in the car."

"How is that different from waiting at home?" asked Tino.

"Because once you and Zack determine Johnson's not a threat, I can join you to speak with him."

"You don't trust us to speak with him?"

"Three heads are better than two," I said. "I might think of questions to ask that neither of you would."

"I doubt it," said Tino. "I was a Marine. I'm trained in interrogation."

"And I'm a woman."

"What difference does that make?"

"We have genetically superior communication skills."

Tino shared a look with Zack who grimaced at me. Then he released a heavy sigh before finally acquiescing. "Can't argue with that. But you stay in the car until I signal you that it's safe to enter." Then he turned to the boys. "You guys okay with that?"

"I suppose," said Nick, although his expression said otherwise.

"Ditto," said Alex.

Score one for the estrogen contingent of one.

~*~

The next morning Zack and I drove through intermittent snow flurries to the North Plainfield address Tino had supplied us for Darnell Johnson. When we arrived at the building, a mid-century three-story brick apartment complex, Zack pulled into a parking space across the street.

A moment later Tino exited a black Mercedes SUV parked two spaces in front of us and walked toward Zack's Boxster. He wore a navy pea coat with a black knit ski cap pulled low over his forehead and ears, reminding me of the hired "muscle" from every gangster film or TV show I'd ever seen. Good thing I knew he had a heart of gold.

"I'm going to leave the engine running to keep you warm," Zack said. "Lock the doors when I leave." I bit back the snappy retort itching to roll off my tongue and smiled sweetly. Zack hopped out of the car, but instead of walking toward Tino, he stood with fists on hips, glaring at me through the driver's side window, until I reached over and engaged the lock.

By this time Tino had made his way to Zack. He shook Zack's hand, then waved hello to me before the two of them turned and headed across the street. I watched as they entered the building's vestibule. Then with nothing to do but twiddle my thumbs and wait, I switched on the radio to chill out with some Christmas tunes.

The radio station had finished airing a rendition of "We Need a Little Christmas" and was halfway through "Little Town of Bethlehem" when my cell phone rang. "Everything okay?" I asked, after seeing Zack's name pop up on the display.

He chuckled. "Absolutely. Come on up. Second floor, first apartment on the right."

I couldn't imagine what was so amusing, but before I could ask, Zack disconnected. I turned off the engine, grabbed the key, and stepped from the Boxster. After closing the door, I hit the lock on the remote.

Once inside the small vestibule, I located Darnell Johnson's name on the intercom board, pressed the button, and was immediately buzzed through the door that led into the lobby. Although in need of an update, the interior was well lit and clean.

An elevator stood directly across from the entrance, a staircase to its left. I opted for the stairs, deciding the climb would counteract at least a few mouthfuls of last night's chocolate cake. I had no idea how many calories I'd burn hiking up two flights of stairs, but I figured every little bit helped.

I arrived on the second floor slightly winded but feeling virtuous. The Johnson apartment door stood open. Friendly sounding voices spilled into the hallway from within. I knocked on the doorframe.

A petite woman with bouncy strawberry curls and a splash of freckles across a flawless latte-colored complexion stepped into the entryway. She held a newborn in an infant carrier strapped to her chest. "You must be Mrs. Pollack," she said, extending a hand and offering me a huge smile.

I shook her hand. "Anastasia."

"I'm Serenity Johnson. Come on in." She looped her arm around mine and led me inside. Zack, Tino, and a man I assumed was Darnell Johnson sat in a crowded living room filled with toys and a portable crib. A toddler played at a Thomas train table off to one corner. A massive Christmas tree took up the floor space in front of the double windows that faced out onto the side street.

Darnell Johnson rose from his chair next to the sofa and extended his right hand toward me. "Pleased to meet you, Mrs. Pollack. I am Darnell Johnson." He spoke with a thick Jamaican accent. His construction worker physique matched Tino's ex-Marine body muscle for muscle, making me wonder who'd come out ahead in an arm-wrestling contest.

I shook his hand. "Likewise, Darnell. And please call me Anastasia."

"Have a seat," said Serenity. "Coffee should be ready by now."

"Would you like some help?"

She chuckled. "With two little ones I never turn down an offer of help. This way." I followed her into a dated but immaculate kitchen. "If you take that," she said pointing to a tray on the small kitchen table, "I'll grab the coffee pot."

I carried the tray containing milk, sugar, spoons, and mugs back to the living room, noting she'd already included me in the count. Serenity followed with the coffee pot. As we placed everything on a small coffee table, the newborn let loose a sound every mother recognizes. Serenity scrunched up her nose. "Help yourselves to coffee," she said. "Doody duty calls."

While Serenity scurried down a hallway, I took a seat on the sofa next to Zack and played substitute hostess, pouring coffee for everyone. "You all look like you're getting along famously," I said, eyeing each of them as I passed around the coffee.

"Darnell was telling us why he turned down Dion's offer to find him another construction job," said Zack.

I poured a splash of milk into my coffee. "So the brothers did live up to their promise of finding jobs for everyone?"

"They did," said Darnell. "Dion was a great boss for the short time he ran things after his father passed away."

"What about Paul?" I asked.

Darnell shrugged. "I know he owned half the company, but whatever he did must have been behind the scenes. He never interacted with the crew while I worked at Parthenon."

I took a sip of my coffee before asking, "Why did you turn down Dion's offer?"

Darnell fought to control an unabashed grin but failed miserably. "I had a better offer that starts next month. I was planning to give notice when I learned we were all getting laid off, so I opted to collect unemployment for six months. My unemployment runs out next week, conveniently right before the start of my new job."

"So Dion ran the company for about six months before hiring Jesse Konopka?"

Darnell nodded. "Between you and me, as nice a guy as Dion was, I don't think he was cut out for construction management. He was smart to hire Jesse. And I don't blame Jesse for wanting to bring on his own crew."

"Did your coworkers feel likewise?" asked Zack.

"No one seemed to care since we were all guaranteed new jobs. Plus, Dion generously sweetened the sting by handing out thousand dollar bonuses to everyone."

"With a new baby on the way, that extra money really helped," said Serenity, returning to the living room. She sank into a corner of the sofa. "Unemployment helps, but it doesn't stretch anywhere near as far as a paycheck."

"Everything okay?" Darnell asked his wife.

"El Stinko is once again baby fresh." She turned to me. "It's amazing what comes out of such a sweet little bundle, isn't it?"

I laughed. "It's been a long time, but I do remember." I turned back to Darnell. "So what will you be doing come January?"

Serenity answered for him. "You're looking at D.C. United's newest assistant coach."

"Soccer?"

Serenity beamed. "Darnell retired after playing his last World Cup in 2018. He was an amazing player. He's going to make a great coach."

"We'll be packing up and moving to a home outside of Washington right after Christmas," said Darnell. "I won't be sorry to leave this shoebox of an apartment, but it enabled us to save quite a bit of money while we were here."

Every instinct in my body told me we could definitely rule Darnell Johnson from our suspects list.

I raised my mug in a toasting gesture. "Congratulations."

"Thank you. The construction work was never meant to be anything but temporary until the right coaching offer came along."

"Was Dion able to find jobs for everyone else?" I asked.

"Everyone who wanted one," said Darnell. "Gonzalo decided he hated the winters up here and moved back to Florida, and Weldon went into business for himself."

"Dealing prescription drugs?"

He shook his head. "Damn fool. I tried to talk him out of it, but he wouldn't listen."

"He got what he deserved," said Serenity. "I'm an emergency room nurse. I've seen firsthand how opioids destroy lives."

I wondered if Darnell or Serenity had something to do with ending Weldon Smith's short tenure as a drug kingpin but decided to stifle my curiosity.

That still left one ex-Parthenon employee unaccounted for. "What about Mateo Garza?" asked Tino. "You have any idea how we can get in touch with him?"

Darnell and Serenity exchanged a worried glance. "He took off months ago," said Darnell. "No one knows where or why."

"Before or after the layoffs were announced?" asked Zack.

Darnell mulled the question over for a moment. "To be

honest, I'm not sure. Right around that time, though."

"Are you certain he left?"

Serenity's eyes grew wide. She grasped her baby a little tighter. The infant squirmed under her arms before settling back down. Serenity gently patted the baby's back. "What do you mean?"

"Could something have happened to him?" asked Zack.

"I suppose that's a possibility," said Darnell. "One day he just failed to show up at work. Dion voiced his annoyance, questioning all of us, but no one knew anything."

"Did Dion report him missing?" asked Tino.

"I don't know, but he'd only been working with us a short time. Not everyone is cut out for construction work. Sometimes guys just leave without notice."

"Anyone ever come around asking questions about him?" asked Zack.

"You mean like the cops?"

"Or anyone else."

He shook his head. "Not that I know."

"What do you know about him?" I asked.

"Not much. Mateo kept to himself. Everyone else on the crew got along. The guys went out to lunch together or grabbed a beer after work. Mateo never joined us. He rarely spoke to any of us."

"Something was off with him," said Serenity.

EIGHTEEN

"What do you mean?" I asked.

"We bumped into him once at Target. He had this furtive look about him."

"Furtive?"

She nodded. "He never made eye contact and seemed ready to bolt. At first I wondered if he suffered from autism, but I quickly changed my mind."

"Why?"

"The way he kept his arms wrapped tightly across his chest, as if he was hiding something under his coat. I suspected he was shoplifting."

"It sounds like Mateo probably had more than a few secrets," I said.

Serenity shuddered. "Do you think he had something to do with Dion's death?"

"I don't see it," said Darnell. "There was never any indication that Mateo had a beef with Dion. And even if he did, why would he wait months to kill him? It doesn't make sense."

I couldn't disagree with his assessment. From everything we'd learned, it appeared Dion's death had nothing to do with his former employees. "You're probably right."

We'd learned as much as we could from the Johnsons. Zack apparently read my mind because he placed his empty coffee mug on the tray and stood. "Thank you for your time and hospitality," he said. "We won't impose any longer. You've been extremely helpful."

"Good luck with the new job and the move," said Tino, reaching across the coffee table to shake Darnell's hand. "I'll look for you on the sidelines."

"I hope you find Dion's killer," said Darnell as he and Serenity walked us to the door. "He was a fine man."

"Thank you," I said. "And Merry Christmas." I patted the baby's back and nodded toward the toddler. So absorbed with his wooden trains, he'd ignored us throughout the visit. "You have much to celebrate this year."

Serenity's face lit up. "I know. We're truly blessed. Merry Christmas to all of you, too."

"Nice family," said Tino as we took the stairs down to the lobby.

"Yes," I said.

We continued downstairs, no one mentioning the elephant following silently behind us. Once outside I asked, "If we agree that Mateo, as sketchy as he sounds, most likely had nothing to do with Dion's murder, who else could the killer be other than someone connected to Lawrence?"

"What do you know about Dion Leonides?" asked Tino.

"Mama may know more about him, but as for us, other than

what we saw on the news and what Darnell just told us? Not a thing."

"Exactly," said Tino. "Everyone has skeletons in their closet. Dion may have had one that got him killed. I'll see what I can dig up."

I raised an eyebrow. "Legally?"

Instead of answering, Tino glanced at his watch. "Would you look at the time! I told Ira I'd be at his place by ten. See ya!" With that he trotted across the street to his SUV, waving good-bye without a backwards glance.

As much as I appreciated Tino's desire to help me, I felt guilty drawing him into a murder investigation, especially since he had no qualms about resorting to unscrupulous methods of acquiring information. "I hope he knows what he's doing."

"He's a big boy," said Zack. "He knows exactly what he's doing."

"Breaking the law. For me."

"He knows that."

"I wonder if he also knows he probably can't order bespoke prison jumpsuits."

"Do you think that would deter him?"

"Probably not."

~*~

Zack and I arrived home to find Harriet Kleinhample's battered VW bus parked in front of my house. I followed the sound of the TV and glanced into the den where half a dozen commie comrades were devouring the contents of my refrigerator and pantry while camped in front of a rerun of *What Not To Wear*. A rather ironic choice, given Lucille's entire wardrobe consisted of circa nineteen-seventies polyester pantsuits. Her minions, garbed in a selection of decade's old outfits considered unfashionable even back in the day, scored equally low on the fashion barometer.

I made my way back to the kitchen where Zack had started a fresh pot of coffee. "Good thing I had the foresight to place our contribution for tonight's potluck dinner in the apartment fridge. The commies have cleaned us out." I had also moved the gift basket items to the apartment after realizing they weren't safe in the pantry.

"I know we've joked about this in the past, but you might want to get serious about a padlock for the refrigerator and pantry. Either that or resign yourself to a dozen freeloaders."

"A baker's dozen. What Lucille pays me each month doesn't come close to covering what she and her dog consume."

Zack nodded toward the kitchen table. "The boys left a note."

I picked up the piece of paper and read:

> Walked the dog.
> Locked up Ralph.
> Fled the commies.
> You better still be alive.
> See you later.
> Love,
> Your sons

"Everyone's a comedian," I said, knowing the boys had volunteered to help set up the church dining room for this evening's dinner.

Mama phoned as the last drips of coffee fell into the pot. I answered with a forced cheeriness, "Hello, Mama."

In her best Blanche DuBois imitation, she said, "Anastasia,

dear, I'd like you to do me a favor, please."

"What kind of favor, Mama?"

"I really should pay my respects to Dion's brother and his wife. Would you drive me to their home?"

I caught Zack's attention and executed an eye roll. "It's Christmas Eve, Mama. Do you really think today is the best day to pay a condolence call?"

Zack's eyebrows rose halfway to his hairline. "Leonides?" he mouthed.

I nodded as Mama said, "Well, I can't imagine they have holiday plans under the circumstances."

I tried another tack. "Wouldn't it be more appropriate to wait until funeral arrangements are announced and attend the viewing?"

"With reporters, detectives, and curiosity seekers crashing the funeral home? Certainly not! The place will be a zoo. Besides, I'm not just anybody. Dion and I were in a relationship. I'm sure he mentioned me to his family."

Suddenly we'd leaped from *dating* to *relationship*? In Mama-speak *relationship* was code for something firmly entrenched in TMI territory. I'd heard and seen enough when she'd gotten involved with Lawrence Tuttnauer. Before she went into graphic detail regarding her exploits with the recently departed Dion Leonides, I said, "I'll pick you up as soon as I grab an early lunch."

I hung up and dropped onto one of the kitchen chairs. Zack handed me a steaming mug of dark roast with a splash of milk and asked, "You need a shot of whiskey in that?"

I glanced at the wall-mounted clock above the sink. "Tempting. It is five o'clock somewhere, isn't it?" Then I came to my senses and declined the offer. "If I grabbed a drink every time

Mama or Lucille created havoc in my life, I'd wind up an alcoholic. Besides, I now have to play chauffeur."

"Valid points. How about a less inebriated solution?"

"And that would be?"

"You could have said no."

"And never hear the end of it?" I shook my head. "Best to get it over with as soon as possible."

"Maybe they won't be home."

I laughed. "And how likely is that, given my luck?"

"Want me to come along for moral support?"

"Thanks, but I love you too much to subject you to Mama twice in one day."

"Twice?"

"She always joins us for the Christmas Eve family service and covered dish dinner."

Zack grimaced. "Lucky us."

After a quick lunch of sliced apple, cheese, and crackers, I kissed Zack good-bye, and headed back out.

A few minutes later I pulled into a parking spot in front of Mama's condo. Before I could turn off the engine, she sashayed out the front door and in a pair of black suede high-heeled boots, gingerly navigated the light coating of snow on the path that led to the parking lot.

"Those are hardly snow boots," I said when she settled into the passenger seat.

"But they're so *au courant*, and they were on sale for only a hundred dollars at Lord & Taylor."

Only a hundred dollars? What a steal—not! I wondered if Ira was also paying her L&T credit card bill along with the other expenses he picked up, but I bit my tongue. Instead I said, "They have no traction. You could slip and break something."

She waved her hand dismissively. "You worry too much, dear."

One of us had to.

Fifteen minutes later I pulled up in front of Paul and Octavia Leonides' home. "Wait there," I told Mama as I killed the engine.

"Whatever for?"

"I'm coming around to help you out of the car. You're not breaking a hip on my watch."

"Don't be ridiculous," she said. "I'll have you know, according to my last bone density test, I have calcium to spare. My doctor said I have the skeleton of a thirty-year-old."

"Even thirty-year-olds slip on the ice and break bones, Mama." I already dealt with a semi-invalid mother-in-law. I didn't need to add a semi-invalid mother to my list of responsibilities.

I engaged the child lock, making it impossible for her to open the door on her own. She glared at me but finally gave in. "Fine. Have it your way."

"I will."

I helped her out of the car and held onto her arm as we navigated the slippery walkway that no one had bothered to salt this morning. If Mama slipped, she'd most likely pull me down on top of her. Luckily, that didn't happen. We made it up the porch steps without disaster striking in the form of bruised flesh, sprained ankles, strained muscles, or broken bones.

Loud shouting greeted us from within the house as we approached the front door.

NINETEEN

"Oh, dear," said Mama, placing her ear to the door. "They seem engaged in a rather heated argument."

That was an understatement. I assumed the angry, raised voices, those of a man and woman, were Paul and Octavia Leonides. However, I found it difficult to make out most of what either yelled back and forth with the exception of a few choice expletives.

I pulled Mama away from the door and said, "I don't think this is a good time for a condolence call."

She directed a frown toward the doorbell. "I suppose." But instead of moving toward the porch steps, she walked over to one of the windows and peered inside. "Should we call the police?"

I dragged her away from the window. "Stop that! Do you want them to call the cops on you?"

"Whatever for?"

"For being a Peeping Thomasina."

"Don't be ridiculous, dear. I'm concerned for their welfare."

"I don't think there's any reason for concern. After all, couples fight all the time, some louder than others."

"But—"

"Mama, if people called 9-1-1 whenever they heard their neighbors having an argument, the police would never have time to deal with real crimes."

"Really, Anastasia? How do you know a real crime isn't occurring inside as we stand here? Are you now clairvoyant?"

I shook my head and sighed. "No, Mama, but I'm not hearing anything to indicate that what's going on inside this house is more than a couple having a loud disagreement over something that's none of our business."

I latched onto her elbow and gently tugged to get her to leave. She dug in her designer boot heels but finally turned around and allowed me to help her off the porch. At the bottom of the steps she stopped and glanced over her shoulder. "You're sure we shouldn't—?"

"Positive. Didn't you ever fight with any of your husbands?"

"Of course, I did."

"And did anyone ever call the cops on you?"

"Of course not! Why would you suggest such a thing?"

I clamped my lips together to keep from uttering something I'd regret the moment the words escaped my mouth.

She muttered under her breath as I led her back to the car and settled her into the passenger seat. As I pulled away from the curb, she smacked her hands onto her thighs and said, "Well, that was a waste of my time."

Her time? I bit my tongue so hard I'm certain I left permanent teeth marks.

~*~

I drove Mama back to her condo. "We'll pick you up at four-thirty," I said after helping her to her front door. "Please wear more appropriate footwear. The weather report calls for flurries this evening."

She glanced down at her high-heeled suede footwear, then at my practical snow boots. "I'm not wearing clunky snow boots to church on Christmas Eve."

"Wearing clunky snow boots on Christmas Eve beats wearing leg casts on Christmas Day, Mama."

She let loose a long-suffering sigh. "I have no idea where all this pessimism and negativity come from. Certainly not my side of the family, and your father was such an optimistic soul."

"Are you suggesting I'm adopted, Mama?"

She pursed her lips and squinted at me. "I think I'd know if that were the case. What I do know is you never used to be such a Negative Nelly. You've changed."

"And not for the better?"

Mama shoved her key into the lock and opened her door. Before stepping inside, she turned and said, "Exactly. I blame that mother-in-law of yours."

She was right, of course, but given all that had happened to me throughout the past year, losing my Mary Sunshine outlook on life was inevitable. I kissed my mother good-bye, then my clunky snow boots and I walked back to my car.

I arrived home to find Harriet Kleinhample's VW bus still parked in front of my house. Entering through the back door, I was greeted with a loud, rather graphic, narrative from *Dr. Pimple Popper*, which had replaced *What Not to Wear*.

I slipped off my wet boots and went in search of Zack. Not finding him in the house, I stepped back into the boots and made my way to the garage and up the stairs to the apartment. I discovered Zack tapping away on his computer. Ralph, perched on his shoulder, followed every keystroke as if he could read the text on the screen. Given Ralph's other talents, this hardly seemed beyond the realm of possibilities.

"Something looks yummy," I said, spying half a dozen cold salmon and capers pizzas on the counter. I grabbed a slice and took a large bite. If Zack ever tired of gallivanting around the world with his camera (or his gun?), he'd have no trouble securing a gig as a top chef at a five-star restaurant.

"Hey, those are for tonight." He closed his laptop and strode across the room, positioning himself between the counter and me.

"No one will notice."

"Really?" He pointed to the void in the circle of pizza. "How do you explain the missing slice?"

I grabbed a spatula and quickly nudged the remaining slices closer together to shore up the empty spot. "What missing slice? Besides, I needed to sample one to make sure they're good enough to serve at church tonight."

"And do your taste buds approve?"

I cocked my head to garner a view of the pizzas lined up behind him. "Not sure. I think I need one more slice in order to make a determination."

"No you don't." He grabbed my hands before I could reach around him to snag another slice.

"Shouldn't they be refrigerated?" I asked.

He nodded toward a stack of pizza boxes. "I was about to do that. Had to take care of something first." Then he changed the subject. "Was your trip successful?"

"Not even slightly." I told him about the aborted condolence call and how Mama wanted to report the arguing couple to the police.

Zack rolled his eyes. "At least you talked her out of that."

"It wasn't easy. You know how stubborn Mama can be when she sets her mind to something."

I opened the refrigerator to pull out the salad ingredients for another of our dinner contributions. However, instead of finding heads of lettuce, cucumbers, broccoli, cabbage, and cauliflower, I discovered an enormous bowl of tossed salad. "You've been busy," I said.

Zack shrugged. "I had the time."

"So what should we do the remainder of the afternoon?"

He shot a glance over his shoulder toward the bedroom. "I'm sure we'll think of something."

~*~

As expected, Mama had defied me. When we arrived to pick her up for church, she was wearing her not-meant-for-snow-and-ice designer boots.

"You called it, Mom," said Alex as he and Nick jumped from the car. Before Mama had finished locking her door, each boy had taken hold of one of her arms to escort her down the path.

We arrived at church in time to grab one of the few remaining parking space in the church lot, which was large enough for most Sundays but never big enough to handle the number of cars for Christmas or Easter services. Those who arrived later would have to jockey for spots on the adjacent streets.

Zack and I carried the pizzas and salad, along with a large platter of Christmas cookies, into the church kitchen while the boys and Mama headed for the sanctuary to claim a pew for us.

A few minutes later we joined them in the sanctuary. Shane

and Sophie sat with Mama and the boys. To my surprise, Ira, his kids, and Tino occupied the pew directly behind them. Had I given it any thought, I should have known Ira would show up. After all, Mama and Lawrence had tied the knot here last summer. It didn't take an Encyclopedia Brown to deduce this was our family church.

"Those kids better not kick the back of our pew," I whispered to Zack after nodding hello to Ira and Tino.

"Relax. Knowing Tino, he's probably threatened to break their legs if they don't behave."

Still, I wasn't taking any chances. Christmas Eve is one of my favorite times of year, and I didn't want Ira's kids ruining the evening for me. Before taking my seat, I graced Melody, Harmony, and Isaac with my sternest former-schoolteacher expression, silently warning them to misbehave at their own peril. All three responded with devilish smirks and began swinging their legs, stopping a fraction of an inch before making contact with the back of the pew.

Tino reached over and clamped his arm across their thighs. "What did I tell you?" he said.

"Not to kick," said one of the twins. "We didn't."

"Sit still. Hands in laps. No fidgeting."

They immediately complied. After I settled into my seat, Zack squeezed my hand and whispered, "See?"

Maybe Tino *had* threatened to break their legs. Either that or take away all their electronic gadgets until they turned twenty-one since all three were currently gadget-less, a rarity for Ira's kids.

As the organist struck the first chords of the prelude, stragglers quickly found seats, the buzz of conversations ended, and the Christmas Eve service began.

~*~

An hour and a half later, having worked our way through the buffet line, the twelve of us were gathered around one of the dozens of tables set up in the church dining room. Christmas carols played in the background, competing with a multitude of conversations and the clicking of utensils on dishes.

At one point Mama excused herself to powder her nose. Upon her return, she tapped me on the shoulder and asked, "Do you know if Dion's brother and his wife attend church here?"

"Why do you ask?"

"I thought I caught a glimpse of Dion's sister-in-law on my way to the powder room."

When I'd seen Olympia Leonides on the news after Dion's murder, I'd tried to place how I knew her. However, I know I would have at least recognized her name had we belonged to the same church.

Perhaps I'd noticed her at a school function or around town at some point in the past. Then again, I'd only seen her briefly on TV. I couldn't remember her possessing any outstanding features that would set her apart from any of dozens of other middle-aged Westfield women with a medium build and shoulder-length bleach blonde hair. "I don't think so, Mama."

She shrugged. "Maybe I'm mistaken. After all, I only saw her that one time on the news."

"Where she was only briefly onscreen," I said.

Mama nodded. "Besides, I was focused more on Dion's murder and your involvement in it."

"She's not involved," said Zack.

Mama turned to him. "She found his body, didn't she?"

I sighed. There was that.

"Anyway," she continued, once again speaking to me, "with a name like Leonides, they probably attend the Greek Orthodox Church."

"I suppose."

"So much for that, then. The woman probably didn't look anything like Dion's sister-in-law." Mama strode down the length of the table. However, at the last moment instead of taking her seat, she dropped her purse onto her chair, pivoted, and proceeded to the dessert table for a third round of grazing.

"At least she didn't accost the woman," I told Zack.

He nodded. "No telling what she would have said."

I shook my head and heaved a sigh as I watched my mother heap her plate with enough sweets to feed half our table, no mean feat, given the three kids and two teens seated with us.

"I don't suppose she plans to share any of that," said Zack, following my gaze.

"Doubtful. The woman doesn't have a sweet tooth; she has thirty-two of them. She's worse than a child. She never knows when to stop."

Zack chuckled as he offered me a forkful of chocolate cherry cheesecake. "Open up. This should help you mellow out."

I thought I was pretty mellow this afternoon, but that could lead to a conversation I didn't want overheard by anyone else at the table—especially my sons. So I parted my lips, and he slipped the fork into my mouth. If the way to a man's heart is through his stomach, the way to this woman's heart is with chocolate cherry cheesecake. I closed my eyes and savored the rich confection. When I had finished, I pulled Zack's plate in front of me. "You'd better hope there's more on the dessert table because I'm confiscating this piece."

After the meal, Reverend Carmichael gathered the younger children to read them *The Night Before Christmas*. When he finished, people said their good-byes, donned their coats, and drifted toward the parking lot—all except those of us on cleanup duty.

On orders from Tino, Ira's kids assisted Alex, Nick, and Sophie in clearing our place settings. The teenagers, having worked set-up earlier in the day, decided to walk the half-mile back to Shane's house. Ira, his brood, and Tino left shortly thereafter. While one group of volunteers wiped down, folded, and stored the dining room tables and chairs, Zack, Mama, Shane, and I moved on to kitchen detail.

However, as we were about to enter the kitchen, Mama let loose an extremely loud and decidedly un-Mama-like belch. She then grabbed her stomach with one hand, covering her mouth with the other, and raced toward the ladies' room as quickly as her high-heeled boots allowed.

"Some people just can't handle their sugar," I muttered before rushing off to follow after her.

Ten minutes later we returned to the kitchen, Mama still slightly green-around-the-gills. I found Zack and Shane working in tandem, Shane scraping plates as Zack loaded the industrial dishwasher. "Would you mind driving Mama home?" I asked him. "She's in no condition to help with cleanup. I'll take over for you."

He stepped aside and grabbed a towel to dry his hands as I took over loading duties. "It shouldn't take me more than twenty minutes," he said.

"No need to return," said Shane. He indicated the beehive of activity in the kitchen. Half a dozen church members were making quick work of the aftermath of the meal, wrapping and storing leftovers as well as hand washing, drying, and stowing away those items that weren't dishwasher safe. "We have more than enough help. I'll drop Anastasia off as soon as we're finished."

An hour later the church no longer showed any signs of the large gathering that had taken place within its walls earlier that evening. Leftovers had been stored, recycling sorted, trash bagged and deposited in the Dumpster, counters wiped, floors swept.

Shane offered to retrieve our coats while I dashed to the ladies' room. By the time I returned, we were the only two left in the church besides the minister, who was waiting to set the alarm and lock up before heading across the street to his residence.

As I slipped into my coat, I noticed an overlooked trashcan full of garbage sitting in a far corner of the kitchen. I pointed it out to Shane. "Looks like we need to make a trip to the Dumpster on our way to your car."

He pulled the plastic bag from the can and knotted the drawstring. "Sophie and I didn't arrive in time to get a spot in the parking lot. My car is on the next block. Wait here while I get it."

I held out my hand. "No point keeping the minister waiting. I'll take the trash while you bring the car around and meet me at the Dumpster."

"Thank you both for your help this evening," said Reverend Carmichael. "And Merry Christmas."

"And Merry Christmas to you," said Shane. He handed me the trash bag before making his way to the main entrance of the church.

"I'll wait here with you, Anastasia," said Reverend Carmichael, fighting to suppress a yawn and failing miserably. "It will take Shane a few minutes before he returns with his car."

Noting the bags under his eyes and his drooping eyelids, I

refused to keep him from his bed a moment longer than necessary. I glanced out one of the kitchen windows. A few stray flurries danced in the beams of the parking lot lights, but other than that, the night appeared calm. "No need. It's so peaceful outside. I don't mind waiting by myself."

He glanced at me, then out at the empty parking lot. "Are you sure?"

"Of course. Shane's on his way, and you look beyond exhausted."

He nodded. "It has been a long day. Goodnight, Anastasia."

I again wished him a Merry Christmas before pushing open the door and stepping outside.

The Dumpster was situated as far from the church as possible to keep the stench of garbage from seeping into the church during the heat of summer. I made my way across the parking lot to the Dumpster, flipped open the metal lid, and tossed the trash bag inside.

When I turned around, a gun was pointed inches from my chest.

TWENTY

My assailant stood backlit by one of the parking lot lights, making it impossible for me to identify who was threatening to shoot me. However, judging from the stature and build, I was dealing with a woman. Recent experience suggested rather than a random mugging by some young punk looking for drug money, this had Lawrence's fingerprints all over it. Had the mob entered the twenty-first century and was now recruiting members of the opposite sex? I doubted Betty Friedan and Gloria Steinem had considered *made women* on equal footing with *made men* when they were organizing the women's liberation movement back in the sixties.

I needed to buy time until Shane arrived, hoping my gun-wielding mob wannabe would panic and run off once she saw his car pull into the parking lot. Thankfully, I knew Reverend Carmichael would have exited the church by way of the front entrance after activating the alarm. At least I didn't have to worry about him startling this modern-day Bonnie Parker and have her open fire.

I held my purse out to her. "All I have is twenty dollars and some change in my wallet."

"Drop the purse," she said.

For a brief second I considered swinging it at either the gun or her head, but if I failed to knock her off balance and dislodge the weapon, she'd shoot me before I got a second chance. And at such close range, no matter how bad a shot, odds favored her hitting her target—me.

As I opened my hand to let the purse fall to the pavement, someone grabbed me from behind, clapping a massive gloved hand over my mouth and pinning my arms to my sides. I fought to break free, kicking at his legs, but he only gripped me tighter, making it impossible for me to breathe.

He lifted me off the ground and growled in my ear. "Keep it up, and I'll snap your neck."

I ceased struggling.

The woman picked up my purse and rifled inside. "No phone," she said.

"Check her pockets."

With the gun pressed into my ribcage, she stuck her hand first in one coat pocket, then the other. "Nothing," she said. Yanking my coat up over my hips, she patted me down until she discovered my phone in my left blazer pocket. "Got it." She turned back to the Dumpster, lifted the lid, and tossed my purse inside.

"Hurry up," said the man.

He dragged me over to an SUV parked in the shadows at the far corner of the lot. The woman opened the back door. The man tossed me onto my stomach across the backseat, pinning me with one hand firmly on my neck, his knee digging into my lower back.

His female accomplice came around to the other side of the vehicle, opened the door, and shoved a rag in my mouth, securing it with a strip of duct tape.

The man grabbed my hands and yanked my arms behind me while the woman bound them together with another length of duct tape.

"Give me the tape," he said. A moment later my legs were also bound at my ankles.

"Let's get out of here," said the man. They slammed the car doors, leaving me lying across the backseat, unable to leverage myself into a sitting position, while they climbed into the driver and passenger seats.

A moment later we sped across the empty parking lot toward the driveway, but before we'd reached the street, bright lights suddenly shined through the windshield, filling the interior of the SUV. Brakes squealed. A car horn blared. The woman screamed. The driver cursed as he yanked the steering wheel to the right to avoid a head-on collision. The SUV swerved onto the sloping embankment alongside the driveway, nearly flipping the vehicle onto its side.

The woman screamed again. "You're going to kill us!"

"Shut up!" He jerked the wheel in the opposite direction. Two of the tires went airborne, and I was tossed to the floor before all four wheels landed back on the driveway. Peeling rubber, the driver turned out of the parking lot and sped down the street.

"Slow down," shouted the woman. "The last thing we need is a cop pulling us over."

"Don't tell me how to drive."

"I wouldn't have to if you weren't so reckless."

"What the hell are you doing? Is that her phone?"

"I'm trying to crack it. Some people have easy passwords, like 1234."

"Are you freaking nuts? Get rid of it. Toss it out the window."

"Why?"

"Because I don't want anyone tracking us."

"You don't have to yell."

"Give me that! If you weren't so stupid, I wouldn't have to yell. Use your brain for once."

A rush of cold air entered the car from the driver's side, indicating the man had lowered his window to toss my phone. After he raised the window, the two of them sat in silence for a few minutes until the woman finally said, "What are we going to do with them?"

"Them?" Who else had they kidnapped?

"We're going to serve them tea and crumpets. What do you think we're going to do?"

"How?"

"I haven't figured that out yet. We'll stash her with the old lady for now."

Old lady? Did he mean Mama?

"How can we be certain one of them didn't already rat us out?"

Rat them out? The pieces began to fall in place. Could I have been more wrong? Lawrence wasn't behind my kidnapping. My abductors were Paul and Olympia Leonides. And they already had Mama.

"There you go acting stupid again. If they had, the cops would have come after us already. The bodies have to disappear without a trace. We'll be sunning ourselves on a beach in Ecuador—just you, me, and our millions—way before anyone figures out what happened."

"I told you I don't want to go to Ecuador. I don't speak Spanish. Neither do you."

"We'll learn. We're going to Ecuador."

"Why?"

"Because Ecuador doesn't have an extradition treaty with the U.S. The Feds can't touch us there."

Why would Paul and Olympia Leonides want Mama and me dead? Only one reason sprang to mind. They knew Mama and I had been to their home earlier in the day. Either they'd heard us on the porch or had a security system that had alerted them. What had they fought over that freaked them out enough to want us dead?

Then it hit me. Lawrence might not have anything to do with my current situation, but it certainly smacked of his standard M.O. of covering up evidence of one murder by committing another. Had Paul Leonides killed his brother Dion?

Mama hadn't been mistaken when she thought she saw Olympia earlier at church. She and Paul had been following us, possibly ever since we'd left their house, waiting for the perfect time to strike. And we'd handed it to them. They must have followed us to church and later followed Zack and Mama, grabbing my mother after Zack dropped her at her condo. Then they returned to the church for me.

The bodies have to disappear without a trace.

Was Mama already dead? *Don't go there, Anastasia!* I banished the thought from my brain. I needed to focus on figuring a way out of this situation. I'd done it before; I could do it again.

Only the last time I'd found myself tied up and dumped in a car, I'd had a tool to MacGyver my way out of my restraints and a phone to call for help—all because my captor wasn't anywhere close to the sharpest X-Acto knife in the crafting toolbox.

However, neither of those options currently existed. My only hope was for Paul and Olympia to commit a major slipup, allowing me to take advantage of their lack of experience as practitioners of violent crime.

I shot off a desperate prayer that the God of Reluctant Amateur Sleuths would smile down on me once again. Even though I may not have gotten myself into this mess by playing Jessica Fletcher and hadn't broken my promise to Nick, it hardly mattered if I wound up dead anyway. I needed to find a way to save Mama. And me. I didn't want my sons associating Christmas with the murder of their mother and grandmother.

~*~

Minus a clock or watch, I've never been able to determine the passage of time, and I wasn't positioned on the floor in a way to notice a dashboard clock through the space between the front bucket seats. My pounding heart and racing adrenaline didn't help. We either sped along in the dark for a few minutes or as much as half an hour. And since I couldn't see any landmarks, I had no idea of the roads we traveled. I only hoped that when we arrived at our destination, I'd find Mama alive.

Paul and Olympia remained silent. I suspected Paul was plotting their next move while Olympia stewed over his verbal abuse. Should the opportunity arise, maybe I could use her anger toward him to my advantage. After all, why would anyone want to move to Ecuador?

Eventually Paul parked the car and yanked me out, hoisting me over his shoulder. The area was poorly lit, but it looked like a large industrial park comprised of one-story buildings. I saw nothing to indicate location. We could be in Linden, Rahway, Carteret,

Plainfield, or a dozen other towns in Union County or beyond.

Olympia unlocked a door in the middle of one of the buildings opposite where Paul had parked. They both stepped inside, closing and locking the door before flipping on the overhead lights.

Judging from the furnishings, we had entered the reception area of Parthenon Construction. A fake wood Formica counter that had seen better days stood on the far side of the room with a row of four folding chairs lining the outer wall. A few before-and-after photos from the company website hung in cheap plastic frames on beige walls that looked like they hadn't received a fresh coat of paint in decades. The room made no pretext to impress.

Olympia opened a door in the far corner, and we entered a hallway, passing several doors along the way until we arrived at the end of the hall and a final door. She unlocked the door and flipped on a light to a large utility and storage closet. A hot water heater stood in one corner. Rows of metal shelving lined three of the four walls. Some contained thick binders and large cardboard tubes that probably held blueprints. Others held office, cleaning, and coffee supplies along with several cases of bottled water. A massive copy machine filled the remaining wall.

Mama lay in the corner between the copy machine and a shelving unit. She moaned.

"Shut up!" said Paul. The moaning quieted to a muffled whimper. "I said shut up, or I'll kill you right now!" He then dumped me on the floor partially on top of her. Mama's frightened eyes stared back at me.

"Now what?" asked Olympia.

"I'm working on it."

"Well, work faster. The longer you dither, the more likely the cops will figure out you killed Dion."

"I wouldn't have had to kill him if you weren't so sloppy. How the hell did he find out about the second set of books?"

"How should I know? I certainly didn't tell him! And how is this my fault? Did it ever occur to you that maybe killing Dion wasn't such a good idea? Now we'll have three dead bodies? Four if Jesse had died. If we're caught, we'll fry."

"No, we won't. New Jersey doesn't have the death penalty. Besides, they won't be able to touch us in Ecuador."

"So, you say. What happens if the U.S. and Ecuador sign an extradition treaty? Maybe you shouldn't have gone off half-cocked until we learned whether or not these two heard anything."

"There you go being stupid again. If they didn't hear us, why did they leave before ringing the doorbell?"

"I don't know, but it hardly matters now, does it, *Mr. I'll Handle Everything*? You're handling us into life sentences."

"I'm handling us onto a one-way flight to Ecuador, unless you'd rather stay here. I'm going whether you come with me or not."

"You'd leave me to take the rap?"

"Your choice. I've got everything under control. Now let's go."

"Where?"

"Home." He grabbed her arm and pulled her toward the open door.

She glanced over her shoulder at us. "Wait! They won't be able to get out, will they?"

Paul laughed. "Not even if one of them was the reincarnation of Houdini." He flipped off the light as they exited.

Through the closed door I heard Olympia ask, "Why are we going home?"

"We have a long road trip ahead of us," said Paul. I heard the lock click. Then he added, "I want to catch a few hours of sleep before we set off in the morning."

"A road trip where?"

They began to walk back down the hall, their voices fading. "I haven't decided yet. Somewhere up in the Catskills, I think. Maybe farther."

"And do what?"

Before the door to the reception area closed behind them, I heard him say, "We'll toss their bodies over a steep ravine. There's more snow on the way. They won't be found until spring if they're found at all. With any luck the wolves will get them."

Beneath me, Mama's body began to tremble uncontrollably.

TWENTY-ONE

No way would I allow Paul to carry out his plot. Step One, I had to break free of my restraints, and to do that, I needed to see.

I rolled off Mama, bent my knees, and pushed myself away from her toward the corner of the metal shelving unit. Grabbing the unit's leg with my hands—not the easiest of feats with my arms taped together behind my back—I maneuvered myself into a seated position. Still holding onto the vertical rail, I aligned my legs at a right angle to the upright by bouncing my butt sideways on the floor.

Now for the hard part. If the shelving unit toppled under the strain of my efforts, I'd probably kill Mama and me. Not my hoped-for result but at least it beat death by wolf pack.

After shooting off yet another prayer, I began the arduous task of pulling myself to a standing position. I moved my hands upward, inch by slow inch hoisting my torso as I crab-walked backwards.

After what seemed like an hour, I'd barely made any progress.

My heart pounded, my head throbbed, and spasms overtook the muscles in my arms and legs. Sweat dripped from every pore in my body, stung my eyes, and saturated my clothes. To keep my sweaty palms from slipping along the metal, I had to squeeze my fingers so tight they grew numb.

I recognized the signs of dehydration setting in. Fighting back the dizziness that threatened to destroy my efforts, I pressed on, refusing to give in to the pain and exhaustion.

Finally, I managed to pull myself fully upright. I leaned against the shelves, closed my eyes, and allowed my limbs a few precious minutes of recovery before forcing them to conquer the next challenge.

My eyes had adjusted to the dark, but I still couldn't see much beyond shadows. However, I had a general idea of where the door was located, and I knew the light switch was on the wall next to the door. Every muscle in my legs and arms screamed in pain, but the spasms had stopped. I began to hop my way forward until I smacked nose-first into the door.

A nosebleed was the last thing I needed, but tell that to my nose. I couldn't even swipe away the blood with a shrug of my shoulder, thanks to the way my arms were bound. I ignored the gush and used my head to feel around the wall next to the door for the light switch. A moment later I used my head to butt the switch up and flood the closet with light.

I turned to find Mama blinking from the sudden glare. Once her eyes focused, she nodded. I took that to mean she was okay. I nodded back, which I hope she took to mean I'd find a way out of this mess.

At least I was making progress. I looked around the room, searching for anything I could use to cut through the duct tape. A quick scan of the shelves containing office supplies found no knife or scissors lying about in the open.

However, Paul's flippant comment about Houdini had given me an idea. He'd made a tactical error by not removing my puffy, down-filled nylon coat before binding my arms behind my back. I was swimming in sweat. If I could somehow manage to lower the zipper, I felt certain I could pull off a Houdini by wiggling out of my sweat-slicked coat.

If only I could communicate with Mama....

Too bad I couldn't reach my nose. I could write a message to Mama with my blood. But the blood had leveled off from a gush to a steady drip that trickled onto the front of my coat, and my hands were tied behind me.

I turned my attention to the shelves of office supplies. Reams of paper filled several rows of shelves but none low enough for me to reach.

I could reach the copier drawers, though. I hopped my way across the floor and turned my back to one of the drawers. Grabbing hold, I yanked the drawer open and felt inside. Paper!

Now I needed a pen or pencil. I hopped back to the office supplies and spied a box of red fine-line markers within reach. I positioned my body with my back to the shelf and grabbed the box. Then I pulled open the flap, withdrew a marker, and hopped back to the copier.

I clicked the marker open and leaned backwards to scrawl a message on the top sheet of paper:

PULL MY COAT ZIPPER

I twisted my neck to read over my shoulder. Not the best

penmanship but legible enough. I dropped the pen and pulled the sheet of paper from the copier. Then I maneuvered myself into position for Mama to read the message. When I looked back, she nodded.

Mama inch-wormed her way on her belly to the middle of the floor and rolled onto her side. I lowered myself onto the floor beside her, positioning my body so that she could grasp my zipper and pull. In tandem, she drew the zipper down as I squirmed in the opposite direction until we'd released it.

I then wiggled my way back down until my shoulders were even with Mama's hands and rolled onto my side. She grabbed hold of my collar, and we repeated our opposite shuffle, pulling the coat off my shoulders. Mama then took hold of my cuffs, and I crawled out of the coat.

As soon as my arms were freed, I ripped the duct tape from Mama's mouth and yanked out the rag.

"I knew you'd save us," she said.

Or die trying. I freed my own mouth and pressed the rag against my nostrils. "Are you okay?"

"I am now. At least this time I didn't have that commie lying on top of me."

"I'm sorry, Mama."

"For what? This wasn't your fault. It was mine. If I hadn't insisted on paying that condolence call, we wouldn't be sitting here."

True. Still I couldn't help but feel partially responsible. Although, I blame Karl for the last time Mama found herself hogtied by a killer.

But I pushed all those thoughts aside. We still had some hurdles ahead of us, and I had no idea when Paul and Olympia would return. How long had it taken me to free us? An hour? Three? More? I had no concept of the time that had passed.

After I released my legs and Mama's bindings, I helped her into a sitting position with her back leaning against the copy machine. Then I retrieved a roll of paper towels and a few bottles of water. I slumped back to the floor beside Mama, handed her a water bottle, and ripped off a sheet of towel.

I replaced the dirty rag with the paper towel and applied pressure to my nose while guzzling a quart of water. I quickly realized it's nearly impossible to drink and breathe at the same time without the use of your nostrils. I wound up alternately gulping air and water. Mama sipped her water in a more lady-like fashion, but then, she hadn't gone through nearly the amount of physical contortions I had and probably wasn't dehydrated.

After a few sips she hauled herself to her feet and said, "Come on. We have to get out of here and call that detective friend of yours."

She marched over to the door, but the handle refused to budge. She rattled it back and forth, alternately pushing and pulling. When that failed, she stamped her foot, and screamed a tirade of four-letter words that would have given her fellow DAR members apoplexy.

"It's locked, Mama."

"I can see that. How do we unlock it?"

I pulled myself to my feet and searched around the shelves until I found a box of paper clips, removed two, and unbent them. "Step aside, Mama."

Her eyes grew wide as she watched me insert the metal wires into the lock. "How did you learn to pick a lock?"

"YouTube."

"Whatever for?"

I shrugged. "I thought it might come in handy someday." I decided against telling her I learned the fine art of lock picking in order to open her ex-husband's lockbox.

After a few attempts, the lock popped, and I opened the door. I grabbed Mama's hand, and we staggered down the hall to the reception area. Then I stepped behind the counter, picked up the phone, and placed a call to Detective Spader.

Since Olympia had tossed my phone and I'm terrible at remembering numbers, I couldn't call Spader's direct line. Nor did I know the number for the Union County Police Department. I had no idea of our location, whether we were even still in Union County. The counter held no business cards or brochures with an address for Parthenon Construction, and I didn't want to waste precious time hunting through desk drawers. So I dialed 9-1-1.

The dispatcher picked up on the first ring. "9-1-1. State your emergency."

"Are you in Union County?" I asked.

"Yes, ma'am. Please state your emergency."

"I need to be patched through to Detective Sam Spader immediately."

"Ma'am, this isn't an answering service. Is this a true emergency?"

"Yes, it's an emergency! My mother and I were kidnapped, and the kidnappers are planning to return and kill us."

"Where are you, ma'am?"

"At Parthenon Construction."

"Do you have an address?"

Jeez! If I had an address, I'd give it to her, wouldn't I? "No, I don't have an address. I don't even know what town we're in, just that we're in an industrial park."

"What's your name, ma'am?"

"Anastasia Pollack."

"Stay on the line, please, Ms. Pollack. I'm patching your call through to Detective Spader."

Maybe I should have started off by giving my name because a moment later I heard the welcome sound of the detective's gruff voice. "Mrs. Pollack, where the devil are you? I've got every cop on the force out looking for you."

Making me persona non grata with all of them, I'm sure. After all, it was Christmas Eve—or perhaps even Christmas Day by now.

"We're at Parthenon Construction. Wherever that is. Paul and Olympia Leonides kidnapped my mother and me. Paul killed his brother and tried to kill Jesse Konopka. He plans to kill us."

"Where are the Leonides now?"

"Hopefully, nowhere nearby. They went home, but they're coming back. They left us tied up, but I was able to free myself and my mother." What if Paul wasn't able to fall asleep? He may have decided to get an earlier start than planned. I stared at the front door. He could walk in at any moment.

"Stay on the line with the dispatcher. I've got officers nearby. They'll be there momentarily."

Momentarily was good—as long as they showed up before Paul returned.

Which, thankfully, they did. Seconds later flashing red and blue lights filtered through the window blinds.

~*~

The officers who arrived insisted on transporting Mama and me to the hospital to be checked out. Arguing with them got me nowhere. "Sorry, ma'am, orders of Detective Spader. You wouldn't want to get us in trouble, would you?"

Since I didn't want to extend their evening any longer than necessary, I reluctantly complied. When we arrived at the hospital, I found Zack waiting for me. After a prolonged hug, he asked, "What am I going to do with you?"

"Hey, this wasn't my fault. Paul and Olympia weren't even on my radar."

"Blame me," said Mama, wringing her hands. She'd grown more and more distressed now that the crisis had passed. "This is all my fault. I'm the one who insisted Anastasia drive me to see Dion's family."

I reached for her hand and squeezed it. "It's not your fault, either, Mama. We had no way of knowing. Up until a short time ago, I believed Lawrence was behind Dion's murder."

Mama shook her head and muttered, "No, I should have listened to you."

The assigning of blame ended when a nurse ushered Mama and me into an examination room. She took our vitals before being joined by a doctor who examined both of us. As expected, I was still dehydrated. So was Mama. Lying on side-by-side beds, Mama and I were each hooked up to IV fluids. The nurse also gave Mama a mild sedative to relax her.

When the hospital staff left the room, I asked Zack, "Do the boys know what happened?"

"Not yet. They're still at Shane's house. I asked him not to say anything."

"So it's still Christmas Eve?"

"It's still Christmas Eve." Zack pulled out his phone and glanced at it. "And will be for another forty minutes."

How could it only be eleven-twenty? Less than four hours had ticked by since my kidnapping? Hard to believe. "You're sure?"

He held up his phone to show me the display. "Smart phones don't lie."

A few minutes later a background soundtrack of soft snores filled the room as Mama's sedative took hold. Zack checked her bed, then turned back to face me, and placed an index finger to his lips.

"Sound asleep?" I whispered.

"Like a baby."

An hour later the nurse was removing my IV when Detective Spader arrived.

TWENTY-TWO

"Did you pick up Paul and Olympia?" I asked Spader the moment he stepped into the room.

"Picked them up and locked them up. And if the D.A. has anything to do with it, Paul won't see freedom for decades, if ever."

"What about Olympia?"

"She's warbling like a diva canary, claiming Paul masterminded everything and forced her to help him."

"I don't know that I believe that," I said.

"I certainly don't," said Spader. "She refused to talk at first, immediately demanding a lawyer, even before she was read her rights." He huffed out his displeasure. "That woman is one conniving cookie. Once she spoke with her attorney, she conveniently came up with an abused spouse defense. They're looking to cut a deal. Whether she does time or not will depend on the D.A."

He reached into his pocket and pulled out a cell phone. "Thought you'd want this back."

My phone! "How did you find it?"

"Complete luck. One of my officers discovered it on the side of the road while driving around Westfield looking for you. His headlights picked up a flash of pink and stopped to investigate. Good thing you have a brightly colored phone case with pictures of your kids on it. Made it easy to identify."

I pressed the button, and my phone sprang to life. "Thank you, Detective. I can't believe that it was found in one piece, let alone in working condition. Paul hurled it out the car window while speeding down the road. I didn't expect it to survive the impact."

"A phone can be replaced," said Zack, holding my hand in both of his. "I'm just glad you and your mother returned in one piece."

"I'll second that," said Spader, albeit gruffly.

From listening to Paul and Olympia verbally battle, I'd pieced together much of the mystery of Dion's death. Dion had accused Paul and Olympia of cooking the books. Paul retaliated by killing his brother, then setting his house on fire to cover up the crime scene, dumping Dion's body elsewhere. Ira's Christmas extravaganza provided a convenient location, given its proximity to Paul and Olympia's home.

While Mama continued to snore away, Detective Spader filled in the blanks.

"According to Olympia, she and Paul ran the day-to-day operations at Parthenon after they hired Konopka, with Paul splitting his time between Parthenon and his real estate office. Dion went back to practicing law fulltime, even though old man Leonides left each of his sons half the business. That annoyed the heck out of Paul."

"So he decided to skim?" I asked.

"Right. Along with being the firm's architect, Olympia

handled the books. Paul got her to doctor them, recording bogus invoices and substituting orders with inferior quality materials."

"Classic double-bookkeeping," said Zack.

Spader nodded. "Embezzlement 101, along with the usual motivator."

"Which was?" I asked.

"Paul and Olympia Leonides live way above their means and are deep in debt—maxed out credit cards, second mortgage on the house, not to mention a habit of frequenting the local casinos where they spent hours in front of the slots."

I wondered if they'd ever crossed paths with Dead Louse of a Spouse during one of their casino junkets. Wouldn't that be the icing on this poisonous cake?

"Jesse's wife told me he'd complained about the quality of some of the materials he was receiving at job sites," I said, "but that he brushed it off as delivery errors, saying mistakes sometimes happen. Sounds like they were happening much more often than sometimes."

"Which is why he grew suspicious," said Spader.

"From what I overheard tonight, Jesse didn't trip and fall at the construction site; Paul pushed him."

Spader nodded. "We think Paul crept up behind Konopka and bashed him in the head with a two-by-four, then tossed his body into the basement, making it look like a trip and fall. Left him for dead."

"Only he wasn't dead," I said. "Did Olympia tell you that?"

Spader nodded again. "Konopka doesn't remember seeing or hearing anyone, though. However, he was more concerned about Paul than he let on to his wife."

"Does he suspect Paul tried to kill him?"

"Not at the time. But in addition to the substandard materials, he wasn't happy with the work of some of the subcontractors. As the general contractor, he should have had control of hiring the subcontractors, but Paul insisted on handpicking them."

"Were they tradesmen his father had used?" asked Zack.

"No, that's why Jesse grew increasingly suspicious. He suspected kickbacks were involved with both the subcontractors and possibly the building inspectors. He contacted Dion with his concerns."

My jaw dropped. "When did you learn all this?"

"When I spoke with Konopka at the hospital Thursday."

"And Dion confronted his brother?"

"He told Konopka he'd look into the matter."

Anger began to build inside me. "Jesse never said a word about any of that when I spoke with him."

"I asked him to keep quiet," said Spader. "I couldn't risk word somehow getting back to Paul and jeopardizing the case."

"So you've subpoenaed Parthenon's books and bank records?"

"We're working on it. These things take time. We want to make sure the case isn't tossed out of court on a technicality."

Was he serious? At that moment I wanted to leap off my hospital bed and strangle him. Zack apparently sensed my anger because he placed a firm hand on my shoulder.

"Let me see if I understand this," I said. "You decided it was more important to dot all your 'i's' and cross all your 't's' than consider you might be jeopardizing additional innocent lives? My mother and I were kidnapped because Paul thought we had overheard something incriminating. He was going to feed us to the wolves—literally."

When Mama stirred in the bed beside me, I lowered my voice

to a seething whisper. "Do you really think I would have taken my mother to pay her respects to Paul and Olympia had I known Paul was a suspect in his brother's murder?"

"We had no concrete evidence to connect him to Dion's murder at that point," said Spader, "and only Konopka's suspicions concerning embezzlement. We needed more proof before a judge would issue a subpoena."

But I'll bet he had plenty of suspicions. "It doesn't take an advanced degree in criminology to connect the dots here."

Spader gritted his teeth. "Mrs. Pollack, I had no way of knowing you planned to visit the Leonides. When you graduate from the police academy and get a job on the force, I *may* consider sharing information about ongoing investigations with you. Until then, consider this conversation a courtesy few civilians are ever extended."

We stared each other down for a moment before I conceded and said, "I overheard Paul admit to killing Dion. Did Olympia confirm that?"

"She did."

"Are you going to share the particulars with me?"

He shrugged and muttered, "In for a dollar...."

I raised an eyebrow, waiting for him to continue.

Spader shrugged again. "According to Olympia, Dion called them last Tuesday night, asking them to meet him at the office. When they arrived, Dion confronted them about the embezzlement and threatened to go to the police if they didn't repay all the money. Paul pulled a gun and shot his brother."

"Just like that?" I asked. "In cold blood? No argument or struggle?"

"Just like that," said Spader. "At least according to Olympia.

She then drove Dion's car into Rahway. Paul followed with Dion's body in the back of his car. They removed the license plates from Dion's car and abandoned it in an area known for drug activity. Then the two of them drove back."

"With Dion's body in Paul's car?" I asked.

"That's right."

"Why not leave the body in the abandoned car?" asked Zack.

Spader offered us a knowing smirk. "A smart perp would have stuck the body in the victim's car and torched the car to destroy evidence. Most perps are caught because they screw up. Those two combined have fewer brains than your average two-bit crook. At this moment CSU is combing Leonides' vehicle, collecting DNA evidence."

"But why dump the body in Ira's sleigh?" I asked.

"A combination of convenience and serendipity, thanks to the circus at Pollack's house," said Spader. "When Paul and Olympia returned to their house, they walked over to Prospect and mingled with the crowd, chatted with a few of the neighbors they knew to give themselves an alibi. They witnessed the attack on Pollack. It was pure coincidence that Pollack's attacker and Dion were wearing similar coats, which gave Paul the idea to dump Dion's body in Pollack's yard. Late that night he placed a ski cap over his brother's head and hauled him into a wheelbarrow. Then he transferred the body to Pollack's sleigh as it made its way around the back of the house."

"Ira has security cameras," said Zack. "Wouldn't he have been caught on them?"

"The camera at the rear of the property points to the back door. It didn't pick up any of the activity."

"What about the fire at Dion's house?" I asked. "Was that just coincidence?"

"No, Paul set the fire."

"How? He was at Ira's the same time we were. We heard the fire sirens."

"Paul and Olympia made a quick stop at Dion's home on their way back from abandoning the car. Because Dion's house stood a distance from any neighbors, no one noticed any smoke or flames until the house was nearly fully engulfed."

"And the fire at Paul and Olympia's house?" asked Zack. "Set by Paul to make it look like someone was targeting both brothers?"

"Exactly."

The nurse returned to take our vitals once again, waking Mama in the process. Mama took one look at Spader and asked, "What did I miss?"

As soon as the nurse departed, the detective gave her a thirty-second recap.

"I don't have to worry about them getting out on bail and coming after us?"

"No, ma'am. They're not going anywhere.

At least not for now. I noted Spader skipped over the possible plea deal for Olympia. However, given that she thought nothing of throwing her husband under the bus to save her own neck, I doubted she'd seek revenge. More likely, if she did get off without any prison time, she'd pack up and move as far away from New Jersey as possible—but definitely not to Ecuador.

~*~

Spader checked his watch. "It's officially Christmas, folks, which means I'm off duty." He directed his next comment to me alone. "Try to stay out of trouble for at least the next twenty-four hours, Mrs. Pollack. After tonight, we all deserve a quiet holiday."

My jaw dropped. I stabbed at my chest with my thumb. "Hey, I'm the victim here, remember? Besides, once again I solved your murder case for you. I'd think a little appreciation is in order, Detective."

"And once again, nearly got yourself killed in the process. But thank you."

"It certainly wasn't the way I planned to spend Christmas Eve."

"Mrs. Pollack, it wasn't the way any of us planned to spend Christmas Eve."

I frowned at him. "So, is this the end of our détente, Detective?"

Instead of answering me, he winked and said, "Merry Christmas," then swung open the door to leave but stopped and turned around. "Almost forgot," he said, snapping his fingers. "You'll be receiving the twenty-five-thousand-dollar reward Paul offered for information leading to the arrest of Dion's killer."

"*What?*" Was Spader making some kind of cop joke? "You can't be serious. *He* killed his brother. He's not going to pay out on the reward."

"He doesn't control the money. Once he made the offer, the funds were deposited into a special account administered by the county."

"He thought he'd get away with it."

"As do most killers, but his hubris was no match for your tenacity."

"Is that a compliment, Detective?"

Spader winked and strode from the room as twenty-five thousand George Washingtons made me forget all about setting up a gift basket business in my nonexistent free time.

A few minutes later the nurse once again returned, this time announcing the doctor had cleared us to leave. As we departed the hospital, I told Mama I wanted her to spend the night with us.

"And share a room with that communist heathen? No thank you, dear. I've had enough pain and suffering for one night."

"You can stay in my room, Mama. Zack and I will sleep in the apartment."

"I appreciate the offer, but what I want right now is a good tub soak and my own bed where I plan to sleep until at least noon. Besides, I was abducted before I had a chance to feed Catherine the Great. She must be starving."

Mama's cat was so fat, she could fast for a week and still need to shed extra baggage. However, no pleading on my part would persuade her to spend what remained of the night with us. I finally gave in, reminded her that the boys, Zack, and I would be working at the soup kitchen in Plainfield tomorrow, and asked if she wanted us to pick her up on our way to Ira's house afterwards.

"I'll think about it," she said. "Call me before you head over there. I may not be in the mood."

I doubted I'd be, either, but Ira deserved to know what had taken place tonight and that he was no longer a suspect in Dion's murder. Besides, I had promised we'd try to drop by after working at the soup kitchen. After all, it was Christmas, he was family, and my middle name isn't Scrooge.

After making certain Mama was safely inside her condo with her door locked, we headed to Shane's to pick up Alex and Nick.

"I know you weren't doing any last-minute shopping," said Nick, arms crossed over his chest, his face filled with skepticism, once we entered the house.

I glanced toward Shane. He shrugged. "Don't look at me."

"I suggested it," said Sophie. "I had a feeling something bad happened and didn't want Alex and Nick to worry."

"Except all the stores closed hours ago," said Alex. "So we humored Sophie."

"Are you going to tell us about it?" asked Nick.

Not if given a choice, but I knew that wasn't an option. My sons deserved the truth. Besides, if I didn't tell them, their grandmother would eventually spill the beans. Mama never met a secret she could keep for more than a few minutes.

"Let's sit down," I said. We all moved to the great room, and once everyone had settled into the sofa, with Alex on one side of me and Nick on the other, I continued. "First, I want to start out by saying your grandmother and I are fine."

"Was it one of Lawrence's guys?" asked Nick.

"Was *what* one of Lawrence's guys?" I asked.

"Whatever it was that happened to the two of you," said Nick.

I shook my head. "No, your grandmother and I found ourselves in the wrong place at the wrong time." I then proceeded to explain how I'd driven Mama to visit Paul and Olympia Leonides earlier in the day and how it resulted in our kidnapping this evening. I spared them the goriest details, hoping Mama was so traumatized by the thought of becoming the main course at a wolves' buffet that she'd wipe the thought from her memory banks.

"So you didn't think the dead guy's brother had anything to do with his murder?" asked Nick.

"Never crossed my mind," I said. "I was Team Lawrence all the way."

He held up his little finger in front of my face. "Pinkie swear?"

I hooked my finger with his. With my other hand I crossed my heart for good measure. "Pinkie swear."

Once again, my sons had almost lost their mother, and this time also their grandmother. In the end, the perpetrator hardly mattered. But I had my doubts we'd heard the last of Lawrence Tuttnauer.

TWENTY-THREE

Given the hour and the evening's events, I suggested foregoing Christmas brunch with Shane and Sophie for a few extra hours of sleep. Disappointment filled Sophie's face. She had no relatives other than her father, and although we'd only recently met the Lamberts, we'd developed a bond that went far beyond Sophie's budding relationship with Alex. I quickly added, "Why don't we plan a late Christmas supper, instead?"

Sophie's smile returned as her father responded, "Under the circumstances, I think that's a much better idea."

The boys, Zack, and I finally arrived home at one-thirty in the morning. Alex and Nick headed to bed, and I proceeded to rendezvous with a steaming shower. Barely awake, I allowed the pulsing water to pummel my sore muscles until I'd depleted every drop of hot water. Then I crawled into bed, nestled into Zack's inviting arms, and waited for the welcome oblivion of sleep.

The sandman had other ideas.

Every time I closed my eyes, instead of visions of sugarplums dancing in my head, hungry wolves feasted on my flesh.

"Want to talk about it?" asked Zack after I'd tossed and turned for at least half an hour.

"I'm not sure." Would voicing the horror help dispel it or make it all the more real? I lay there for a few minutes, waging an internal debate, before finally telling him how Paul had planned to dispose of Mama and me.

Zack let loose a stream of choice words. Then he pulled me closer, taking my mind off the wolves and everything else.

The next thing I knew, it was morning.

~*~

I woke to the aroma of frying bacon and freshly brewed coffee. As I made my way into the kitchen, I noted several additional gift-wrapped presents joining the ones I'd placed under the Christmas tree. I found Lucille sipping coffee at the dining room table, waiting for someone to serve her breakfast. I wished her a Merry Christmas.

Towing the party line, she ignored my greeting, although I had half expected an "opiate of the masses" retort. Instead she said, "If you're going to stay out gallivanting all night, have a little consideration when you arrive home. You woke me up."

If anything had awakened Lucille last night, it was her own snoring, which we heard the moment we entered the house. I ignored her comment and continued into the kitchen where I found Zack scrambling eggs at the stove while Alex manned the toaster. "Merry Christmas," I said, kissing them both.

"Sleep well?" asked Zack, sounding totally innocent despite the twinkle in his eyes.

" I did. Where's Nick?"

"Out walking his dog," said Alex.

I raised an eyebrow. "*His* dog?"

He raised his chin in the direction of the dining room. "Well, *she* certainly doesn't lift a finger to take care of him anymore."

When Nick returned, Zack suggested we hold off exchanging gifts until later in the day, after Mama joined us. "If we're lucky, our resident Bolshevik won't be around to make snide comments."

"Mama will appreciate that," I said. "But as for Lucille, I suspect the other members of the Daughters of the October Revolution plan to spend Christmas with their families. They're nowhere near as militant as their fearless leader."

"Even Harriet?" asked Nick.

"Even Harriet," I said. "No way would she pass up a free meal, even if she doesn't agree politically with her family."

After breakfast, the boys cleaned up while I grabbed a quick shower and dressed. Then the four of us drove to Plainfield to help serve a Christmas feast to some of the county's neediest residents.

Afterwards, we returned home to change clothes and found Lucille nowhere in sight. Zack suggested returning to the house after picking up Mama and before driving to Ira's house. "No telling when she'll return," he said.

An hour later we'd finished exchanging gifts and were ready to head over to Ira's house. Before leaving, I removed the one remaining gift from under the Christmas tree, walked into Lucille's room, and placed it on her bed. She may not believe in Christmas, but I do. It didn't matter that I knew she'd never bother to thank me.

We donned our coats and piled into the car. Zack was backing out of the driveway when Harriet Kleinhample jumped the curb in front of the house and skidded to a stop. "Harriet's driving is improving," he said as Lucille hauled herself out of the passenger seat.

"Doubtful. Even a broken clock tells the correct time twice a day," I said.

"Oh my!" said Mama a few minutes later when Zack parked in front of Ira's house and we were greeted by his over-the-top lights and musical extravaganza. "I had no idea it was such a garish production."

"At least there's no dead body," said Alex.

"We hope," said Nick.

Ira swung open the front door as we climbed the porch steps. "Merry Christmas!" he said, ushering us inside. Before we had a chance to remove our coats, he conveyed his joy by bestowing warm hugs on Mama, Alex, Nick, and me, along with a car salesman handshake for Zack. I grinned at Zack, knowing he was probably relieved Ira hadn't attempted a bro hug.

On the other hand, if their surly expressions were any indication, Ira's kids were less than pleased to see us. Then again, my kids felt the same about them. The difference? My kids hid their displeasure behind good manners.

To my surprise, Tino stood behind Ira's three monsters. When they didn't respond to our greetings, he nudged each of them until in unison they muttered, "Merry Christmas."

At least I'd had the good sense not to agree to stay for a meal.

After I handed Ira the gift basket I'd assembled, and he thanked me, Isaac asked, "What about us?"

"Where are our presents?" asked Melody—or Harmony.

"This is a family gift for everyone to enjoy," I said.

Isaac sneered at the basket. "Food? What kind of Christmas gift is that?"

"The delicious kind," said Mama. "Show some appreciation."

"I don't have to do what you say."

Tino gripped his shoulder. "What did I tell you about manners?" said Tino.

"It's not fair," whined Isaac.

"Neither is life most of the time," said Tino. "Apologize to your aunt and her mother."

Isaac mumbled an insincere apology.

"How long do we have to stay?" whispered Nick to his brother.

"We've already stayed too long as far as I'm concerned," Alex whispered back.

So much for my sons' good manners. Hoping Ira hadn't heard them, I shot Alex and Nick my sternest Mom warning.

However, Ira, as usual, seemed oblivious—both to his son's comments and my sons' conversation. After hanging up our coats, he ushered us into the great room. A sea of torn wrapping paper, ribbons, and toys greeted us. "Someone go a bit overboard?" I quietly asked Tino behind Ira's back.

"Does that surprise you?"

I sighed. "Not in the least." And yet, apparently, the stockpile of goodies wasn't enough for greedy Melody, Harmony, and Isaac since Aunt Anastasia hadn't arrived bearing additional bounty for the three of them.

Tino definitely had his work cut out for him. I wondered how long he'd last, but Tino Martinelli was no quitter. When he set his mind to a task, he followed through. If those kids had any chance of turning into decent human beings, he was the guy to make it happen.

"How are you doing?" I asked Tino. "Any regrets?"

He chuckled. "Mrs. P., my only regret is not being allowed five minutes alone with Paul Leonides."

My jaw dropped. "How do you know about that?"

"I have my sources."

I glanced over at Zack. He'd obviously been busy early this morning while I continued to sleep. "Should I regret introducing the two of you?"

"I don't see why," said Tino, looking far too innocent.

Ira returned from the kitchen with an enormous platter of appetizers. "I didn't know what everyone likes," he said, "so I had the caterer include a wide variety."

Of course, he had. The tray, containing enough finger food to feed a regiment, filled the entire coffee table.

When Isaac reached for a puff pastry confection, Tino grabbed his hand. "Guests first," he said. "Go help your father. He then turned to the twins. "You, too. Into the kitchen, now."

Their attitudes radiated displeasure, but they didn't argue. The three of them headed for the kitchen, returning shortly with plates, napkins, and glasses. Ira followed behind them with a bottle of champagne for the adults and sparkling cider for the kids. "I also have eggnog if you prefer," he said as Isaac, Melody, and Harmony passed around the plates, napkins, and glasses. Ira followed, pouring beverages.

After we filled our plates, Tino nodded to Ira's kids. "Now you may help yourselves." He turned to me and winked. "Slow progress is still progress."

"That it is."

When we had our fill of appetizers, Ira walked over to the fireplace and retrieved a stack of envelopes from the mantle. He then proceeded to hand them out to my family and me. I opened mine and removed a single sheet of paper from within. A giant bowling ball dropped into the pit of my stomach as I stared at the words. I looked up. "A cruise? You booked us *a cruise*?"

"For all of us," said Ira, beaming ear-to-ear. "A family vacation in the Bahamas during winter break."

"What!" shrieked one of the twins.

"They're coming with us?" said the other.

"Of course, they are," said Ira. "You can't have a family vacation without family."

"At least he won't be there," said Isaac, indicating Tino.

"Guess again, kid," said Tino. "Someone has to make sure you don't sink the ship."

"Ira, this is far too generous," I said. "We can't accept this."

"See," said Isaac. "They don't want to come with us."

"Nonsense," said Ira, ignoring his son. "You think too much about money, Anastasia."

And Ira didn't think at all.

"Don't be a wet blanket," said Mama. "A cruise will be fun. Thank you, Ira."

"Shane was going to take Nick and me skiing with him and Sophie over winter break," said Alex.

"You can go skiing anytime," said Ira. He turned to me. "You will all come, won't you?"

Before I could answer, Mama said, "Of course we will."

~*~

I couldn't get out of Ira's house soon enough, but I gritted my teeth and made small talk for another half-hour before stating that we needed to leave.

"So soon?" asked Ira, disappointment written all over his face.

"We promised Shane and Sophie we'd stop by this evening."

"I thought you had brunch with them."

It was then that I realized we had never told Ira about the events of last night. "Is there someplace we can speak in private?"

"You and me?" he asked.

"And Zack." Not knowing how Ira would react when I told him about the kidnapping, I wasn't about to tackle the subject without backup.

With Tino and Mama keeping a close eye on Ira's kids to make sure we weren't interrupted, Ira led Zack and me to his study. "What's going on?" he asked after closing the French doors behind him. "Is this about the cruise? I thought you'd be thrilled. After all, I know you can't afford a vacation and probably haven't had one in some time."

Not exactly true but neither Zack nor I had ever told anyone what really happened in Barcelona. Within hours of landing in Spain, some hapless mobsters had mistaken me for someone else, resulting in a less-than-idyllic getaway. "This has nothing to do with the cruise, Ira. It's about last night. Something happened."

"What? Is it Lawrence? Has he escaped?"

"No, the police arrested the person responsible for killing the guy found in your sleigh."

"But that's a good thing, right?"

"It is, but there's more," said Zack. He looked to me, and I nodded, indicating I preferred he explain everything to Ira.

When Zack finished, keeping the tale as straightforward and violence-free as possible, Ira grabbed me in his arms and began blubbering, "I'm so glad you're safe, Anastasia. I don't know what I'd do if I lost you. You mean so much to me."

I looked over his shoulder to Zack and mouthed, "Help!"

Zack extricated me, and we calmed Ira down. Twenty minutes later we finally departed Ira's home.

"I thought we'd never get out of there," said Alex.

"Do we have to go on that cruise, Mom?" asked Nick. "It's going to be a disaster."

"Of titanic proportions," added Alex.

"Don't be ridiculous," said Mama. "I'm sure you'll have fun. I love cruises."

"We'll discuss it later," I said. Of course, by *later* I didn't mean after we arrived at the Lambert home, but much to my consternation, Ira's Christmas present became the main topic of conversation over supper.

Sophie turned to her dad and said, "Why don't we go on that cruise instead of skiing during winter break?"

"What a marvelous idea," said Mama, clapping her hands together. "That solves everything."

"It solves nothing, Mama."

"Why? Because you don't want Ira spending money on you?"

"Exactly."

She waved her fork at me. "Anastasia, you need to learn to act more graciously. Ira is a generous man. There's absolutely nothing wrong with him wanting to share his good fortune and bestow his generosity on members of his family. I see nothing wrong in accepting his gifts."

"You wouldn't, Mama."

She glanced over at Shane and Sophie. "You accepted an extremely generous gift from the Lambert Foundation, didn't you? What's the difference?"

"The difference is that Ira continues to try to buy his way into our lives. Shane gave Alex a scholarship because I saved Sophie's life. How can you equate the two?"

"I fail to see the difference, dear."

Zack came to my defense. "One comes with strings attached, Flora; the other doesn't."

"Besides," said Sophie, "a scholarship isn't a gift."

"Then what is it?" asked Mama.

"An investment in the future."

Sophie possessed wisdom far beyond her years and certainly greater than my Blanche duBois clone of a mother. Mama shrugged before reaching for her wine glass. "A gift is a gift as far as I'm concerned."

"Speaking of gifts," said Shane, changing the subject, "it's time to exchange some."

EPILOGUE

By the time we returned home after dropping Mama at her condo, the emotional rollercoaster that had defined my life the last twenty-four hours had flown off the rails. Between the kidnapping, Ira, and my mother, I was ready to pull a Rip Van Winkle and sleep for the next twenty years.

One of the few bright spots of the day was not finding Lucille and her commie sidekick camped in front of the den television—or anywhere else in the house—upon our arrival home. I glanced in her bedroom and found the Christmas present I'd placed on her bed earlier was gone. Maybe I'd get lucky, and she'd spend the night with Harriet.

"How about a nightcap?" asked Zack. "I'll make us some Irish coffees and hot cocoa for the boys."

I sacked out on the living room couch. "Sounds wonderful, as long as I don't have to move."

Zack sent Alex to fetch the whiskey from the apartment while Nick walked Devil Dog. A few minutes later Zack called from the kitchen, "Anastasia, I think you'd better come in here."

I sighed. "Do I have to?"

"Hurry, Mom," said Alex.

"It's an emergency," said Nick.

"It had better be." I forced myself to my feet.

But when I arrived in the kitchen, I saw no evidence of an emergency, only all three of them looking extremely guilty. Of what, I had no idea—until Zack dropped to one knee, pulled a small velvet box from behind his back, and flipped it open.

From atop the refrigerator Ralph squawked, "*He, sir, that must marry this woman. As You Like It.* Act Four, Scene One."

ANASTASIA'S REPURPOSED GREETING CARD CRAFTS

For the May issue of *American Woman*, Anastasia selected National Creativity Day to feature as her unusual holiday and chose projects that could be made by recycling greeting cards. These craft projects work especially well for Christmas, but can also be used for other holidays, special occasions, or anytime decorating.

3-D Ball Garlands

Choose cards in colors and patterns that work well together and match your decor. If you have a 2" scalloped circle punch, punch out six circles. Otherwise, use a compass or template to draw 2" circles on the back of the picture side of the card, then cut out the circles with either pinking shears or scalloping shears. You will need 6 circles for each ball and 3-4 balls for every 12" length of garland.

Fold the circles in half, wrong sides together, to form a crease. To make each ball, glue the wrong side of half of one circle to the wrong side of half of the next circle for all but the last two halves. A glue stick will work best for gluing.

Determine the length you want your garland. Add at least 24" (12" for each side) if you plan to tie your garland in place rather than drape it. Cut a piece of ribbon or cord to this length.

Place the ribbon or cord on a flat work surface. Apply glue to the two remaining panels of one ball. Beginning in the center of the garland, sandwich the ribbon or cord against the center of the 3-D ball between the unglued remaining halves. Glue the remaining halves together.

If desired, tie a knot to either side of the ball to add an additional decorative element.

Once you've finished attaching the center ball, determine how far apart you'd like your balls, and repeat the process for the remainder of the garland. You can also thread beads between each ball as you add them.

To display, drape the garland over a picture frame, from a fireplace mantle, over a doorframe, across a window, or along a stair railing.

3-D Ornaments

These ornaments are made using the same technique as the garland balls but can be made in various shapes. Hearts and simple Christmas tree shapes work well, and you can use cookie cutters as templates.

Cut out six shapes for each ornament. When all but the last two halves are glued together, cut a 9" length of ribbon. Fold the ribbon in half, and sandwich inside the remaining halves with the loop extending above the top of the ornament for hanging. Glue together the two remaining halves.

Triangular Flag Garlands

Vertical cards work best for this project. Cut a large isosceles triangle from one card and use it as a template for the other triangles.

Score 3/4" along the right side of the short edge of the triangle and fold over, wrong sides together, to form crease.

Determine the length you want your garland. Add at least 24" (12" for each side) if you plan to tie your garland in place rather than drape it. Cut a piece of string to this length.

Arrange the triangles in the order you want them. Points should touch but not overlap. Turn the flags over so the wrong sides face up. Place a piece of double-sided tape along the top edge of each flag above the crease.

Center the string along the flag crease lines. Fold the top edge of each flag down to tape the flags to string.

Triptych Wall-hanging Photo Frame

On the wrong side of the picture side of six greeting cards, draw a 3-1/2" x 3-1/2" square. Cut out the squares. Continuing to work on the wrong side, on three of the squares, measure in 3/4" from outer edge of each side to draw a 2" x 2" square centered within the larger square. Cut out this center square.

Tape a photo behind each of the square openings.

Cut an 11" piece of 1/4" ribbon. Glue vertically along the center back of the wrong side of the squares without the photos, leaving 1/2" between the squares.

Cut a 9" length of ribbon. Glue to the top of the wrong side of the top square, 3/4" from side edges to form hanging loop.

With wrong sides together, glue the squares with the photos to the top of the other squares.

Greeting Card Wreath

Trace a holly leaf, approximately 2-1/2", on the wrong side of the picture side of a card. Cut out the leaf and use it as the template to trace and cut many more leaves. The number of leaves needed depends on the size of the wreath, but you'll need quite a few for full coverage.

Glue toothpicks centered to the back of each leaf, 3/4" from bottom edge of leaf.

Tie a ribbon around the top of a Styrofoam wreath as a hanging loop.

Beginning at the outer top edge of the wreath, insert the toothpicks at a slight angle into the wreath, working around the wreath with each leaf slightly overlapping the preceding one. When the first circle of leaves is complete, begin the next circle, slightly overlapping the first circle. Continue in this manner until the entire wreath is covered with leaves.

DIY Decorative Gift Bags

Gift bags are expensive, but you can achieve that expensive look for pennies by with a glue stick and recycled greeting cards. Purchase inexpensive solid color brown paper gift bags. You can often find these in bulk at dollar stores, craft stores, and discount stores. Glue the fronts of greeting cards onto the front of the gift bag.

If desired, dress the gift bag up even more by gluing decorative trim or ribbon around the card and tying a bow to the handle.

ABOUT THE AUTHOR

USA Today and Amazon bestselling and award-winning author Lois Winston writes mystery, romance, romantic suspense, chick lit, women's fiction, children's chapter books, and nonfiction under her own name and her Emma Carlyle pen name. *Kirkus Reviews* dubbed her critically acclaimed Anastasia Pollack Crafting Mystery series, "North Jersey's more mature answer to Stephanie Plum." In addition, Lois is an award-winning craft and needlework designer who often draws much of her source material for both her characters and plots from her experiences in the crafts industry. Learn more about Lois and her books, where to find her on social media, and a link for signing up for her newsletter at www.loiswinston.com.